Lost gold, greed, a deadly curse and the quest to solve a hundred year old mystery...

Here's a horror thriller that captivates the imagination with mystery, violence and interest that makes a fast paced read with a dramatic tale . . . If you enjoy a horror/mystery read, don't miss this one.
   -*Daily News*, Kingsport, TN

Action-packed adventure about a college professor, his graduate assistant, and their colorful guide who defy a death curse and go in search of a lost gold mine in British Columbia. A recommended read.
   -*Online Review of Books*, onlinereviewofbooks.com

The story is an interesting one and a temptation to anyone who has ever wondered about gold fever. The author has created very deep backgrounds for the characters so that the reader will truly understand the nature of the curse in the end. A good read.
   -*BookReview.com*

I think it's great! Couldn't put it down.
   -*J. Dunn*, Architect, Seattle, WA

SLUMACH
The Lost Mine

EDGAR RAMSEY

RAMSEY BOOKS
www.RBooks.org

This book is a work of fiction. Names, characters, places and incidents are products of the author's imagination or are used fictitiously. Any resemblance to actual events or locales or persons, living or dead, is entirely coincidental.

RAMSEY BOOKS
20321 Nashua Rd
Sonora, CA 95370-9046

Copyright © 2003 & 2006 by Edgar Ramsey

All rights reserved, including the right to reproduce this book or portions thereof in any form whatsoever. For information, address: Ramsey Books, 20321 Nashua Rd., Sonora, CA 95370

Library of Congress Control Number: 2004115056
IBSN-10: 0-9769592-0-8
ISBN-13: 978-0-9769592-0-5

Publication Date: October 30, 2006

For information regarding special discounts for bulk purchases, please contact sales@RBooks.org

Cover layout and design by L. Portelance.
Cover photo: Pitt Lake, BC, Canada, copyright © 1996, Waite Air Photos Inc. Used by permission. For info, contact:
www.globalairphotos.com

Set in Garamond, 11 point
Printed in the U.S.A.
10 9 8 7 6 5 4 3 2 1

This book is dedicated in loving memory of my father, Leo.

PROLOGUE

"Nika memloose . . . Mine memloose."
(When I die, the mine dies.)

July 5, 2007

THE DENSE FOREST canopy hid the afternoon sun. The tiny bit of light that did trickle through cast a strange net of dark green shadows on the mossy floor. A young woman, her long black hair tied in a single braid, ran down the narrow trail like a deer in flight. Her eyes had that wide, startled look like she was being chased by a hungry mountain lion.

She knew *it* was coming. Heard the snap of dried vines and branches as *it* pursued her.

Her heart pounded in her ears. Sweat glistened on her dark skin. The steep terrain ahead, led back down to the lake. And camp.

She thought of the .30.30 Winchester in her tent. Loaded. It seemed so far away. How far? Maybe a quarter of a mile. Too far, she thought. *It* was gaining. She pushed herself to the limit, the leather hiking boots kicking a flurry of cedar needles and dried leaves. She leapt over windfalls like hurdles. But this mad dash wasn't for a gold medal, just simple survival. She was the prey and *it* was the hunter.

And *it* sounded hungry. And close. Too close!

The young woman lunged off the trail and grabbed a small tree trunk, using it to propel her body off at a tangent. The thick salal and underbrush soon covered her bare legs with deep scrapes and scratches. The pain of the cuts caused her to wince but not to slow down.

The maneuver worked. *It* overshot the mark and now had to double back. That gave her a few precious seconds.

She wove amongst the rotten stumps, remnants from clear cuts made long ago by men who had died before she was even born. The axed notches from the fallers' spring boards were still visible on the sides of the stumps where they had stood for hours and sawed at the giant Douglas Firs with their crosscut saws. Men of steel.

She pushed these and all other thoughts from her mind. Except for the gun. It was the goal, the only goal.

As she got closer to the lake, the ground leveled out making the going a little easier. But she got careless and tripped over a small root. It sent her sprawling.

"Damn!" Her knees smashed into a mossy chunk of granite. She was near the edge of a small stream. Its waters looked peaceful and inviting, but there was no time to stop for a drink. *It* had left the trail above and was following her path. Relentless, still hungry.

She pulled herself to her feet and started down the creek, it was the next best thing to a trail. Her boots splashed through the shallow water as she stuck to the mud and gravel on the sides and avoided the larger rocks.

She pictured the gun: cocking the lever in one swift motion so the bullet slid smoothly into the chamber, aiming at *its* head and pulling the trigger. She pictured *its* brains exploding in a cloud of blood, bone and gray matter. That thought, made her feel better— for a second or two. The problem was, now she could hear *it* splashing behind her. *It* had already reached the creek.

She saw a clearing to the right and headed towards it. Perhaps it opened onto another trail.

Immediately she realized her mistake. Ahead was a dead end with a steep incline on three sides. Too late to double back. She scrambled to the slope and started to climb. It was steep, but climbable. She had been rock climbing several times with one of her boyfriends in college. She felt a sense of relief and triumph as she pulled herself upward. She was going to make it! She pulled herself higher, could see the rock wall level out just above her fingers. Almost there! Then something grabbed her ankle like a steel band. Her fingers screamed as they tried to melt into the rock. Oh, no, NOOO! She fought with every ounce of her being. But it was no use; *it* was stronger and even more determined. Her fingers slipped off the rock and she fell backwards.

She hit the ground hard, knocking the wind out of her. She struggled slowly to her feet and tried to run, but her ankle had been sprained in the fall. She tried to hobble away feebly, but *it* was back on *its* feet, watching her with dead eyes. Then *it* pounced, hitting her at waist level, knocking her back to the ground. She clawed frantically at *its* face, trying to gouge out *its* eyes, but *it* smashed her hard in the groin. She stopped struggling and fell back; felt *its* full weight on top of her, *its* hot, foul breath. Felt *it* clawing at her blouse as buttons popped and fabric ripped.

"You crazy bastard!" she screamed.

The pain was hot, excruciating when *it* bit her. She screamed in agony. Then *it* grabbed her by the throat and began to squeeze, hard. In seconds, the world went white, then black.

* * *

January 16, 1891

IT WAS ALMOST sunup in the Fraser Valley. The only light visible on Blackwood Street, shone from the window of the local parish where Father Morgan stood in his long johns, sipping his morning coffee. His breakfast, two poached eggs, a thick slice of back bacon and a tea biscuit sat cold, untouched. He was thinking of *other* things.

William Morgan was a squat, heavy-set man with wide cheekbones and a rather broad nose. His thick crown of red hair had begun receding when he was only in his early twenties, and now at fifty-one, he was almost bald. All that remained were two small tufts, one above each ear, and a thin band of hair across the back. The scalp on top of Father Morgan's head looked tight and shiny. Two pale blue eyes loomed out intensely larger than life from behind the lenses of his small wire-framed glasses.

Father Morgan picked up a clean, white handkerchief from the oak dresser, quartered it, honked rather loudly, and then inspected the results. Unsatisfied, he honked again twice as hard and pulled the hanky open. This time the result must have been more satisfactory; he dropped the cloth back on top of the dresser and grumbled his way across the room to fix a second cup of coffee. His joints were achy this morning. It must be the weather, he thought. "Or maybe I'm just getting old," he sighed. "C'est la vie."

The living quarters at the rear of St. Peter's were small and sparsely furnished. There was a pine table and chair set crammed in front of a roll-top desk and oak wardrobe, a small alcove that housed a tiny pantry cluttered with dirty dishes, and a threadbare, wing-back chair where Father Morgan liked to do his daily reading. Besides his quota of Scripture, he was currently enjoying

Satires by Horace in the original Latin. The kerosene lamp on top of the table flickered constantly, bathing the ceiling and walls in an ever changing cobweb of light and shadows.

Father Morgan finished dressing and yawned sleepily. Dry alder crackled fiercely in the cast iron cook stove, occasionally spitting out a spark or two from the open draught.

Father Morgan pulled out his gold plated, Hamilton pocketwatch. It read 6:05 a.m. He gulped down the last of the coffee, wishing it was something stronger. It was not uncommon for the good Father to consume an occasional pipe of tobacco or snifter of brandy. A model of convention he was not, quite to the contrary, Father Morgan thought of himself as devout, but not self-righteous and stuffy like some men of the cloth. He was comfortable with his humanity and he liked to think of himself as a practical man. Leave the ritual and dogma to someone else.

"Yaahhh," another yawn escaped him. He was still half asleep. Most mornings, he set his alarm for 7:45, but *this* morning the service was at dawn. Father Morgan walked over to the door with little enthusiasm and pulled his coat from the brass coat rack.

Brisk gusts of icy wind assaulted the open door. It was blowing up the hill from the frozen river below. Father Morgan shivered. It had been an exceptionally cold winter to date. He fixed his overcoat snugly at the collar and wrapped the thick, woolen scarf tightly across his cheeks—one of the ladies in the congregation had knit it for him—there was a fair walk ahead and he didn't cherish the thought of getting frostbite.

Swirls of frost hung on the outside of the parish windows in delicate sculptures of tiny crystals. The churchyard, framed against a background of tall firs, their boughs straining under a heavy burden of fresh snow, looked surreal and foreboding against a pale grey sky. In the graveyard, tombstones poked their heads up defiantly through the thick, white blanket, taunting the living with their grim prophecy: *Nika memloose . . . Mine memloose.* Father Morgan uttered a quick prayer under his breath, and then made his way gingerly down the slippery plank walk to the white picket gate. His breath was frosty.

"Morning, Father."

"Good morning, Jake," Father Morgan replied to a passerby, shutting the gate behind himself.

"Nice day."

"Yes, it is. Awfully chilly though, don't you think?"

"Aye. 'Tis that." The two men stopped and faced each other.

"Today's the day."

"Yes."

"'Bout time, I say."

"Yes. Well, all in God's time, I like to say. I'd better get going though. I mustn't be late. Bye, Jake."

"Bye, Father." Jake turned and started walking away. "See you in church on Sunday!"

Father Morgan smiled and gave a quick wave with his mitten. Then he headed in the opposite direction down Royal Avenue towards Eighth Street.

IT WAS A VERY good dream. The old Indian hunter smiled in recollection. He twisted the long braids of graying hair between his fingers and contemplated the dawn. The angry grizzly bear snoring up a storm on the bunk next to him was only his nephew, Peter Pierre. I must ask him for an interpretation, the old Indian thought. He gave the sleeping hulk a nudge. Peter was the Katsie tribe's medicine man. He had the power to see into dreams. It was strong magic.

SLUMACH – THE LOST MINE

When Peter was fully awake, Slumach described the dream to him.

Through the eyes of a raven, I see a young brave heading out in his canoe. He paddles east, to avoid the sandbars near the mouth of the river, and then heads due north towards Goose Island. Slumach droned on slowly in Chinook, his deep voice measuring each word carefully. *The lake is calm, smooth like the skin of a young child. With a light wind at his back, the young brave makes excellent time over the gentle rippling waters. At the tip of the island, he cuts west, keeping to the windward side of the second island, Little Goose.* Slumach made a canoe with his left hand and dragged it across his blanket in an illustration. The chains on the wrist shackles, rattled against the iron bed frame in the process.

As the young brave approaches the black, craggy rocks, he notices a large break in the face at the waterline. Curious, he paddles up to the sharp, slippery bluff. There appears to be a small cavern so he pulls the canoe closer, eventually slipping inside the narrow opening.

As his eyes become accustomed to the dim light, the young brave sees a large serpent perched on a flat ledge directly in front of him. Although the serpent looks very old and weak, the young brave is terrified; sure that death will come at any moment. Slumach raised his arms in a gesture of submission, but the chains on the shackles limited his movement. He smiled.

"Do not be afraid, my son," the serpent says in a tired gentle voice. "I am the guardian of this place, but I am very old. My body is weary and my heart longs to hunt with the ancestors. You have been chosen to take my place here."

"But what is there to guard here?" The young brave asks the serpent, some of the fear diminished by the thrill of a mystery.

The serpent responds slowly, "deep in this cavern there are many shiny pebbles. They are the sacred treasure of our people. They must be kept safe, especially from the men who wear the pale skin. Very soon now, they will come. If this treasure is lost, it will be the end of the good life as we know it, we the descendants of the great Swaneset." Peter began nodding his head with the rhythm of the story.

The waters begin to rise in the cavern as the lake responds to the call of the moon. The serpent leans over and touches its head to the young brave's shoulder. A blinding flash of blue white light transforms the young brave into a strong serpent. Beside him stands a very old warrior with parched skin and hair the color of dirty snow. Slumach sat up very straight and his brown eyes twinkled. He enjoyed telling stories.

"I entered this place as a young man like you, the old warrior tells the new serpent. I replaced the last guardian as you have now replaced me. If any man enters this chamber, show no mercy. Only death will keep our treasure safe."

The old warrior slowly lowers his legs into the rising waters. "Do you understand your sacred duties, my son," he asks?

"Yes, old one," the new serpent responds proudly.

"That is good," the old warrior replies in a tired voice. "I go now to meet the ancestors. Farewell!" The old warrior slips into the water and is swallowed by the darkness."

Slumach looked over at his nephew and shrugged, waiting for a response.

"An interesting dream," Peter agreed. "The Creator works in many ways." He paused to consider it for a moment. Just then a noise interrupted their thoughts as a metal tray bearing two plates, was pushed in under the metal door. Peter walked over and picked it up. "I see the Transformer at work here. He has come down from his world high above the clouds to continue his great work. He is watching us always, even now." Peter handed one of the plates to Slumach. His voice became very quiet. "And he's listening to us too; he hears every word we speak.

"He could be disguised as a dog on the street, or that spider on the wall." Peter pointed to a small, black spider climbing up the dirty red bricks towards its web in the corner. "Tomorrow when they return you to the ground, the raven will be your eyes and—"

Just then the cell door opened with a clank, and in walked the jailer, followed by Father Morgan whose cheeks were still rosy from the chilly walk uptown.

"—And your ears. You will always walk with the bear, swim with the salmon and fly with the eagle," Peter whispered quickly to Slumach, who smiled again. "You are the raven."

The jailer closed the door and re-locked it.

"Good morning, Slumach. Morning, Peter."

"Good morning, Father!" Peter offered a pleasant smile.

Slumach looked up from his eggs and sausages, and grunted an acknowledgment. Peter acted as the translator, Slumach did not speak English.

Father Morgan rubbed his hands together briskly and blew into the palms. "Brrr . . ." He turned to Slumach. "They will be coming for you soon," he pronounced gravely. "Are you ready to be baptized and accept the Lord Jesus Christ as your savior?"

The old Indian listened to the translation, and then shrugged indifferently.

"Good," Father Morgan replied. "Shall we begin with a prayer?

"Our Father, who art in Heaven . . ."

Slumach slurped down the last of his eggs. They were runny. Some of the yoke dribbled down his chin, onto the grey fatigues. "Let's just get on with it," he replied quietly in Chinook.

THE DAILY NEWSPAPERS hit the downtown streets a few hours later. Paperboys fought each other for the best corners, shouting excitedly to everyone who passed by, "Extra, extra. Read all about it!"

A man in a long overcoat and top hat gestured to one of the young vendors. "Over here, boy."

A six year old, with only a few newspapers left in his shoulder sack, ran over immediately. "Wanna buy a paper!" His grin was almost as immense as his enthusiasm.

The man flicked him a dime. The boy's eyes grew big. He reached into his bag and handed the man a paper, hot off the press. The man opened it to the front page while the boy ran back to his corner, obviously happy with the tip. The man read intently as he walked:

The Daily Columbian, New Westminster, B.C.

Friday, January 16, 1891

PAID THE PENALTY

Slumach, the murderer of Louis Bee, pays the penalty of his crime. Old Slumach was hanged in the yard of the provincial goal this morning at 8 o'clock for the murder on September 8th last, of Louis Bee, a half-breed.

Pierre (the Indian catechist-medicine man) slept in the same cell with Slumach, and prayed with him night and day, and it is satisfactory to know that the labor of the good priest and his assistant was not in vain.

Slumach awakened early and immediately went into devotional exercises with his spiritual attendants, after which breakfast was brought in and he ate a good meal with apparent relish.

A few minutes before 7 o'clock, Father Morgan baptized Slumach, who professed his belief in Christianity and the hope of salvation. Prayers were continued until the arrival of the hangman to pinion him, and to this operation, he submitted without a murmur. All being in readiness a few minutes before 8 o'clock, the procession was formed and proceeded to the scaffold. Mr. Sheriff Armstrong led the way, followed by Mr. Wm. Moresby, governor of the jail and the deputy sheriff, next came Slumach, supported by gaolers Burr and Conner, and followed by the hangman, masked and hooded.

Father Morgan, Pierre, Dr. J.M. McLean, Dr. Walker, and a number of constables brought up the rear of the procession.

Slumach walked firmly up the steps leading to the platform and faced the crowd below. The hangman quickly adjusted the noose, and Father Morgan commenced a prayer. Then the black cap put on, and at 8 o'clock exactly, the bolt was drawn, the trap fell, and Slumach had paid the penalty of his crime.

The hanging was very ably managed, and beyond a few little twitching of the hands and feet, the body remained perfectly still after the drop. In three minutes and fifty-eight seconds, life was pronounced extinct, but it was more than twenty minutes before the body was cut down and placed in the coffin.

Coroner Pittendrigh and a jury viewed the body and brought in the usual verdict. Slumach's neck was broken in the fall, and death must have been painless.

The drop was eight feet five inches. Over fifty persons witnessed the hanging, and a large crowd gathered outside the jail, and remained there until the black flag was hoisted. Among the crowd on the street were several Indian women, relatives of Slumach, who waited around the jail for more than an hour after the execution.

THE LUCHEON WAS held at the Irving house, 302 Royal Avenue, now the home of Thomas and Mary Briggs. The house was built in 1862, by Mary's father Captain William Irving, who was better know to the locals as the "King of the River."

When gold fever struck British Columbia in 1859, Irving moved his steamers from the Willamette River in Oregon to the Fraser River where he earned his nickname.

"Ah, My Lordship, so pleased that you could make it. Good afternoon, My Lady." Thomas Briggs smiled and took Judge Drake's hand. "Little chilly today?"

"No doubt," Drake replied, his huge, handlebar moustache dripping with melting ice, "Chilly indeed!" Drake was a provincial court judge.

"Sarah!" Briggs called impatiently.

"Coming, Sir!" Sarah Mills was one of three maids. She rushed in and helped Drake off with his overcoat, took his top hat, and then attended to Mrs. Drake's mink jacket and scarf.

"Thank you," mumbled Drake almost inaudibly.

"You're very welcome, sir." Sarah beamed. A man of Drake's stature rarely bothered with courtesy to a lowly house maid. His Lordship must be in a fine mood today, indeed!

"This way, sir," Tom invited. He was pleased that Drake had shown up. It gave the gathering that little extra shot of prestige that had been sorely lacking. "The men are having a drink in the library. Sarah, show Mrs. Drake to the parlor."

"Right away, sir. Mrs. Drake, please follow me." Sarah led Jennifer Drake into the large parlor, a spacious room with textured wallpaper, a square grand piano and an Italian marble fireplace.

The ladies, dressed in their Sunday best, were sipping tea, munching on an assortment of pastries and discussing the finer points of the morning's hanging. They exchanged brief pleasantries with Lady Drake and then resumed their blow by blow commentary on the execution.

"Did he have any final words?"

"Well not officially, but June Conner's husband swears that he heard him whisper some gibberish while they were putting the noose around his neck. He couldn't understand a word of it, but Pierre was there. I'm sure he must have heard what was said."

"Hmmm, I'll have to ask Pierre when I see him next."

"Yes," someone agreed.

"He's here you know."

"Who?"

"Pierre?"

"What? Here at this house?"

"Yes. He came with Father Morgan."

"No! You've got to be kidding..."

"I'm not!

"Really!"

"What a faux pas!

"You'd think a priest would know better..."

Briggs and Judge Drake left the ladies to their gossip, and continued down the spacious hallway.

The Irving house was a large, wood-framed mansion in the San Francisco-Gothic Revival style that was popular at the time. Mary's father had it built by the Royal Engineers. At Captain Irving's insistence, all of the structural lumber was redwood, imported from Northern California at considerable expense.

Drake walked in to a chorus of "Your Honor." They were all here, the cream and elite of New Westminster's fledgling society.

The library was separated from the main hallway by a curtained archway, the heavy draft drapes pulled to each side. Elegantly embossed volumes of the classics covered three walls in mahogany bookcases, and a stained glass window, near the ceiling on the end, allowed in diffuse light from the southwest. Mr. Pittendrigh, Dr. McLean and Dr. Walker stood in front of the pump organ, chuckling as if someone had just told a funny joke.

Bill Moresby was talking to a stranger, over by the smoking table, Bill's pipe billowing out clouds of smoke like one of Captain Irving's steamers. And there was Father Morgan with Peter Pierre, off in a corner, examining a leather bound volume of Milton.

Absolutely disgusting, Drake thought as he spied Pierre with Father Morgan. A paddy priest! And bringing a savage to the home of a gentleman, how utterly thoughtless!

Thomas Briggs returned with a double scotch neat, hoping it would be to Drake's liking. "Well, here's to the end of a rather distasteful matter," Briggs proposed.

"Aye, I'll drink to that," Drake agreed as the two long stemmed glasses clinked together.

"To the end of it!"

PART ONE
The Lost Creek Mine

"Mutato nomine de fa Febula narratur..."
(Change the name, and it is of yourself that tale is told)
 -Horace, *Satires*

Time present and time past
Are both present perhaps in time future,
And time future contained in time past...
 -T.S. Eliot, *Burnt Norton*

Beware!
His guardian spirit, the raven
That watchful scavenger
Sits at the gates of death
And curses all who enter there.
 -Simon George, from an unpublished poem

Chapter 1

May 14, 2007

Beverley Dayton walked down the hallway of the Anthropology Building, carrying an armload of books from the UBC library. More than one head turned as she passed, Bev was a very attractive young woman with straight, black hair and big brown eyes. Her light cotton dress made no attempt to conceal her shapely figure. She stopped at a door bearing a small bronze plaque engraved: DR. PAUL GREGORY, shifted the books to one arm, and knocked softly.

"Come on in." The office was a disaster area, the decor an exercise in chaos theory. "Hiya, Bev. Just set them down over there." Paul pointed to the handsome, burl coffee table that one of his students had made for him as a gift. It was piled high, overflowing with essays, papers and an assortment of textbooks. Book shelves, also crammed to their limits, lined one wall from floor to ceiling and the light oak paneling on the other two featured several limited edition prints of Haida art by the late Roy Vickers, one of Canada's premier native artists. Paul's desk was covered in more books, articles and loose sheets of paper, the tools of academia, and some Salish artifacts including a couple of carved wooden masks. A large, woven basket was filled with an assortment of office supplies: pens, pencils and paper clips. How he could find anything in this mess amazed Bev, but Paul always seemed to know just where everything was.

Paul himself was a sensitive looking man in his mid forties, with short cropped, brown hair graying slightly at the temples, a tidy beard—a little too tidy for Bev's taste—and clear hazel eyes that sparkled with a good sense of humor. "Thanks for the favor!" The grin showed off Paul's even white teeth.

"No problem, Doc," Bev replied with a wink. She plopped the books down on the heap and then sat down on the tan Naugahyde loveseat. "All part of being a graduate student and your personal slave!"

Paul chuckled at her outburst. Bev was one of Paul's graduate students, but lately their interest in each other had become more than just scholarly. This type of liaison was most definitely frowned on by the university's board, so Bev and Paul kept their affair as discrete as possible.

Bev picked the latest issue of *Archeology Today* from the pile on the table and started skimming it. "And by the way Paul, are you starting a new project or something?" Her insatiable curiosity had been aroused the moment he had handed her the library list.

"Well, yes ... and no," Paul teased elusively.

Bev frowned and crossed her legs. Her look said, "You better tell me more or else!"

Paul cleared his throat and continued. "Actually, I'm planning a hiking and canoeing trip for the summer break."

Bev put the magazine back on the table, got up and walked over to the window, where a lush fern hung in a macramé hanger. "Hmmm ... That's funny." She observed, rubbing the long leaves slowly between her fingers. "I never pictured you as one of them crunchy granola, back to nature, fresh air types." Bev turned back towards Paul and gave him a puzzled look. "Besides how could that possibly relate to your work?"

"I'm afraid, dear, that that's a secret!" Paul responded, pausing just long enough for Bev to fake a pout. "But I tell you what. For the honor of escorting such a beautiful woman to dinner this evening, I just might take you in to my confidence."

"Oh, gee, big talk!" There was that pout again. She came over to the desk. "Promise?" she asked, fluttering her long eyelashes at him.

"You betcha!" Paul's voice dropped to a whisper. "But how do I know you won't spill the beans?"

Bev leaned over the desk, grabbed Paul by his tie and pulled him closer. "My lips are sealed," she vowed as she kissed him.

"Mmmm... You taste good." They kissed again.

"So where are you taking me for dinner?"

"How's a little Greek sound?"

"Oh, you pervert! You should be ashamed of yourself," she scolded, and let him go.

Paul laughed. "Yep. I got this terrible craving for some fruit of da vine, Greek salad, Moussaka and for desert." This kiss was longer.

THE ONLY WOMEN that frequent the Raleigh Hotel Pub on Main Street are the exotic dancers (they don't like being called strippers or peelers anymore) and a few hookers who pop in and out looking for potential johns.

The Raleigh is a strip joint, just a few blocks north of Hastings Street on the border of Gas Town, one of Vancouver's main tourist traps with its quaint, turn of the century, cobbled streets, steam clock, antique lamp posts and hanging baskets filled with colorful flowers, and the East End slums, a scene from T.S. Eliot's, "The Wasteland."

The Raleigh is fortunate enough to sit on the sunny side of Main, so to speak, that fine line of black asphalt that separates the world of affluence from brown, paper bag country.

In the pub, a regular crew of bored businessmen, chronic alcoholics and hardcore rednecks guzzle Molson's lager by the pint, shoot the shit and watch the continuous tits and ass show.

All day long, the girls descend the spiral staircase to the stage below, their slinky, sequenced costumes glittering under a barrage of multi-colored flashing lights, mirror balls, black lights and strobes. The DJ moans their wares in his deep drawl. "I say, gentlemen, its time to direct your attention back up to center stage. Won't you give a big round of applause for the luscious Miss D cup herself, the lovely Lona Prince!" The loud music, heavy on the bass and kick drum, soon drowns out the cheers, whistles and catcalls.

The three bouncers all look more or less alike, they might have been triplets: white shirts—the Raleigh coat of arms embroidered on the front pocket—open to the chest, with their sleeves rolled up to the elbows, tight black jeans, cowboy boots, and they all look like maybe they pump iron on a regular basis, they're big mean-looking suckers. Many a drunk has found out the hard way that you don't cause trouble in the Raleigh, no sir, not unless you want to wake up on the sidewalk missing a few teeth.

All of the waitresses are good looking; it must be a prerequisite for getting hired. Short, skimpy skirts and a low cut bust lines are their uniforms.

Lona was taking a shower in a glass shower stall that had been constructed on one corner of the stage. The guys in "Gyno Row," as the ring-side seats were called, howled and hooted as she generously lathered soap all over her body.

"Want another beer?"

No reply. The guy seemed to be in la-la land.

"Do you want another beer, sir?" the waitress asked again politely.

"Huh? Oh, sure."

Randy Smith peeled his eyes away from Lona's crotch and handed the empty mug to the waitress, who set down a fresh pint glass of beer on the table.

"Four seventy-five, please."

Randy handed her five dollars. "Keep the change."

"Thank you SO much," she replied, stuffing the bill into her apron. Randy wasn't much of a tipper.

Lona finished her shower and was wrapping up her fifteen minute act with a floor show. She spread her quilted blanket on the stage, and spent the next four minutes doing rolls, back flips and splits. The whistles and yelling was deafening as she climbed back up the staircase carrying her costume under one arm.

The next girl up was Simply Charming, a cute blonde about five feet nothing with really big breasts. Randy took a long pull of the foamy brew and belched loudly. It was his third pint of the day. The ills of last night's party and this morning's hangover, a real killer, had begun to subside. Randy's head was starting to mellow out. It no longer felt like someone was sticking hot needles into his eyeballs. No more dry heaves either, thank God. It had been almost an hour since Randy was in the bathroom puking up air. All in all, Randy was almost feeling human again. He was even getting a little buzzed. One sure cure for a hangover was to start working hard on the next one, postpone the real pain for another day. The only hard part was getting down that first drink; after one you got your rhythm back. By the third or fourth you were right back in the saddle.

Simply Charming removed her bra and G string. Randy debated whether her breasts were silicone or the newer technology, fat cell injections. Probably silicone, he decided, but she was a natural blonde alright, no doubt about that.

Someone let out a loud wolf call right next to Randy's ear. Randy jumped about a foot high in his chair, slopping beer down the front of his T-shirt. "Damn it!"

"Hey, Randy! How's it going, pal? You getting a hard on yet?" A pair of gorilla sized hands seized him from behind by the shoulders.

"Wha—?" Randy turned. He wanted to smack the guy for causing him to spill his beer. "Oh! . . . It's you." Randy recognized the intruder. "Hi, Kev. I thought you were working today."

"I was." Kevin Macarthur sat down on the empty chair beside him. "But I had a misunderstanding with my boss."

"Err, uh, what about?" Randy wasn't sure if he wanted to know or not.

Kevin flashed Randy a wicked grin that showed off the absence of a front tooth. He had lost it playing hockey. "That fucker will think twice before he messes with me again."

Randy couldn't for the life of him imagine anyone wanting to mess with Kevin who was six foot four and two hundred and fifty pounds.

"He's just lucky I didn't shove my framing hammer up his crapper, claw end first!"

"Owww! That would smart!" Randy's rear end puckered up in sympathy. "So what happened? Did he fire you?"

"Huh? Are you kidding? I quit! That son of bitch was riding me all day long, telling me to hurry up, let's hustle, that kind of bullshit. Finally, I just got pissed off and told him to stick his job where the sun don't shine. He's real lucky he didn't taste HATE." Kevin had LOVE tattooed on his left knuckles and HATE on his right ones.

"Good move," Randy agreed, trying to sound as serious and enthusiastic as possible. Sometimes it was hard not to laugh at Kevin's crazy antics, only Randy was afraid that Kevin might take it the wrong way. Randy had no desire to kiss HATE; he liked his teeth just the way they were. "So what are you going to do now, eh?"

"I don't know. Maybe I'll collect UI for a while. I paid my dues." Kevin smiled coyly. "Besides, I've got a plan. By the end of the summer, I'll be rich, guaranteed."

Oh, no, Randy thought, not another one of Kevin's get rich quick schemes, the last escapade had gotten Randy a long lecture from a hard nosed, woman judge, plus sixty days in the slammer.

"So what do you say?" Kevin asked. "You just stick with old Kev here and maybe I'll cut you in for a slice of the action." Kevin stuck out his hand. "Deal?"

"Ah, I don't know. Maybe. I, I—"

"Look pal, this plan of mine is foolproof, a sure fire way to the easy life. Come September, we'll both be driving brand new Cadillac's, snorting the finest Columbian blow and licking the sweetest muffs in town." Kevin gave Randy a thumbs-up and a playful jab in the ribs with his elbow. "What do you say, huh?" Deal?"

Randy sighed, and stuck out his hand. "Deal."

They shook on it. "So what's the action?" Randy finally asked, more out of politeness than genuine interest.

"You ever hear of Slumach?"

Chapter 2

The city shone jewel-like, hugging the skirts of the Coastal Mountains to the north, spilling over into the rolling hills of the town proper and then out to the lush flat valley of the suburbs to the south and east—following the muddy Fraser River on its snaky course up the delta to Hope and Hell's Gate.

Bev pushed open the rear doors of the bus and stepped down to the curb. The large LED clock on top of the Molson's brewery read: 6:40. She was late. All because I missed the damn bus, she thought.

She hurried up Burrard Street. The sun setting over Vancouver Island gave the skyline a reddish tinge, and the domed conservatory on top of Queen Elizabeth Park sparkled in the twilight like a gigantic diamond waiting for the stars.

Bev crossed at the lights and turned right onto Broadway. The Greek Village Restaurant was only a couple of more blocks, but Bev was breathing heavily by the time she made it to their door.

The maitre d' escorted her over to Paul's table.

Paul rose while she was seated. "Sorry I'm late, Doc," Bev apologized. "I missed the frigging bus by about five seconds!"

"No problem. I haven't been here all that long myself. The traffic's pretty hectic out there this evening."

"Simply horrendous!" They both laughed.

"Would you like something from the bar while you're looking over the entrees?" their waiter asked. He handed them both a menu and gave Paul the wine list.

"Yes, please," Paul responded. He ordered a bottle of Napa Valley chardonnay.

Bev admired the slender figure of Domenic as he retreated back down the aisle to the bar.

"Quite the moustache," Paul quipped cocking his eyebrows in mock wonder.

"Quite," Bev agreed. "And rather nice buns too!" She ran the tip of her tongue back and forth over her top lip just to tease him.

He did that thing with his eyebrows again, and then they both smiled. It was a private joke.

"Say, Paul, we're in a Greek restaurant, so why not order a Greek wine?"

"Well, as fond as I am of Greek cuisine, I find their cellars a bit heavy. I prefer a lighter bouquet, less acidic, fruitier."

"Oh, you snob!" Bev chastised him in good humor. "On the reservation where I grew up, they used to drink California red by the gallon, and they didn't give a damn about the bouquet, only the alcohol content and the price, cheap!"

Paul looked into Bev's feisty eyes with admiration. She was a real spitfire, nothing at all like his ex-wife, Carol.

BEVERLEY DAYTON GREW UP on the Yakima Indian Reserve in Washington State, near the town of Wapato. Her father, George Dayton, was from a large family of nine brothers and sisters. Her mother, Marie Dayton nee Hennerman, was from Seattle and parents of German extraction, staunch Roman Catholics.

Marie and her older brother Ralph were both educated in the private school system of the church. The strict and sometimes harsh discipline at St. Anne's Academy rubbed Marie against the grain. She was a free spirit at heart. She wanted to live and have a good time, not rot away in some stuffy old convent. At the age of thirteen, Marie began to rebel against her strict Catholic upbringing. She ran away from home for the last time the next spring. A late period had caused her to panic, but thankfully it was only a false alarm.

Marie spent the next couple of years drifting from one small town and man to another. She found out the hard way that absolute freedom wasn't all that it was cracked up to be. Like the song says, "Freedom's just another word for nothing left to lose." Sometimes, she surmised, when her belly grumbled from lack of food, and she sat feeling lonely and sorry for herself on a cold bench at some forgotten bus station, life sucked the big one.

Marie met George Dayton when she was working as a barmaid in Yakima. It was a class-A dive, little more than a truck stop. It was a place where a guy could grab a greasy burger and a beer before heading out on another long haul.

One afternoon, this guy walked in and ordered a Coke. He was a big handsome man with an easy going sort of charm that was infectious.

"Hi, my name's George." He looked Marie straight in the eyes and smiled. "I'll have a deluxe burger, hold the tomato, and some gravy on the fries." He became a regular and it wasn't long before Marie discovered, much to her own surprise, that she was madly in love with him.

Although the tribe neither condemned nor condoned the marriage, they gradually accepted Marie, and after a few years, their cold indifference melted into warm friendship and eventually real love. Unfortunately, Bev and her two older brothers, Luke and Matthew, grew up in that gray area between lukewarm prejudice and outright hostility. They were half-breeds, never totally accepted by the tribe or the white folks in Yakima. For the three of them, life was a never ending battle, one fist fight or name-calling match after another. They were forced to grow up tough and independent.

The thing that redeemed Bev, and probably saved her from a hard life on the reserve, was her mind. She was a bright child, way above average intelligence.

Beverly Dayton became the first member of George's family to graduate. She was awarded several scholarships and had the honor of being the valedictorian.

At seventeen, Bev left home to attend the University of Washington. The loans and scholarships didn't cover all expenses, so Bev took a variety of evening and weekend jobs. They were dull and mundane for minimum wage: delivering pizzas, sitting at a motel desk, janitorial work. She would read as much as possible during her coffee and lunch breaks, and then after work, go back to her dorm and study well into the night. It was a tough four years, but Bev persevered. She didn't mind hard work.

The major decision, to study the anthropology of the Northwest Salish Indians, was made during her sophomore year. Bev had a deep desire to learn more about her father's people and their culture. So much of the rich, Salish heritage had already been lost. Bev wanted to document and preserve what was left of their language, rituals and customs.

At the university's convocation in June of 2000, Bev was

awarded a Bachelor of Arts degree with distinction. George looked so proud, Bev was afraid he might burst at the seams. It was a happy day for the Dayton family.

Bev's advisor recommended that she apply to the University of British Columbia graduate degree program. One of their professors, a Dr. Gregory, was a leading man in her field. In her mind, Bev had pictured Dr. Paul Gregory as a little, somewhat decrepit, old man, with horn-rimmed glasses and perhaps a walking stick. In reality, she was pleasantly surprised. They became lovers in her third semester.

"So WHAT'S THIS deep dark secret?" Bev asked between bites of Greek salad.

"Have you ever heard the story of the Lost Creek Mine?" Paul replied as he topped off their glasses.

"No. I don't think so."

"How about an Indian by the name of Slumach?"

"Hmmm... That name sounds vaguely familiar." Bev sipped her wine, and thought about it. "Didn't he have a buried treasure?"

"Getting warmer."

Bev scratched her chin, sometimes it helped her to concentrate. "Was it out near Chilliwack somewhere?"

"Close, but no cigar. It was Pitt Lake actually."

"Where's that?"

"Not far. Just out of town, near the mountains beyond Pitt Meadows.

"Oh. I don't think I've ever been out that way."

"That doesn't surprise me, you being a Yank and all," Paul teased. "Besides, no anthropologist in their right mind would

SLUMACH – THE LOST MINE

touch this story with a ten foot pole!"

"Ha! Now I know why you're so enchanted," Bev teased back. "Tell me more."

"The story begins in the township of New Westminster. The Caribou rush was pretty much over, but gold fever lingered on. Prospecting was still by far the main topic of conversation in all the saloons.

"There was an Indian named Slumach who worked as a hunter for one of the local logging companies. He provided them with deer and other fresh game for their cookhouses. People described Slumach as being about sixty to seventy years old, of medium build, with coal black or snow white hair, depending on whose account you're following, and an ugly, weather beaten face."

"Ugh!" interjected Bev.

"What?"

"He sounds like my uncle, Sam."

"Sam?"

"Sam... He wasn't my real uncle. He was a friend of my father. He was the ugliest man in Yakima, always gave me the creeps." Bev shuddered. She didn't want to think about Sam. "Sorry to interrupt. Go on with your story."

"One day, Slumach blew into Queen's City, as New Westminster was called at the time, with an amazing treasure, a shot bag crammed full of raw gold nuggets. Apparently, they ranged in size from a pea to a walnut. Some were even reputed to have been as large as a hen's egg or a man's fist."

"Oh, come on!"

"Hey! I'm only telling the legend as it's been passed down over the years. Every good fisherman knows that the size of a catch is always in direct proportion to how many times it's been bragged about."

"That's true," agreed Bev. "Like most guys and their dicks."

"Oh, yeah?" Paul stuck his leg up under the table and tried to coax her knees apart with the tip of his shoe.

Bev pushed his foot away. "I'll have you know, I'm not that kind of girl." Then she smiled and added, "At least not until later." Paul raised his eyebrows again.

"As soon as Slumach got to town, he hit the saloons, buying food and drinks for the house, and tossing handfuls of gold nuggets onto the floor just to watch the white men scurry after them like hungry dogs. Prospectors poured Slumach whisky after whisky, hoping the booze would loosen his lips. Women bestowed their favors on the ugly, old hunter with the same motive. But Slumach wasn't talking." Paul paused for a mouthful of moussaka and a sip of wine. Bev had ordered a rack of lamb, her favorite.

"Meanwhile, on the Fraser River, a fisherman discovered the body of a pretty, young Indian maiden tangled up in the webbing of his nets. In the girl's pockets were several gold nuggets, similar in size and shape to the ones Slumach was using to entertain his new friends in town. The police immediately brought Slumach in for questioning."

"She was murdered?" Bev asked, wrinkling up her small pug nose.

"During the interrogation, Slumach admitted the girl had accompanied him on his last trip. She had gone along to cook and keep him company. Slumach gave her the gold nuggets as payment for these services. Unfortunately, on the return trip down the river, the girl fell out of his canoe and drowned. Slumach stated that he hadn't bothered to report the mishap, as he considered it such a trivial accident."

"Boy, he was a cold one, wasn't he?"

"Yes."

HEIDI SPUN AROUND the shiny brass pole, her erect nipples circuiting the room like the needle of a compass caught in a violent magnetic storm. Then she abruptly stopped her dizzy twirl and suspended herself in limbo by one leg, her long red hair dangling down onto the carpet. The whole room applauded.

"Where was I?" Kevin asked when the noise had died down.

"Some chick drowned," Randy replied.

"Oh, yeah! The police have no evidence of foul play, so they take Slumach at his word and let him go. The next day, he disappears.

"Everyone is left scratching their heads until three weeks later, when Slumach comes back with his shot bag once more bulging with gold nuggets.

"Just like the first time, Slumach blows his booty quickly, having one hell of a good time. Lots of booze, pussy... Hey, Randy! Are you still listening?"

"Uh?" Randy was quite drunk now. His head was spinning almost as fast as the tall brunette, Wicked Wanda, who had taken Heidi's place on center stage. Kevin's story had caught him though, hook, line and sinker. "I'm still with you, Kev."

"Pay attention then! After a few days of continuous partying, Slumach's getting low on cash again."

"Sounds like you and me."

"Yeah. His bag is almost empty, there's only a few nuggets left in the bottom.

"So what happened next?"

"Well the big rush is definitely over, gold is getting scarce. Most of the local prospectors are down on their luck, and everybody's having a hard time, so they decide to follow Slumach on his next trip, but like a phantom he slips out of town right under their noses."

"Bet they were pissed off."

"Very. This scenario goes on for a whole year. Slumach disappears for a few weeks, then hits town again with another sack of gold, which he spends in the saloons and whorehouses."

"Sounds like fun," Randy mumbled, his eyes glued to the stage where Wicked Wanda was doing her floor show with a bottle of baby oil. She was smearing it on all the right places.

RANDY SMITH WAS born at the old Queen Daughter's Hospital in Duncan, on Vancouver Island. He missed being British Columbia's first baby of 1962, by a mere seven minutes. That honor went to some girl in Kelowna. Randy's father, Jack Smith, a logger with Crown Zellerback at their Cowichan Lake Division, didn't care. When they paged him to the phone at the Commercial pub to tell him the good news, he was already well on his way to oblivion.

"Got me a son!" Jack slurred as he hung up the phone and staggered around the room handing out White Owl cigars. There's nothing much prouder than a first time daddy.

"Hey, Suzie," Jack yelled at the bartender, "What are you doing back there, tapping beer, or playing with yerself?"

"Wouldn't you like to know, Butch," Susan Mason replied good naturedly.

Jack's nickname came from his burly build, thick neck and a short crew cut that showed off a variety of scars, some of them earned in brawls.

"What can I do for you, dad? Last call."

"A round for the house, I'm buying!"

"Coming right up," replied Susan. "Sure hope you ain't driving, Butch!"

Under his rough exterior, Jack had a real soft spot in him. He just about loved his newborn son to death. And Randy grew up adoring his father.

Every weekday afternoon, about 5:15, little Randy could be found sitting patiently on the front steps or just inside the porch if it happened to be raining out, waiting for the beat up, yellow crummy to pull up in front of the house. Out would come Jack wearing grey, sweat stained Standfields, a hardhat spray-painted orange—just to bug the foremen who were the only ones who were supposed to wear that color—his red suspenders supporting a pair of tattered faller's pants, padded on the thighs to protect the legs from kick backs, and a pair of muddy cork boots. He would be carrying his yellow rain slick over his arm and a tin lunch pail in the other hand—a sticker on one side read, I.W.A. LOCAL 180, UNITED WE STAND, with "scabs bleed" scratched in underneath. There was also a round hole cut in one end of the lid to allow for an extra large, stainless steel thermos. Jack loved strong, black coffee.

"Daddy! Daddy!" Randy would squeal with delight as he ran down the board sidewalk to greet Jack at the gate, hugging him around the knees. Randy just loved the smell of sweat, chain oil, gasoline and sawdust that always lingered on his father's work clothes. Jack would pat his son on the head and pluck his cheek affectionately. Then Jack would ask young Randy if he had been a good boy that day. Randy always answered in the affirmative.

One fine spring day, while five year old Randy was enjoying his lunch, a big bowl of Campbell's Chicken Noodle soup with crackers busted up in it, a Cheese Whiz sandwich, and a glass of ice cold milk, and daydreaming about the wonderful vacation to Disneyland that Jack had promised, the crummy pulled up onto the gravel in front of the house. Randy heard the crunch of the tires and looked out the window. He knew instinctively that something was wrong. Something was out of sync. Daddy never came home at lunchtime.

Randy watched curiously as his mother ran out the front door. Two men Randy knew vaguely, jumped down from the crew cab to greet her.

"Why are you crying, Mommy?" Randy asked with much concern, as the men helped Elaine back into the house. "Where's my Daddy?"

The crew had been working a steep side hill all week. Just after the morning coffee break, when Jack had been telling the guys for the umpteenth time about his planned vacation, and how excited little Randy had been when Jack told him that he was going to meet Mickey Mouse and Donald Duck, a large limb snapped off the huge Douglas Fir that Jack had been undercutting. It came down from the seventy foot mark, butt end first. For all of the good it did him, Jack's hardhat might as well have been made out of Styrofoam.

It was a closed casket service. Nearly the whole town showed up at the Sand's Chapel, Jack had been an active member of the community and a volunteer fireman.

Randy sobbed and cried during the eulogy. His uncle Bill, his favorite uncle, finally took the little fellow off of Elaine's knee and up to the crying booth. When the service was over, the family members climbed into the back of two limousines and led the solemn procession out to Mount Benson Cemetery.

RANDY'S HEAD LURCHED up. "Huh?" He had been daydreaming again, almost nodding off.

"Quit sleeping and pay attention!" Kevin growled. He downed

the rest of his beer in one angry gulp, and then slammed the empty glass down on the table. Kevin whistled and held up two fingers to the nearest waitress, who acknowledged the order with a nod.

"Sorry," Randy blurted out sheepishly.

"Aw, that's okay. I thought you were passing out on me." Kevin lit up a smoke and continued the story.

"All attempts to follow Slumach fail. Heck, anyone knows you can't follow an Injun if he don't want you to.

"By this point, some of the prospectors are desperate. There is even talk about torturing the secret out of Slumach, but luckily for him, it never happened. I guess the prospectors didn't want to get their butts thrown into jail. Most folks though, were content to just sit back and enjoy the party while it lasted."

"That makes sense," Randy agreed, "Why pass up a good time?"

"Indeed. The cops start getting more and more interested in this Slumach character. When they check out their missing persons file, they find that every time Slumach splits town, some chick disappears for keeps. So far, five squaws and three white women are unaccounted for. Very suspicious definitely, but still only circumstantial evidence, nothing you could nail the guy with. So they assign this fuzz named Constable Grainger to the case, hoping maybe he can dig up something more concrete so they can charge the old bugger."

"Where'd you learn all this stuff?" Randy asked. Kevin never ceased to amaze him.

"From books, where did you think? If you spent half as much time reading as you did playing with your wand, you'd be a fucking genius by now. Now don't interrupt me, I'm getting to the good part."

"Hey, no problem!" Kevin's eyes could sure look crazy sometimes.

"In 1890, this half-Irish, half-Chinese call girl by the name of Molly Tynan arrives in town from somewhere in the United States. Molly hears the incredible story of Slumach and his gold, and vows then and there to snag him and his glory hole.

"The cop, Grainger, has keen ears. He hears Molly's bragging, so he goes to her to warn her of his suspicions. Molly just laughs it off. She tells him that she's handled the biggest, toughest, meanest men all the way from the Barbary Coast to Alaska. This Slumach will be a piece of cake."

"Sounds like a tough cookie."

"She was. And apparently Molly was pretty good looking too, a little plump maybe, but she was a pro. It didn't take her long to get the old Indian by the short hairs. One night with Molly, and Slumach promises her all of the gold she can carry, all she has to do is come with him on his next trip, cook his meals and keep him warm at night, if you get my drift. 'It's a deal!' Molly tells him.

"Grainger hears through the grapevine about this cozy little arrangement, so he tries one last time to warn Molly. Foolishly, she pays no heed to the paranoid cop. She's too busy thinking about all the fancy dresses and jewelry she can buy down in 'Frisco with the gold. Grainger sees its useless arguing with her. The only course of action left is to put Molly and Slumach under close surveillance. As usual, it's fruitless. Come morning, Molly's hotel room is empty.

THE CANDLE IN the amber tinted jar flickered seductively, bathing the white tablecloth in a soft glow. Paul coughed. He took a sip of water to sooth his throat.

"Constable Grainger anxiously awaited the return of Slumach and Molly. Slumach finally meandered back into town a couple of week's later, with a sack of gold in hand, but no sign of Molly. Grainger immediately confronted Slumach and demanded to know of her whereabouts. Slumach calmly told him that Molly had changed her mind at the last minute, and decided to go back to the United States rather than accompany him on the trip. Slumach swore that the last time he had seen Molly was in her New Westminster hotel room the night before they had left."

"A likely tale!" surmised Bev. They were on dessert now.

"Grainger thought so too." Paul topped off their glasses with the last of the wine. "So he immediately organized a search party. One group of men was sent out to drag the Fraser River. Just before nightfall, they pulled up the body of Molly Tynan with you guessed it, Slumach's hunting knife buried in her heart right up to the bone handle."

Bev started whistling the theme from the old TV serial, Dragnet.

"The old Indian hunter cum prospector was hauled in and charged with capital murder."

"Can I get you folks anything else?" Domenic interrupted.

"Bev?"

"No, thank you."

"Nothing for me either, thanks. I'm stuffed." Paul waited for Domenic to take their dessert plates.

"After a quick trial, a mere formality I would think, Slumach was found guilty and sentenced to death. Just before the noose was put around his neck, Slumach admitted to killing Molly as well as several other women. The motive was obvious; he had to keep them quiet. He also put a curse on his mine and anyone who tried to find it. His last words were, 'Nika memloose . . . Mine memloose,' which translates roughly to, 'when I die, the mine dies with me.'"

"Wow! That was quite a story."

"That was only part of it, a small part."

Domenic dropped off their bill as they prepared to leave. Paul signed the credit card receipt, making sure to leave a generous tip, and then helped Bev on with her coat. "I've started a journal on Slumach and the Lost Creek Mine. I'll let you read it sometime. The whole thing is really quite fascinating."

EXCERPT from the journal of Paul Gregory, PhD:

Like most legends, there are many twists and turns to the colorful tale of Slumach and his lost gold mine. Unfortunately, most of them seem to be in direct contradiction to the few documented facts that we have in the matter. Many of the records of the period, including police reports and court transcripts, were destroyed in the great fire that devastated New Westminster on September 20, 1898.

An Indian named Slumach did exist, and he was hanged for murder, but not for killing a woman. Slumach marched into documented history on September 9, 1890. The headlines that evening read: **SHOT DEAD**.

According to an account in the New Westminster Daily Columbian newspaper, a half-breed Indian named Louis Bee and two other Indian companions, were trout fishing on the Lilooet Slough, not far from Sheridan Hill. They heard several gunshots nearby, and a little while later, Slumach came out of the woods. Bee approached Slumach casually, and asked him what all of the shooting was about. Without any warning, Slumach leveled his

SLUMACH – THE LOST MINE

shotgun at Bee and fired point blank, killing the man instantly. While Slumach calmly proceeded to reload his rifle, Bee's companions fled in terror, figuring they might be shot next. They quickly reported the crime to the nearest authorities, describing Slumach's behavior as that of an incarnate demon, a man who was obviously totally insane and capable of anything.

The Indians stated that Slumach had always been somewhat of a queer sort. Sometimes, he would start acting very strangely, and then he would retreat into the dense forests, and stay there by himself for weeks on end. Slumach usually returned from these long sojourns into the wilderness looking wild and unkempt, more like a savage animal than a human being.

Slumach was described as a very powerfully built man, who was dreaded even by his friends. The police warned all hunting and fishing parties heading into the area to beware, as Slumach was armed and probably had plenty of ammunition. There was no telling what the desperate old hunter might do if he was cornered. The two Indians who had witnessed the killing reinforced this by stating that from Slumach's demonic looks, they were sure he might gun down anyone he met.

The local coroner, Captain George Pittendrigh, set out for the murder site to take charge of the body and to prepare for the coming inquest. Several heavily armed parties began searching the area for some sign of the killer. When they arrived at Port Hammond, they heard a loud chant coming from the Katsie village. It droned on and on into the night. The Indians were mourning the death of their comrade, Louis Bee.

Upon Pittendrigh's arrival at the scene, a group of Indians informed him that, after the murder, Slumach had placed Bee's body in a canoe and paddled it towards Pitt Lake, probably intending to dump the body in deeper water. Pittendrigh ordered the Indians to start dragging both the river and the lake for the corpse. Soon after, it was recovered drifting in a canoe. Some of Bee's friends made the grisly discovery.

Two days after the murder, an inquest was held at the city hall in New Westminster. Dr. Walker had performed the autopsy. He stated that death was caused by a shotgun ball entering the upper left arm, shattering the fifth rib, tearing through the left lung and heart, and finally embedding itself in the wall of Bee's right lung. In the doctor's expert opinion, death must have been instantaneous. Charlie Simon, one of the eye witnesses, described the killing in gruesome detail. The verdict of the inquest was a charge of willful murder against Slumach.

Deputy Sheriff William Moresby and two other police constables formed a posse and set out for Pitt Lake. They reached Slumach's cabin the next day and burned it to the ground, in case Slumach was desperate enough to return there for provisions. The posse then started combing the woods around Lilooet Slough, working their way north towards Pitt Lake.

They caught sight of Slumach only once. He was standing on a rocky bluff in the distance, wearing nothing but a red shirt with a handkerchief tied around his head like a bandanna. Slumach was out of shooting range, and by the time the posse reached the spot, he had vanished into the dense forest.

The search went on for several weeks with no luck. The bush wise old Indian managed to evade all pursuers. Most of the Indians believed that Slumach was a crazy psychopath, but some claimed that he was only a blood thirsty old villain. It was reported that Slumach had committed at least five other similar murders in the preceding quarter of a century.

Slumach's run from the law ended on October 15, 1890, when he contacted his nephew Peter Pierre, and asked him to bring the

Indian Agent, Mr. P. McTurnan, who arrived a short time later, accompanied by two native policemen. Slumach surrendered to them quietly. The headline that evening was: **STARVED OUT**.

Slumach was emancipated and extremely weak from his long ordeal in the bush. He had not eaten for days, as he had run out of ammunition, and there was nothing left of his clothing but filthy rags. The doctor attending Slumach did not expect him to live long enough to stand trial, but the old Indian must have been a lot tougher than thought, because Slumach recovered quickly, regaining most of his strength.

The trial took place on November 15th and 16th, 1890, with the Honorable Judge Montague W.T. Drake presiding. It came out in the evidence, that the deceased Louis Bee had been a troublemaker, and that he was in the habit of hassling with and threatening nearly everyone he came into contact with. Towards Slumach, Bee held a sort of grudge. When Slumach emerged from the woods on the day of the murder, an altercation had broken out between the two men, with Bee calling Slumach a sorcerer, a witch and a devil, the most severe insults in the Chinook language. In the scuffle that followed, Slumach shot Bee dead.

The evidence of guilt was overwhelming. It took the jury only fifteen minutes to return a verdict of guilty. Judge Drake sentenced Slumach to death. On Friday, January 16, 1891, at 8:00 a.m., Slumach was hanged at the provincial jail in New Westminster, British Columbia.

Chapter 3

It was dark, the eight o'clock cannon had already boomed in Stanley Park. Randy and Kevin finally stumbled out of the Raleigh. They were both drunk, staggering a bit. Kevin's truck was parked several blocks away, in a residential area where there were no parking meters, he being too cheap to park in a paid parkade.

"So the way I see it," Kevin was slurring his words badly, "We gotta—hiccup—go out there and find us the gold."

They walked past the ghost of Bob Dylan standing in front of the liquor store. He was wearing a floppy brown hat and picking an out-of-tune flattop guitar covered with an array of stickers from all over the world. In a nasal, off-key voice, he was crooning an old Dylan tune, something about "Cinderella sweeping up on Desolation Row." On a good night, the poor guy might have enough spare change and small bills in his battered case when the store closed to buy himself a Big Mac with fries and half a gallon of Okanogan Estates, a cheap red wine guaranteed to rot your socks off.

"W-What, uh, makes you think we can f-find it?" Randy asked

as they staggered along Hastings Street. His speech wasn't any better than Kevin's.

"Positive thinking!" Kevin put his hand on Randy's shoulder. "You just gotta—hiccup—think positive, my friend." Kevin turned towards Randy and looked at him with two very bloodshot eyes. "Besides I've got a nose for money, I can smell dat gold from 'ere!" They staggered on.

Three elderly ladies stood like statues in front of the Cenotaph, watching the unfolding street scene with complete indifference. Their bony fingers held copies of the Watchtower and Awake! Either their shift for salvation was nearly over, or they were the night crew; God working overtime.

"Awake! Awake! The watchtower is falling!" Randy screamed at them.

The women didn't even bat an eyelid, just stood there like three wooden Indians.

"Cool it," Kevin warned. "There's a pig car—hiccup—coming this way."

"Have a very gooooood night, ladies!" Randy bowed to them as he walked away. "Bet they ain't had sooo much fun in years!" he said to Kevin. The police cruiser passed them without incident.

"Prob'ly not," Kevin agreed.

They walked on in silence. Kevin's thoughts were consumed by lust, but not for the usual sex, drugs and rock and roll. Tonight, all he could think about was gold. He picked his nose subconsciously, pulled out a big booger, and said, "All we've got to do when we find the gold, is stake ourselves a claim, play let's make a deal with some big mining company, and voila! The cash will start rolling in." Kevin took aim and flicked the snot onto a storefront window.

"Sounds simply m-marvelous! I'm in."

They did their buddy handshake, a complicated gesture of bangs, pulls and slaps.

"When's this going down?"

"Oh, I dunno. We gotta round up some camping gear, a tent . . . pick up a few bags of grub, maybe swipe a boat from somewhere. Let's see." Kevin pulled on one end of his huge moustache. "How about the weekend after I get my first unemployment check? That should be here in about six weeks or so."

"Right on!" Randy pulled a package of Player's Filters out of his shirt pocket and lit two cigarettes.

"Thanks."

They passed by Pigeon Park on the way to Kevin's pickup. Half a dozen derelicts were sprawled out on the benches and grass. One of them was covered up with a copy of yesterday's Province newspaper. He must have fished it out of a trash bin. It made a cheap blanket. Another bleary eyed old man with stubby, grey whiskers looked up at them and puked up his Sally Ann dinner. It poured down his chin, all over his tattered overcoat.

"Yuck! What a loser," Randy said, disgusted by the spectacle.

AFTER DINNER, PAUL TOOK Bev for a relaxing ride along Marine Drive, before taking her home to her West End apartment. When they finally pulled up in front of her building in English Bay, Bev asked him up for a nightcap. There were half a dozen ice cold Heinekens in her refrigerator dying to get cracked.

"You promise not to take advantage of me?" Paul asked her, ever so seriously.

"I give you my word, sir!"

"Hah! I saw you cross your fingers."

"Just be thankful I'm not going to cross my legs instead."

Soon they were on Bev's waterbed, sweaty and exhausted from lovemaking.

Bev's suite was on the ninth floor. The bedroom window faced due west, providing them with an unobstructed view of the bay. They could see the lights of ships out in the Georgia Straight. It was a perfect backdrop to cap a perfect evening.

"So," Paul said, as he lightly massaged Bev's neck and back with his fingertips, "I'm hoping to write a book about Slumach and the lost mine. That's why I'm keeping a journal." Paul had brought the book up from his briefcase in the car. Bev had skimmed through it briefly, before their thoughts had turned to more physical activities. "I'd like to go out to Pitt Lake this summer. Take a good camera, portable tape recorder, and kind of get a feel for the place. They say you can't really write about something until you've experienced it."

"Like a virgin trying to write a screenplay for a porno?" Bev interjected mischievously.

"Exactly!" Paul laughed. Bev could be such an imp sometimes. "I plan to paddle up the lake in a canoe and camp for a night or two at the head. I was wondering, perhaps you would like to come along? The scenery is supposed to be absolutely breathtaking, and it might be fun roughing it for a few days, keeping each other warm at night. What do you think?"

"Sure. I'd love to come with you," Bev replied. Her long hair tickled and caressed Paul's chest before her tongue slithered down the length of his belly. "When?" She paused at his belly button, teasing it with her tongue. "Hmmm?" She continued on lower.

"Sometime in July!" Paul gasped.

EXCERPT from the journal of Paul Gregory, PhD:

The big question concerning the authenticity of the lost mine, is this: if Slumach did bring as much gold as he was reputed to have brought into New Westminster during his wild spending sprees, why is there no mention of it in the newspapers of the day? Gold discoveries were big news, front page material. Surely such an amazing find would not go unnoticed by the local media who then as now, were always eager for a good story. Also there is no record of any disappearances or unsolved murders of young women in the press or surviving police reports and court documents during the decade preceding Slumach's execution in 1891.

While it is easy to dismiss the murders as pure fantasy, a little spice added over the years, it is not as easy to write off the existence of the lost mine itself.

By the turn of the century, the tale of Slumach's gold had traveled up and down the West Coast. It was convincing enough to catch the attention of John Jackson, a seasoned prospector and miner on his way back to the United States from the Alaskan gold fields. He arrived in New Westminster in the early spring of 1901, and swore that he would find the lost mine or die trying. As soon as the weather warmed up, Jackson headed for the headwaters of Pitt Lake, then out into the bush to begin his search in earnest. No one saw him again until late that autumn.

Jackson came out of the bush a sick, broken man. He stayed in his hotel room in New Westminster, and barely spoke to anyone. After resting a few days, he checked out and headed for California. A rumor soon filtered back that upon his arrival in San Francisco, Jackson had deposited nearly ten thousand dollars in gold nuggets at the Bank of British North America. Unfortunately, this deposit cannot be verified as the bank's records were destroyed some years later in the firestorm that devastated San Francisco following the 1906 earthquake.

The long ordeal in the rugged Coastal Mountains was too much for the ailing Jackson, his health deteriorated rapidly. Three years later, Jackson sent a letter to a friend of his in Seattle. He died shortly thereafter.

Exhibit ONE, a copy of Jackson's letter:

I had been out over two months and found myself running short of grub. I had lived mostly on fresh meat for one can't carry much of a pack in those hills. I found a few very promising ledges and colors in the little creeks, but nothing I cared to stay with. I had almost made up my mind to light out the next day. I climbed to the top on a sharp ridge and looked down into a canyon or valley about one mile and a half long, and what struck me as singular, it appeared to have no outlet for the little creek that flowed at the bottom. Afterwards, I found that the creek entered a crevice and was gone.

After some difficulty, I found my way down to the creek. The water was almost white, the formation for the most part had been slate and granite, but there I found a kind of schist and slate formation. Now comes the interesting part. I had only a small prospecting pan with me, but I found colors at once right on the surface, and such colors they were. I knew I had struck it right at last.

In going upstream, I came to a place where the bedrock was bare, and there, you could hardly believe me, the bedrock was yellow with gold. Some of the nuggets were as big as walnuts and there were many chunks carrying quartz. After sizing it up, I saw there was millions stowed around in little cracks. On account of the weight, I buried part of the gold at the foot of a large tent shaped rock facing the creek. You can't miss it. There is a mark cut in it. Taking with me what I supposed to be ten thousand dollars in gold, but afterwards proved to be a little over eight thousand dollars.

After three days of hard traveling, it would not have been only two days good going, but the way was rough and I was not feeling well, I arrived at the lake and while resting there was taken sick and have never since been able to return, and now I fear I never shall, I am alone in the world, no relatives, nobody to look in after me for anything. Of course I have not spoken of this find during all this time for fear of it being discovered. It has caused me many anxious hours, but the place is so well guarded by surrounding ridges and mountains that it should not be found for many years, unless someone knew of it being there.

Oh, how I wish I could go with you to show you this wonderful place, for I cannot give you exact directions, and it will take a year or more to find. Don't give up, but keep at it and you will be repaid beyond your wildest dreams. I believe any further directions would only tend to confuse it, so I will only suggest further that you go alone or at least take one or two trusty Indians to pack food and no one need to know but that you are going on a hunting trip until you find the place and get everything for yourself.

When you find it and I'm sure you will, should you care to see me, advertise in the 'Frisco Examiner and if I am living, I will either come to see you, or let you know where to find me, but once more I say to you, don't fail to look this great property up and don't give up until you find it.

SLUMACH – THE LOST MINE

Now goodbye and may success attend to you,
W. Jackson

Jackson's friend, a Mr. Hill or Mr. Shotwell depending on whose account you are following, and there are many, subsequently sold the letter and the accompanying map to a group of Seattle businessmen. They made several unsuccessful attempts to find the creek. After abandoning the quest, they in turn must have sold the letter and map to some other treasure seekers for soon after, copies of the map began popping up everywhere.

According to the Canada West Magazine, there is sufficient evidence to conclude that Jackson's letter is genuine, although it is impossible to prove this conclusively. The map is another story. Nowhere in Jackson's letter is the existence of the map mentioned. He states that he cannot give exact directions to the treasure. Fraser McDonald, who was the gold commissioner in New Westminster for twenty-five years, stated once, that he had seen at least a dozen different versions of the map, each one claimed by its owner to be a true copy of the original. One enterprising American had thousands of maps printed, which he sold by mail order for twelve dollars and fifty cents each.

In view of the many discrepancies and the lack of any documentation whatsoever, it is likely that the map never existed and that all of the copies were fakes.

Chapter 4

THE GIRL WAS standing on the corner of Pendrell and Jervis Streets. She didn't look much older than fifteen. She was dressed for work, wearing a short, wrap around skirt, with black, fishnet stockings and a braless sequined top, her nipples poking against the fabric because it was chilly out, and she wasn't wearing a jacket. Her heavy makeup was intended to make her look elegant and more mature than her years, but it wasn't successful. Even in the dim light of the street lamp, her acne showed through the heavy powder. She was carrying a small white purse on a long strap.

A car slowed, then stopped. The girl opened the passenger door, spoke a few words to the driver, and then climbed inside. The car sat motionless for a minute while the girl and the driver talked, then it pulled away from the curb and drove slowly up the street. The blinker came on and the car turned into an alley, went about a hundred feet, finally pulling in to a dark parking stall behind the Gladstone United Church. The car cut its lights and faded into the blackness.

"How are you doing?" the man asked.

"Alright." The girl eyed him up and down, but it was pretty dark. She was chewing her stick of Doublemint like it was the last piece of gum on the planet. She pulled a small penlight out of her little purse, and turned it on. "You ain't a cop are ya?" She shone it at his face.

"No," the man responded impatiently. "Do I look like one?"

"Nah." The girl eyed him up and down again. "You look okay." She blew a tiny bubble and licked the stickiness off of her top lip. "So are you looking for a good time?"

"Maybe. Depends. Now get that damn light out of my eyes."

"Sorry." The girl set it on the seat cover between them, pointed at the dash, more than enough light to conduct their business by.

The man glanced nervously in the rearview mirror. No one was there.

"Well, for fifty, I'll blow you," the girl suggested, chomping her gum even faster. "But if you want to fuck me, it'll cost you more, and you gotta wear a party hat." The girl's eyelashes fluttered like a moth fighting a strong headwind. "And I don't do no kinky stuff. Okay?"

The man pulled a hundred dollar bill out of his shirt pocket, and handed it to the girl. "A straight fuck will be just fine."

The girl smiled and crammed the bill into her tiny purse. Then she fished around inside it for a moment and pulled out a bright blue colored prophylactic. She picked at the package with her long fingernails while the man removed his trousers.

Randy's hands were shaking badly when the girl passed him the condom. He fumbled with it for a moment trying to put it on inside out.

"Here, let me do it," the girl volunteered. She carefully rolled it over Randy's semi-erect penis, pinching the air out of the reservoir end. Then she unfastened her skirt and let it fall open. Her underwear popped off with two snaps. She gave it a tug and it slipped out from between her legs. "There you go mister," she said. She leaned back against the armrest and arched her body towards him. She was still chewing her gum at an incredible pace. "Just try not to take too long, okay? I've got a busy schedule tonight."

She had nothing to worry about; Randy came in less than a minute.

AFTER THE DEATH of Randy's father, Elaine and Randy moved to Burnaby, to live with Elaine's sister, Velma, and the cats, seven females, all spayed.

Velma Curry was deeply religious. She belonged to the Sisters of Grace, a renegade and fanatical sect of the Catholic Church. SOG, as they were called for short, was founded by the Reverend Mother Carla Benson, a former nun who had left the overbearing mother church after having strange visions. Benson claimed that Christ had already returned and was roaming the planet incognito, marking sinners on the forehead with an invisible X. UFOs flown by angels—there were thousands of them waiting just outside the orbit of Pluto—would descend on Judgment Day, and carry the faithful and pure of heart to Heaven, but anyone bearing an X on their forehead would be left behind to be consumed by nuclear bombs dropped from the departing starships.

The blood of the Lamb, the X, could only be washed off a sinner by prolonged chastity, pious acts, diligent prayer and of course, generous donations to SOG's bank account. Benson went on to claim that this was what the Bible really meant when the Apostles referred to being washed in the blood of the Lamb.

Reverend Mother Benson had even spotted Christ once. The Lord was boarding a bus on Hornby Street. He was dressed up just like any other businessman, in a three piece suit, carrying a black leather briefcase and wearing designer shades, but she could tell that it was Him by the halo and sandals.

Every Tuesday night, SOG would hold a bingo in the White Eagle Hall in East Van. Velma always volunteered her help. She was proud of the money she helped raise for SOG and its Holy crusade. She was very relieved, when the Reverend Mother told her that the X Velma had been sporting when she first joined SOG, had faded considerably, soon it would be completely gone. "You're walking the straight and narrow path to Christ's door now!" Benson would tell Velma with a wink and a pat on the bum. The Reverend Mother was a bit of a dyke.

Little Randy didn't like living at Aunty Velma's house. He hated it.

The house itself was creepy, cold and unfriendly, more like a mausoleum than a home, the dark wood paneling and plastered ceilings, the stiff uncomfortable furniture that belonged in a museum. There was a Madonna or Crucifix in every room, including the john. Scrolls in ornate frames spoke of the coming King, and the wrath that will befall the wicked and sinful. A print of Leonardo da Vinci's Last Supper hung on a wall over the thick, black walnut dining-room table that must have weighed several hundred pounds.

The bathroom was huge by modern standards. It had a large, free standing bathtub, supported on cast-iron lion's paws, with brass facets and bone handled taps. The white enamel, pedestal sink and toilet were so clean, they sparkled. The toilet's lid and tank were covered with chocolate brown, flannelette slip-ons.

Aunty Velma made Randy go pee sitting down on the toilet.

She didn't want his peter dribbling all over her nice clean floor. Little Randy was humiliated and a bit confused. His daddy had been so proud of Randy, the first time he had peed in the toilet standing up like a man. Jack had patted his son on the head, and told him he was growing up to be a big boy. Randy remembered the warm glow of his father's praise like it was yesterday. How he longed to be back at their real home with both his mommy and daddy. He kept asking Elaine when daddy was coming to take them home, but she would just give him a queer look and say, "Soon, Randy, soon. Now run along and play."

If Randy got caught peeing in the toilet standing up, he got his bare bottom tanned with a thick leather strap by Aunty Velma. A few times, he had tried to get away with it, carefully inspecting the floor and rim of the bowl for any spots, then wiping them up with a Kleenex or some toilet paper, but Aunty Velma wasn't fooled. Randy was beginning to think that she could see right through walls like Superman. The consequences of trying to deceive Aunty Velma were severe indeed.

Once, Randy had tried appealing his case to a higher court, his mother, hoping she might have a little sympathy for his predicament, but Elaine had merely told him to, "Mind your Aunty Velma, Randy. She's right, you know. Little boys shouldn't be allowed to make a mess." She pointed a stern finger towards the stairs. "Now go to your room and tell Jesus you're sorry."

Randy cried for nearly an hour. His mother had gotten more and more distant since they'd moved to the city. She acted a lot like Aunty Velma now, often attending the SOG meetings or bingo nights, but it was more of an imitation than the real thing. Underneath the surface, Randy could sense something darker brewing inside Elaine, something cold and hard. She seemed to be losing her capacity to love.

Randy's room was the smallest of the four upstairs bedrooms. His maternal grandfather had died in it several years before he was born. The spare room across the hall was Aunty Velma's sewing room. Randy wasn't allowed in there under any circumstance, with threats of severe punishment from Aunty Velma, should he ever be foolish enough to disobey this rule.

Randy had a roll down cot to sleep on, fitted with a plastic bottom sheet. Velma insisted on the plastic even though Randy hadn't wet the bed for several years. She was paranoid.

There was a three drawer, painted dresser for Randy's clothes, and a toy box—one of the few items Randy had been allowed to bring from the old house—which was almost empty. Elaine and Aunty Velma had gone through it, and thrown out all of the toys they considered too violent or worldly for a growing child. The few toys left were the ones Randy never played with anyway.

The dormer window looked out onto a back alley. It provided a bleak view, in sharp contrast to the lush, well manicured front lawns facing Cambridge and Oxford streets.

The big Crucifix over Randy's bed gave him the spooks. It was a large, ceramic statue of Christ on the cross, the skin painted a pale yellow except where the spikes stuck out from the palms and feet. These areas were painted bright red, like the color of ketchup. Randy often imagined that he could see blood dripping out of the wounds. He would blink and the illusion would go away. The Savior's eyes looked sad and forlorn, more like a lonely puppy than the King of the Jews. The framed scroll of *1 Corinthians,* Chapter 13, on the wall beside it, spoke of love, but all Randy ever felt in this room was overwhelming oppression. It wanted to smother him, the room; it was evil. Sometimes, it actually seemed to get hard to breathe in here, like something was sucking the very life out of him.

The closet was the scariest place of all. It was long and narrow. The ceiling descended at an angle where it met the roof line. And it was dark. Randy didn't know what a black hole was, but if he had, he probably would have compared his closet to one. When Randy was bad, really bad, like if he got caught swearing, lying or stealing, his aunt or mother would lock him in the closet for hours on end, so he could talk to Jesus without any distractions. When the door shut and the world went black, Randy would kick and scream until there was nothing left inside. When they finally came back to let him out, they usually found him huddled in the corner asleep, his thumb in his mouth and his eyes red and puffy from crying. They would shake him awake and ask, "Are you going to be a good boy now, Randy? Huh? Did you tell Jesus you were sorry?" Randy would nod his head frantically in silence, too afraid to speak, terrified he would say the wrong thing and they would lock him up again.

R<small>ANDY DROPPED THE</small> girl off on Hastings Street, and headed home to his suite in Burnaby. He felt relieved and sick at the same time. His mouth was very dry. It was going to take at least a six pack to wash away the sour taste.

Despite Randy's big talk with his buddies, his sex life was nearly nonexistent. He had never had a steady girlfriend, and his only sexual release came from daily masturbation and the occasional prostitute, when he could afford one. The feeling after paying for sex was always anticlimactic and dirty. Randy would go home and shower with hot, hot water, scrubbing his skin vigorously over and over until long after the water ran cold. He would step out of the shower, feeling ashamed, his body covered in angry red welts. Unfortunately, guilt did not wash off with mere soap and water.

PAUL GREGORY GAVE the starter cord a tug. The motor sputtered, and then died. Paul adjusted the choke and pulled again. This time, the Lawnboy mower roared to life.

Paul lived on West Sixteenth Avenue in Point Grey, near the entrance to the university. Paul had bought the place two years ago, when he was tenured. It was a good size, Cape Cod with white, vinyl siding, louvered shutters and a shake roof. It sat on an oversize lot, which was to Paul's liking. There was room to breathe, but that also meant it required a lot of upkeep.

Paul started mowing the front yard first, weaving in and out of the hedge and shrubs. Then he worked his way down the side yard to the back.

When Paul finished cutting the grass, he went back into his two car garage to fetch the Weed Eater and a cold beer from the beer fridge.

"Phew!" Paul exclaimed as he wiped the sweat from his forehead with the bottom of his T-shirt. "Here's to summer!" He toasted the warm breeze and chugged down a third of the bottle in one gulp.

Paul loved the summer season, three months of freedom from the daily grind of teaching. A chance to spend lazy days at Wreck Beach, soaking up the sunshine and sipping cool margaritas served by bronzed maidens. Equally tanned fellows traipsed along the beach with Styrofoam coolers full of ice cold suds which they sold for a few bucks a can. Wreck Beach was the local nudie beach, clothes and bathing suits optional, but most people hung out there in the buff. And there were always people selling a wide variety of food from burgers to gourmet. Illicit drugs were also available, if you were into that scene. Wreck Beach in the summer, a Mecca for sun worshipers, crowded with people of all age groups. The gay crowd also had their own hang out by the log booms that demarked the edge of the industrial area to the south.

Paul unraveled the hundred foot extension cord. Somehow, it always managed to piss him off. No matter how carefully he coiled it up and tied it when he put it away, it always came out looking like Goedian's Knot.

"You piece of shit!" Paul swore at the cord as it resisted his efforts. "Damn it!" he hissed. Finally the last knot fell apart.

Paul plugged the cord into the exterior receptacle and strung it over to the hedge. Then he went back in the garage for the Weed Eater, brought it out and plugged it in. Before he hit the ON switch, Paul bent down and plucked a long strand of grass. He stuck it in his mouth and chewed on it. It made him look like some country bumpkin, right off the farm. And it reminded him of when he was a kid, growing up in Richmond. Soon he was daydreaming . . .

PAUL WAS ONLY ELEVEN years old again. He bent down and plucked a long blade of grass. He liked to roll them between his fingers and chew on the ends. It was another Indian summer, the third in a row, and the forecast, according to CFXM's morning news, was for more of the same with highs in the mid-seventies. Not too shabby for early October in the Pacific Northwest. Normally by now, it was socked in with heavy clouds and rain. Paul was on his way to visit Marty Vanderkoff, his second best friend after Billy Taylor, who was his absolute, number one best friend in the whole wide world.   Marty lived on a dairy farm on Steveston Highway.

Richmond was a major farming community, supplying the surrounding area with fresh vegetables and dairy products. Some of the lower lying areas also grew blueberries and cranberries. The rich, silt laden topsoil seemed to grow almost anything.

Paul turned south off Williams Road, onto Number Four Road, walking slowly past the Roberts' house, carefully inspecting the boarded over windows, peeling paint and wild overgrown yard. It used to be one of the nicest vegetable farms in all of Richmond, the pride of its former owner, Jack Roberts, who used to set up a stand on the side of the road, and sell fruit and fresh produce out of wooden bins. Most of his customers had been city folks from Vancouver. Now, there was no sign of life, only neglect. Marty once told Paul the place was haunted, but Paul knew that Marty was just full of poop.

Marty had told Paul that Jack's son, Stevie Roberts had come back from the war in 1945, half a deck short with a pair of built in binoculars for eyeballs that seemed to look right through you like x-ray vision. Apparently, the shell-shocked Stevie wasn't interested in farming, so he took up a job with the McKiver Brothers, driving a dump truck. They hauled gravel and topsoil for local builders.

Stevie didn't last long. He came in late and often smelled like the night before. Some days, he didn't bother to show up at all. They felt bad about it, the McKivers. They wanted to help the kid out, his being a veteran and all, but he was just too damn unreliable.

Stevie seemed to exist in his own little universe. He was on another planet, a different dimension. If you asked him to do something, he would look right through you with those eyes of his, and then walk away like he hadn't even heard you. He was kind of spooky, definitely a weirdo.

Stevie tried several other employers. Like the McKivers, most folks wanted to give the boy a break, but Stevie just couldn't hold down a job. He took to hanging around Kal's Pool and Billiards on Number Three Road. One day, in the middle of an important shot—they were playing pea pool with ten dollars riding in the pot—something snapped in Stevie's head. He started balling his eyes out and smacking the side of his head like it was a punching bag.

"No! No! I can't look. Please don't make me look! I don't want to see NO MORE!!!"

The hustlers and pool sharks laughed him clear out of Kal's. They didn't want some crazy, loony tune hanging around fucking up their game. Pool was serious business. It took concentration. Sometimes the afternoon pot got as high as a hundred bucks. Stevie was just a basket case anyway, no loss.

Stevie climbed into his Ford pickup, revved the motor into the red, popped the clutch and sprayed gravel so hard a stone smashed one of Kal's windows, landing in the middle of a snooker game.

"You stupid moron!" Kal Brown screamed from the sidewalk, shaking his fist at the cloud of dust. "I'll get you for that one, Roberts! You hear me?"

Stevie wasn't listening; he had other things on his mind. He pulled into the driveway of the family farm, made a brief stop at the woodshed, and then proceeded into the house where he methodically hacked his mother, brother and two sisters into pieces with a double bladed axe. The police found Stevie huddled in the corner of his bedroom. He was mewling like a frightened kitten, his shirt covered with dried gore. In the palm of each hand, they found one of Stevie's eyeballs. He didn't want to see no more, nope.

Jack Roberts died from a heart attack a few months later. The shock and grief must have been too much for him. Stevie is still alive somewhere, living in a nice padded cell, and the ghosts of his mother and siblings walk the farmhouse at night, restless, lost souls. Yes, that house was definitely haunted . . .

Marty's story had upset Paul so much, he began having recurring nightmares. He even started wetting the bed again. Marge Gregory noticed the puffy bags under her son's usually bright blue eyes. She took Paul into her arms, and asked him if something was bothering him. Paul shook his head at first, nothing was wrong, Mom; but, then the whole story spilled out like water from a busted dam.

"Oh, my poor baby! That Marty's been feeding you a crock, 'e 'as. That boy should be ashamed of himself, scaring you 'alf to death like that. Why I have a mind to—"

Marge then went on to explain the truth to Paul. Yes, Stevie Roberts had come back from the war with some problems, a lot of boys had, but they sent Stevie away to a good hospital. As for Molly Roberts and the kids, why they were alive and just fine, thank you. They had packed up years ago and moved to Kenora, Ontario where Molly's sister lived. The farm had become too much for them after Jack passed away from a heart attack in 1953, at least that much of Marty's story was true.

"Really, Mommy?" Paul asked.

"Would I lie to you, sweetheart?"

"No. I love you, Mommy."

"I love you too, son," Marge replied. She wiped the tears from his cheeks. "Here, blow your nose on this," she added, handing him a Kleenex.

"Thank you, Mommy. I feel much better now. Just wait 'till I get my hands on Marty!"

The next day, Paul confronted Marty. Paul's little fists were buckled up so tight the knuckles were white. "And that's the truth!" Paul sputtered through clenched teeth. "My Mommy told me so!"

Marty just stood there and shrugged. "Could be, I guess. I jus' told ya what my pa told me . . . Course he's about as nuts as ol' Stevie Roberts any day of the week."

Paul's anger subsided quickly. Everyone in Richmond knew how crazy Marty's dad was. They called him the Crazy Dutchman. He had crazy eyes too. Paul still remembered the day he and Marty sat in the barn, watching Frans Vanderkoff tinker with an old hay maker. He told the boys how he had been instrumental in bringing about the great stock market crash of '29 and how he was going to move to America to run for President once his term as Prime Minister was over. Then he was going to retire to the farm and build a big stone castle where he would entertain heads of state. People would come from all over the world to see his flower gardens.

"The Ministry of Tulips, boys! Think about it! Hail to the Ministry of Tulips! That's what I'm trying to tell you!"

The two boys just sat there and nodded their heads. Mr. Vanderkoff was way out there alright.

PAUL PUT THE blade of grass to his lips again and blew hard across it. The high pitched shriek sent a flock of angry crows scrambling skyward like a squadron of Spitfires. Paul blew again. He was practicing his duck call, not warning of incoming Stuka bombers. His dad had shown him how to hold the blade between his two thumbs. It made a loud squawk if you stretched it tight and blew just the right way.

When he got to the Vanderkoff place, Paul planned to help Marty out with his chores so they could finish up early and head down to the South Arm to play on the dike.

Paul took another glance at the Roberts house. It still gave him the heeby-geebys. He wouldn't set one foot in that creepy, old rat-hole for a whole dump truck full of his favorite chocolate bar. A glint of sunlight caught his eye, just a sparkle at the corner of his peripheral vision. The distraction came from the far side of the field adjacent to the Robert's house.

It was a short hop across the drainage ditch to the tall grasses on the other side. Paul almost stepped in a fresh cow pie. "Yuck!" The herd was over by the north fence, chewing their cuds and flicking flies off their rumps with their tails. "Nothing much dumber than a cow," Paul mused as he held up a loose strand of barb wire and crawled under the fence. It was a good thing it wasn't electrified. Paul had gotten a good zap from one of the Vanderkoff's fences once, and he didn't cherish the thought of a repeat performance. It had made his teeth tingle and he felt like he was going to puke, but after a few minutes all he had was a pounding headache.

Paul spit out the blade of grass and walked across the field towards the shiny thing. Sapling alders and tall thistles, real mean-looking ones, with long pointy prickles hid most of it from view. Now that he was closer, Paul could see that it was some kind of a big box.

Paul wasn't in the mood to get pricked by those mean old thistles, no way Jose, so he looked about for a stick or something to knock them back with. He found a long lump buried in the grass. He had to give it one heck of a yank to pull it free. It was one of the Roberts old pea stakes, still tangled up in a long strand of binder twine. Paul removed the string. It came off easily it was so rotten, but the wood underneath seemed solid enough. He poked it between the bottom two strands of barb wire running the length of the perimeter fence. With a look of intense concentration on his freckled young face and his tongue hanging off to the side, Paul began the task of clearing away the foliage.

The thistles were easy, a piece of cake. One good swat and they fell over in a heap. The half inch thick alders were a lot tougher though. They kept bouncing back up like a punch drunk boxer who won't stay down for the count, even though the fight is over. Paul leaned into the fence as far as he could without impaling himself on the barb wire. His mom would crown him if he ripped his brand new bomber jacket. He put both hands on the stick and slashed away with all eighty pounds of his might. The effort caused him to grunt like when he had to take a mean dump but nothing would come out. Constipation, his mom called it. With a final parlay that would have made Zorro proud, Paul beat back the last of the defenders. Ha, now I know what it is, he thought, pleased by the discovery. "It's a 'fridgerator."

The old Iceman chest freezer didn't seem so shiny now that it had been stripped of its camouflage. In fact the white, baked enamel finish had a dull texture like the ice at a hockey game at the end of a period, before the zamboni has a chance to gloss it over again. Brown patches of surface rust had peeled back the finish in several small patches, and there was a big dent in the lid with a long gash in the center where the insulation poked through the sheet metal like pink moss. Looks like an axe hole, Paul thought. He shimmied under the fence for a closer look.

Wonder what's in there? Paul gave the lid a tug. It didn't budge. There might be something bad in there. He reconsidered his options. Maybe I should leave it alone, he finally decided. It sure looks like an axe hole. Then it dawned on him, maybe Marty was right after all. Paul took a step back to think about this. There could be a dead body in there or a horrible monster just waiting to grab him and drag him inside.

"Ah, don't be silly," Paul chided himself out loud. He gave the lid another pull. "There ain't no such things as monsters." I hope. This time the lid came up with a squeak, groaning on its rusty hinges.

"Pheeew!" Paul turned his head in disgust as the stale, musky air hit his nostrils. "This sucker sure stinks!"

The freezer was completely empty, except for an inch or so of slimy green water that had accumulated over the years.

"Sure wouldn't want to get trapped in there and get fixated." His mom and dad had warned him about the dangers of abandoned refrigerators and freezers, and how little children who didn't know any better could get trapped inside and die. Paul pictured someone opening the freezer and finding him there, lifeless eyes staring at nothing, his skin blue like the color of the veins on Mrs. Oliver's legs. He had asked his mom why Mrs. Oliver had those blue things on her legs and his mom had told him. They were varicose veins.

Every time a new word came up, Paul's mom got out the dictionary and read Paul the word, explained what and where it was derived from, and then gave him all of its meanings. "Some words though," she said, "Aren't in the dictionary. Like the cuss words."

Paul knew about cuss words. He had watched his daddy hit his finger with a hammer while trying to drive a nail. His daddy had called the hammer a 'cocksucker.' But when Paul had gotten mad at his dog, Mandy, and called her a 'cocksucker,' his mother had dragged him into the bathroom, and put a bar of soap in his mouth, which didn't seem fair. Mommy never washed daddy's mouth out with soap and he said cuss words too. The soap had tasted bad, worst than broccoli and that was about as bad as it gets. Now Paul only used cuss words when he was absolutely sure his mother wasn't listening.

Paul couldn't figure out how there could be no air in the freezer, especially since it had a big hole in its lid. Axe hole? One thing was for sure though, he wasn't going to test fate just to prove his parents wrong. "I don't want to be a goner." Paul muttered.

He let the lid slam shut. Suddenly the idea of playing around with an old piece of junk seemed rather silly. A waste of time, and time was precious even when you're a kid and you've got all the time in the world.

Paul crawled under the fence and ran back across the field to the road. Marty was waiting and the days were already getting shorter.

Chapter 5

IT WAS A spectacular fire. The old wood framed building was tinder dry and the insides of the walls and attic were full of dust. By the time the Burnaby Fire Department arrived, the roof had exploded sending a huge orange fireball and thick black smoke spiraling into the night. The heat was intense. The firemen had to hose down the walls and shingles of two neighboring houses, to prevent them from catching fire too.

Inside the burning home, a crucifix blackened as the flames licked up the wall where it was hanging. The Savior looked like He was crying as the paint melted off of the ceramic statue and ran down His cheeks like wax on a candle. On the same wall, a scroll of *1 Corinthians,* Chapter 13, browned, blackened, then disintegrated in the heat of the burning.

The upper story collapsed. The interior was now an inferno, the inside of a blast furnace.

All that remained when Police and Fire inspectors sifted through the debris the following morning, was a charred, gutted shell with bits of barely recognizable furniture, appliances and other household items sticking out here and there, from piles of ash that were still smoking. A poignant image: a single fluffy blue slipper sat on the lawn; it had survived what its owner had not.

The cause of the fire was difficult to pinpoint conclusively. After a painstaking investigation, always intense when there's a fatality involved, the Fire Commissioner attributed it to a probable short circuit in the electrical system, the favorite catch-all that meant, who knows? Most of the older homes in the city had outdated and substandard electrical services. The only time city hall could force a homeowner to upgrade the electrical, was if the homeowner applied for a building permit for a major renovation or addition to the structure.

The shriveled, charred remains of flesh and bone had to be identified from dental records.

The Vancouver Sun, Vancouver, B.C.

Monday, February 4th, 1980

TWELVE-YEAR-OLD SURVIVES KILLER FIRE

A twelve-year-old boy escaped a spectacular fire that devastated a home in the forty-two hundred block of Cambridge Street in Burnaby last night.

Fire officials were summoned to the scene at 11:45 P.M., after a neighbor noticed smoke pouring from the eaves of the older, two-storey home. By the time firefighters arrived to combat the blaze, the building was beyond saving. Firemen focused their attention on saving the two adjacent homes.

The boy was found in his night clothes on the front lawn. Fire officials are puzzled as to how the boy managed to make it out of the inferno which claimed the lives of two adult occupants, believed to be the boy's mother and aunt. It appears the adults were asleep when the fire started and that they probably died of smoke inhalation. The names of the victims are being withheld pending notification of kin. A full investigation into the blaze has been ordered by the fire commissioner.

EXCERPT from the journal of Paul Gregory, PhD:

One of the most colorful characters in the saga of the lost mine, was a tough, grizzled old prospector named Robert Allan Brown, who was more commonly referred to as Volcanic Brown.

Brown was a dabbler in many trades. During his long life, he tried sailing, logging, railroad building, prospecting, mining and developing. He was also an herbalist and he practiced many home remedies, such as bleeding himself regularly, claiming that this kept him in good health. Brown prospected the Maritimes, led a logging strike in Ontario, found a rich gold claim near the Lake of the Woods, which he later covered up due to a dispute between the provincial governments of Ontario and Manitoba over jurisdiction, and he followed the Canadian Pacific Railway west on its long trek to the Pacific, prospecting both sides of the tracks as he went.

Brown earned his nickname, Volcanic, in 1885, when he found a mountain near the town of Grand Forks, capped with red iron, a sign of great mineral wealth to an experienced miner. Brown dubbed his claim 'Volcanic,' and founded Volcanic City nearby, a place from which to process and distribute the thousands of tons of ore that Brown envisioned his mountain producing. Brown predicted that Volcanic City would become a great metropolis with hundreds of smelters and at least six railroads. With his fantastic riches, Brown planned to do away with banks and churches. In their place, he proposed magnificent centers dedicated to the study of science. The ever generous utopian would also share his fortune with the masses, bringing an end to hunger and poverty.

The Oliver Mining and Smelting Company incorporated with assets of over twenty million dollars, most of the money coming from American investors, was formed. Brown was one of the major shareholders. Unfortunately for all concerned, Volcanic Mountain was a total dud. The dream of Volcanic City fizzled before the cornerstones were even laid. Brown lost sixty-five thousand dollars of his own money in the fiasco, but he was always an optimist and he took the setback in stride. The new nickname stuck with him for the rest of his life.

Volcanic Brown heard a rumor about an Indian claiming to have stumbled across a mountain of copper on a hunting trip near Princeton. Brown decided to check out the story and the Indian was telling the truth. Brown quickly staked a claim and other prospectors followed suit. Brown named his claim, 'Sunset Claim.' He told reporters, "The Sunset beats anything I ever saw. The Sunset today is the greatest property in the world!"

This time history proved Brown correct. Copper Mountain, as it became known, was one of the greatest copper mines in the world, and continued yielding high-grade ore on a grand scale until it was closed in 1957. Brown's success was short lived though. He was forced to sell his claim in the mine for only forty-five thousand dollars, a small percentage of its true value. Apparently Brown had some legal problems to clear up, but he managed to keep enough money to have some false teeth made out of solid gold!

The newspapers of May, 1925, tell of one of Brown's more notorious misadventures.

It had begun two years earlier when a World War I veteran named Bill Brown, who was no relation to Volcanic, moved to Grand Forks. Bill Brown built himself a cabin next to Volcanic Brown. The mental scars of Bill Brown's tour of duty in France were obvious to everyone; he was a bit crazy and very paranoid.

On the evening of May 9, 1925, Bill Brown and his wife were returning home from town in their buggy. As they passed Lynch Creek, where Bill Brown had recently purchased some property from Carl Jepson, Bill Brown flew into a violent rage. A cabin on the property which Bill Brown had assumed went along with the deal had been removed by Jepson without Bill Brown's knowledge. Bill Brown figured he had been swindled. The couple then stopped at the Cooper house, some friends of theirs, to pick up their children. Bill Brown threatened Jepson's life in front of his wife and Mrs. Cooper. Without permission, he removed a rifle and some shells from the Cooper home.

As soon as Bill Brown left, dragging his helpless wife with him, Mrs. Cooper ran to a neighbor's house to call the police.

The Browns returned home to their cabin where an altercation broke out between Bill, who was still in a foul mood, his stepson, Danny and one of Danny's friends. Mike Andersoff, the other boy's father, heard the ruckus and came over to see what was going on. He took one look at Bill Brown and decided that the man was insane and dangerous. Andersoff sent the two boys over to Volcanic Brown's place and told them to stay there until Bill had cooled down.

But Bill didn't cool down. At about 10:00 p.m., he paid a visit to Volcanic Brown's house, carrying a big club and acting crazy as could be. Volcanic Brown heard Bill Brown's approach and went outside to talk to the troublemaker. Without warning, Bill Brown struck Volcanic Brown across the side of his head with the club, inflicting a deep flesh wound.

Mike Andersoff and two other men arrived at the scene. Andersoff grabbed Bill Brown from behind and held him until Volcanic Brown could crawl to the safety of his cabin. Unfortunately, the two men accompanying Andersoff refused to help restrain Bill Brown. They did not want to get involved in the dispute.

Bill Brown then went berserk, broke Andersoff's hold and charged the cabin, trying to break down the door with his club. The door didn't budge, so Bill Brown vented his fury on one of Volcanic Brown's windows.

Volcanic Brown had come around sufficiently to pick up and load his .30.30 Winchester rifle. He leveled it at the window and ordered Bill Brown to back off and leave him alone. Bill Brown responded by assaulting a second window. Volcanic Brown decided to pull the trigger. The slug caught Bill Brown in the heart and killed him instantly.

Volcanic Brown was detained by the police while they investigated the shooting. A short inquest was held. It found that the shooting had been in self defense.

"I hated to do it," testified Volcanic Brown. "We had been good friends, but the man was crazy, he had a knife in his possession and I knew if I did not get him first, he would get us, so I fired. I make no bones about it."

After a quick review by the Attorney General, Volcanic Brown was released. The next summer, he left Grand Forks for good and set out on the quest that would obsess him for the remainder of his life, the search for Slumach's gold.

Chapter 6

Bev boarded the Skytrain at the Victoria Street Station. She was going to New Westminster to meet Fran O'Day, an old school chum from Yakima. The double doors opened automatically with a gentle swoosh. The red and blue trimmed car was almost empty, the afternoon rush still two hours away. Bev settled into one of the bright vinyl covered seats. A chime sounded a warning and the doors slid shut.

The four car train pulled away from the elevated station with the whine of electric engines shifting gears. It accelerated quickly, but it was a smooth ride. There were no drivers on board, the trains are operated by a central computer in Burnaby, and it is a completely automated system.

"The next stop . . . is Broadway," a female, computer voice announced in its flat, monotone sing song. The air brakes came on with a squeal.

Bev, like most passengers, had hated that voice at first, it was so artificial and lifeless, but now, a veteran of quite a few trips, she simply blocked it out of her consciousness.

Another traveler got into Bev's car, a fat man with bowed

legs. He waddled down the aisle and sat down directly across from her, his huge fanny covering an entire seat designed for two.

The doors closed with another swoosh. The train got underway again, Bev's head began to bob back and forth, the Skytrain always made her sleepy. Just like the clickety-click-clickety-click of passenger trains of old, there was something hypnotic about the monotonous whine of the electric engines and the sway of the coach from side to side.

THE WHITE CADILLAC DeVille floated down Interstate 90 like a glider on wheels. George Dayton was taking the family to Spokane for the spring carney. Bev, Luke and Matthew sat in the back, the two boys fighting over how many red or green cars had gone by going the other way. Luke was counting reds and Matthew, greens. Bev sat in the middle, a kind of buffer zone between the two boys by order of the big boss up front. Bev had tried to count blue cars too, but the boys had just ignored her, so she gave up. It's a silly game anyway, she thought, who cares? Bev just sat there with Cathy on her knee, her and the doll chatting up a storm in Bev's imagination. Boys can be so immature sometimes, right Cathy?

"That wasn't green, it was blue!" protested Luke.
"Wus too!
"Are you color blind or something?"
"No, you're the one who needs glasses." Matthew retaliated.
"Do not!"
"Do to!"
"No way..." Bev got crushed under the onslaught of squirming flesh, fists and flying elbows. A stray knuckle caught her near the right eye.

SLUMACH – THE LOST MINE

"Daddy, daddy!" Bev screamed, "They're hurting me!" She started to cry.

"Cut it out back there, RIGHT NOW!" Big George warned. His angry eyes burned from the rearview mirror. "Or I'll have to pull over and give your hides a good tanning." George turned his head to look at them directly. "You hear me?"

"Yes, sir!" the boys replied.

George's stern warnings usually kept the peace for a few miles. Inevitably, he would have to pull the Caddy over sooner or later and give the boys a couple of good wallops just to show them he meant business.

They arrived in Spokane shortly before noon, and stopped at Marie's brother's place for brunch and a short visit. The kids protested sullenly, they were restless, anxious to get to the carnival.

Rolf Hennerman lived in a two bedroom apartment overlooking the Spokane River. He taught English and Drama at Theodore Burns Junior High School. He was a bachelor even though he was already in his mid thirties. George thought secretly that Rolf looked a little too feminine to be interested in women. In fact, George wouldn't have been the least bit surprised to learn that Rolf went the *other way*. Rolf's roommate, some guy named Carl, was never around when the family visited. Convenient, thought George, Carl's probably went the *other way* too. George would have bet money that Rolf and Carl didn't really need a two bedroom suite. That thought revolted George. He sure wouldn't want a pansy like Rolf teaching his boys.

"Oh, little Bevy! Aren't you just adorable! Come and give your uncle Rolfie a great big hug and kiss." Bev hesitated then finally obliged him, looking like she didn't quite know what to make of the situation. "And boys! My have you grown! Pretty soon you'll be just as big and strong as your daddy." George's neck hairs bristled as Rolf gave him a dead fish handshake. "My, my my..." Luke and Matthew both turned their heads in disgust as Rolf gave them each a wet kiss on the cheek. He patted the top of their heads like they were a couple of cute little puppy dogs. Yuck, they both thought in unison as they wiped their cheeks with the sleeves of their jackets. They liked to visit Uncle Rolf about as much as Dr. Carlin, the family dentist. At least Dr. Carlin didn't kiss them.

"Marie, darling! It's so good to see you!" Rolf gave his sister a hug and a peck on the cheek. "I've got so many marvelous things to tell you, well, you just won't believe it! I've been..."

George sat in silence and listened to them gab. A real hen party, he smirked to himself.

Brunch consisted of poached egg cups with a light garnish, fluffy pancakes, raisin bread toast, and mint tea, and then for desert, butterscotch pudding. The dessert the kids didn't mind; they all asked for seconds. Rolf would have complied if Marie had not intervened—the kids would be having more than their fair share of sweets at the fair—she didn't want them getting carsick on the trip home.

"Have you heard the one about, what do you call a woman without an asshole?" Rolf asked while the kids were playing in the next room.

George smirked again, almost laughing out loud. He knew what you would call a queer without one, frustrated.

"I give up, what?" Marie asked.

"Single! Hee, hee, hee," Rolf giggled. "Isn't that rich? Why I tell you..." He let his wrists fall forward in a gesture that never failed to irritate George.

George finished the last of the hard pear cider. He had been nursing it for almost an hour. He would have preferred a cold

SLUMACH – THE LOST MINE

beer, but Rolf didn't have any. That figured. It was time to go. "Well, I hate to break up this reunion," George said flatly. "But its one-thirty and the kids are dying to get to the fair." He had almost slipped and said, "Dying to get out of here."

"I'm gonna ride on the roller coaster!" Matthew added.

"And the Salt and Pepper!" Luke continued.

"I wanna see the clowns!" Bev got her two-cents' worth in.

Let's get the fuck out of here! George thought. He got up from the table and grabbed his brown leather bomber jacket from the back of the chair.

"Oh! I really wish you didn't have to run off like this," Rolf fussed, close to tears. "You will come again soon, won't you?"

"Of course we will." Marie reassured him.

"I hope so," Rolf sniffed.

Marie gave him a hug. "I promise. Okay?"

George looked up at the ceiling and whistled softly. Don't hold your breath, Rolfie, my boy.

George finally mumbled a barely audible, "See you," when they were already out in the hallway.

"Bye. Love you!" Rolf blew them a kiss as the elevator doors closed, cutting their parting short.

Marie turned and gave George a sharp look that meant, "Why couldn't you have been nicer to my brother?" George just shrugged and pushed "M" for the Main Floor.

THE CARNIVAL WAS in full swing when the Dayton's finally arrived; the promenade crowded with merry fairgoers, the barkers shouting to be heard above the din of the games and the chatter.

"Step right up folks! Win a teddy for the little lady," one of the barkers shouted as the Dayton family walked by. George spent five bucks to win Bev a black-and-white teddy bear.

Balloons of all colors, shapes and sizes floated above the heads of wide-eyed children, the air alive with the smell of hot dogs, hamburgers, candy apples and fresh corn-on-the-cob.

The kids wanted some pink candy floss. The vendor smiled as they watched her twirl the cotton candy cones around the metal canister, the fluffy threads of sweet fiber growing with each revolution.

"There you go," the candy floss lady said, as she handed them each a cone. "That'll be a buck twenty please." Marie paid her, and then they headed over to the rides.

George took the boys on the Mad Mouse. Marie and Bev settled for a spin in the Cup-n-Saucer. Bev had taken one look at the miniature roller coaster and shaken her head violently, clutching both Cathy and the new teddy a little tighter. "Unugh. No!" Bev had squeaked before her thumb found her mouth.

The two cars hit head on. George and Marie laughed at the tragedy. Luke and Matthew were driving bumper cars, wreaking havoc on the tiny court. Bev had cried when the ticket vendor informed her that she was too little. There was a cartoon character with hands to show how tall you had to be, by the ticket booth window. Children who were too short were not allowed on the bumper cars. Marie assured Bev that she would almost certainly be big enough to drive the cars next year.

"I will?" Bev's face brightened noticeably.

"Yes, dear. Come here, let me wipe your face." Bev still had candy floss all over her cheeks. She made her usual faces as Marie licked the corner of a handkerchief and scrubbed Bev's face like she was trying to peal the skin off.

"Oh well, I guess that's good enough. I'll have to give you a bath when we get home."

Then Bev and her parents stood there, watching the boys. The expressions on their faces were priceless. Marie snapped a few pictures with her Kodak Instamatic.

Luke got his car going round and round in circles, the sparks flying in all directions from the pole above. He couldn't seem to figure out how to straighten out his wheels until one of the other cars broadsided him, correcting his trajectory, his head thrown back and forth like it was on a Slinky. George laughed until the tears ran down his cheeks. "Reminds me of Seattle at rush hour!" he snorted, "The future safe drivers of America." He looked to one side, then the other. Then he spun around in a complete circle—

"Hey! Where's Bev?"

"Huh? Well, I don't know," Marie replied, a worried look washing the humor from her face. "She was here just a second ago."

"Wait here and keep an eye on the boys," George commanded. He was suddenly feeling sick to his stomach. "I'll go and look for her. She couldn't have gone very far."

EXCERPT, from the journal of Paul Gregory, PhD:

Every summer Volcanic Brown, now in his eighties but tough as ever, armed with a copy of Jackson's famous letter, journeyed deep into the headwaters of Pitt Lake to search for the lost mine.

In the autumn of 1926, Volcanic Brown got trapped in a blizzard and suffered severe frostbite. He had to retreat to lower ground to recover. Fearful of gangrene, he amputated one of his toes and trimmed the flesh from two others using only his hunting knife, a feat in itself since he had no anesthetic or pain killers. A search party organized by Constable Spud Murphy of the RCMP found Volcanic Brown hobbling back towards civilization, his foot bundled in a makeshift bandage. Undaunted by the narrow escape, Volcanic Brown continued his meticulous search with renewed vigor every summer thereafter.

In 1931, he failed to return on schedule to the Alvin Fish Hatchery, his usual starting and rendezvous point. Constable Murphy once again rounded up a search party. Apparently, the now eighty-eight year old Volcanic Brown was last seen on August 17th by another prospector returning from the bush. He had sold Volcanic Brown some unused rice and beans from his pack. Then, before they parted company, he had wished the old prospector good luck on his journey.

The search for Volcanic Brown lasted twenty-seven days and became a grueling trial of stamina and courage for the men involved. Many times the hardships of the trek nearly forced the rescuers to give up. Over some of the most rugged terrain in the world, they combed the mountains, battling freezing snowstorms and navigating treacherous glaciers. One of the searchers lost thirteen pounds during the ordeal. They found Volcanic Brown's last camp on the edge of Stave Glacier. A pup tent that had collapsed in a storm, some cooking gear, a notepad with a few hand written herbal cures jotted down in it, a loaded shotgun, and a fruit jar containing eleven ounces of raw tracer gold. Neither Volcanic Brown nor his body were ever found.

Chapter 7

KEVIN UNLOCKED THE door to his two-door garage and opened it. He switched on the overhead fluorescent lights. The inside of the garage was neat and tidy, everything in is allocated place. Kevin knew where every tool and spare part was kept, and God help anybody who happened to be around if Kevin discovered something missing or misplaced.

A long bench spanned the entire length of the garage on one wall. It had a sheet-metal top. Mounted on it were several vices and a small double headed grinder. More tools hung from hooks on the pegboard wall above the bench.

The opposite wall had two large windows covered in heavy steel mesh. Kevin didn't want anyone breaking in and ripping him off.

The empty bay below the windows had a grease pit for doing oil changes and other under-carriage work. When it wasn't in use, as was the case now, Kevin kept it covered with loose two-by-twelve planks.

Kevin opened several drawers on his red tool dolly, took out a flathead screwdriver, a crescent wrench, a quarter-inch ratchet and a half-inch hex socket. There was a late model Camero parked in the second bay next to the work bench. It belonged to one of Kevin's buddies, Larry Pepin. The fuel pump was toast and Kevin had agreed to throw in a decent used one for fifty bucks plus a twenty-four pack of cold brewskies.

Kevin undid the hose clamp on the fuel intake and popped off the fuel line. The outtake was quarter-inch copper pipe with compression fittings. Kevin loosened the fittings with a crescent wrench and bent back the line, careful not to crimp it. Now he concentrated on the pump itself.

Kevin put a socket on one of the bolts holding the pump to the body of the motor and gave it a twist. The bolt was stiff, it didn't budge one iota. Kevin gave it a shot of WD40, placed both hands on the ratchet, and pulled harder.

"Com'on, you prick!" He put his body weight into it.

"Squeeeeak, squeeeeak..." the bolt squealed as it turned on rusty threads.

KEVIN GREW UP in Surrey where his parents owned a wrecking yard. His father, John Macarthur, whistled through two fingers, "T'weet . . . t'weet," summoning Duke, a two-year-old black lab. "Com'on, boy!" John clapped his hands.

Duke ran up, his tail wagging happily. He loved to go for a ride. He jumped up onto the tow truck and took his favorite spot on the low metal tool box, right behind the rear window of the cab.

The truck's starter chug chugged the flywheel around, grinding a bit, and then disengaged with an accelerated whine. "Gonna have to get that cocksucker rebuilt one of these days," John commented. He pushed the starter button again. The engine sputtered feebly then died. "Com'on baby!" John coaxed the aging vehicle, a little more choke and this time the motor sputtered, coughed three or four times, and then roared to life. "That a girl!"

Young Kevin Macarthur sat beside his father in the cab, feeling smug and rather important. He enjoyed these outings with his father, especially when his younger siblings were not included. They were watching from the doorway of the house, looking rather sad and dejected. Tough luck, Kevin stuck his tongue out at them as the truck lurched into gear. The clutch was going too. John sighed and bypassed second, the long stick shift rattling back and forth from the vibrations. I'm going to have to replace that sucker too, one of these days, he thought absently. John and Kevin were taking a set of truck rims over to John's brother.

Derrick Macarthur owned a small acreage near Ladner. It had a rumbling old rancher with aluminum siding, the roof covered in moss, a large unused chicken coop that still stunk to high heaven and a red cow barn which doubled as a garage. Derrick lived with his only child, Leonard. Derrick's wife, Joyce, had died in a car accident when Leonard was only a baby. One Saturday morning, she had jumped in her car and sped off to Joan's Market, only about a mile or so down the road. All she wanted was a pack of smokes. She was having a really bad nicotine fit. No one ever knew why she lost control of the car and hit a power pole. The road was straight, the weather had been fine and Joyce was not a drinker. Sometimes shit happens.

Derrick had his share of live-ins since then, but none of them lasted long Derrick was not a patient man. He had a mean temper when somebody or something pissed him off, and it didn't take much to piss off Derrick. He had a very short fuse.

There was an immense lawn on the property, over an acre in total. Derrick had one of those lawn mowers you rode like a go-cart. Kevin thought it was cool. He wished his uncle Derrick would let him ride it sometime, but Kevin didn't have the nerve to come right out and ask him. His uncle was not a patient man, maybe he would get mad.

"Hiya, Cous." Lenny greeted Kevin as he hopped down from the cab. "How are things?" The two boys were almost the same age, Kevin being just ten months younger than Lenny, and they got along famously.

"Can't complain I guess," Kevin replied. "Now that school's out for the summer."

"Yeah!" Lenny paused and looked a little sheepish. "Did you pass?"

"Of course. And you?"

"Nah, I failed math and English. Now I gotta do fourth grade all over again."

"Sorry Cous, what a drag." Lenny had already failed grade two.

"School sucks."

"You got that right. School sucks the big one."

Lenny took off towards the scrub surrounding the south side of the property. "Com'on, Kev. Let's go play!"

"Sure!" Kevin replied, running to catch up. "Whatta ya wanna do?"

"Let's play hide and seek."

"Yer on, numb nuts!"

Kevin raced after his cousin. John and Derrick were sitting in the front yard in a ratty pair of lawn chairs, sucking back some moonshine and smoking their pipes. Derrick had a still in the barn. "Be back here in an hour, max," John called after Kevin, before he got back to reminiscing about the good old days with Derrick.

The boys flipped a nickel for who's its, Lenny lost. Kevin ran deeper into the bush while Lenny hid his eyes against the trunk of a maple, "1 . . . 2 . . . 3."

Where to hide? Kevin thought as he skirted some brambles. He couldn't see any good looking spots, what to do? He ran on through the scrub forest, searching, ". . . 38 . . . 39," Len counted on, time was running out.

A rotten stump caught Kevin's eye, it would have to do, he squeezed in behind it and crouched down low like he was going to relieve himself number two, "98 . . . 99 . . . 100! Here I come, ready or not!"

Lenny soon came traipsing through the alders, his head bobbing back and forth, inspecting the landscape carefully for any sign of prey. "Hey, Kevie. Come out, come out, where ever you are!" Lenny broke into the clearing on the other side of the stump. "I spy with my little eye . . ."

Kevin leaned back as far as he could to avoid detection. Shit, Leonard had spotted him, now it was his turn to be it, but wait? Lenny was shouting something at the top of his lungs and waving his arms frantically. Kevin couldn't quite make out what he was saying, was it "trees" or "please," but that didn't make sense, maybe it was "squeeze" or "bees?" Suddenly it felt like he'd rammed the back of his neck against some nasty prickles. Kevin jumped up in a hurry, only it didn't feel like just a prick, it hurt like Hell! His neck was on fire, the pain white hot, burning down his back. Now, he could see them buzzing around his head like tiny dive bombers—Len was gone, he had split the scene in a big hurry—Kevin's eyes opened wide and he screamed, the full realization finally dawning on him.

"BEES!!!" That was what Lenny had been yelling.

Suddenly they were everywhere, not bees, but wasps, yellow jackets, those mean ones with long bodies and yellow and black stripes. They tangled themselves in Kevin's hair, stinging his scalp. They crawled up his sleeves and pant legs, dangerous territory, and because they were wasps and not honey bees, each one could sting several times in a row. Kevin ran from his hiding place, down the bank and onto the gravel road. His arms were wind-milling like a couple of propellers as he streaked forward, trying to knock the withering mass off of his body. Kevin had never run so fast in all of his life, he might have broken a world record for the hundred yard dash, but no one was timing him. He looked like he was doing some weird ritual dance, shrieking irrationally at the top of his lungs and giving each leg a quick shake in turn, trying to dislodge a wasp that was making a lunar landscape out of his thigh. Another wasp set down on Kevin's cheek and stung him just under the left eye then it crawled up his nose, but got stuck, its angry stinger slashing harmlessly at the air until it got its lower segment turned around enough to plant its stinger on the tip of Kevin's nose. Lower down, a wasp made its way under Kevin's jockey shorts, the soft flesh of his buttocks made an easy target. "Ow! Ow!! OOWWW!!!" Kevin howled as the needlelike stinger inflicted its pain three times in quick succession.

There was no logical plan or direction to Kevin's flight. He was on autopilot, running for the sake of running. One thing was sure, he couldn't out run them, bees and wasps can fly at over thirty miles an hour. The only hope remaining in Kevin's sanity or lack of it, was water, he had to find some water, a ditch, a pool, even a big puddle would do—just something he could jump into and rid himself of this unwanted living jacket.

About half a mile up the road, Kevin came across a farmer watering flower beds in front of his house with a garden hose. Water! Kevin cut across the empty drainage ditch onto the man's property, the farmer looked up at him puzzled, Kevin was quite a sight. Kevin almost stumbled into a row of hives, the farmer was a bee keeper and he had about a dozen wooden hives on his front lawn. This new horror seemed too much to bear. In his irrational state, Kevin was convinced that the farmer's honey bees would now swarm out of their nests too and join the assault on his poor, battered body. The detour around the hives took another fifty yard dash.

The old farmer looked at Kevin and frowned, the kid was hysterical, moaning something about water, over and over. The farmer grabbed Kevin by the collar and beat the few remaining wasps off of Kevin with his huge calloused hand. Most of the nest had given up the chase long ago, only Kevin had been to far gone to realize this. Just then, the cavalry showed up, Len had run home for help, the tow truck appeared in the driveway, Derrick and Lenny both in the cab with John, who thanked the farmer for his assistance, then escorted Kevin back to the truck. Duke hung his head over the tailgate and barked frantically like he knew that something was wrong. John had to give Kevin a good smack across the side of the head to settle him down. He was still hysterical, sobbing in between screams. John felt sorry for his son. Kevin truly looked like Hell. There were red welts all over his face, his left eye had swollen shut, and his nose looked as big and red as a clown's.

"Com'on, son," John said, with more compassion than was usual. "Let's get ya home. Your mom'll fix you up, good as new!"

They arrived home in Surrey about three-quarters of an hour later. Cloe took one look at her distraught son, then ran to the bathroom to draw him a hot Epsom salt bath, and came back carrying a bottle of Calamine Lotion. Kevin felt a little better after the soothing water drew some of the fire from the bites, but the venom caused him to throw up most of the night.

The worst part about healing was the endless days and nights of itching that followed. It was worse than the chicken pox which Kevin had had two winters before. Cloe made up an ointment based on corn starch and baking soda, which seemed to help some, and the bottle of Calamine was now nearly empty. Every night before he went to bed, Kevin would smear his body from head to foot with ointment and lotion. He looked like a strange albino warrior.

Kevin's wounds healed, but his fear of the tiny creatures that had inflicted them would haunt him for the rest of his life.

THE ENCOUNTER WAS brief, it only lasted a couple of minutes, but Bev had nightmares about it for years after.

The clown was tall and skinny as a lamp post. He had a sad sack face topped with stringy, orange hair that looked like a dyed rag mop. An oversized, polka-dotted bow-tie highlighted the white, tuxedo shirt, and a pair of bright red, fireman's suspenders held up the baggy trousers. His shiny, black shoes looked to be about ten sizes too big. He was smoking a big cigar, blowing smoke rings through smoke rings.

"Hello, little girl," he said when he saw Beverly. "What's your name? My name is Bobo. What a cute little doll you have. Will you tell me her name too?"

Bev kept her thumb in her mouth and didn't answer. One, she wasn't supposed to talk to strangers, her mom and dad had made that very clear to her; and two, clowns were supposed to be funny. They did silly things that made people laugh. And clowns loved little children. After all, what good was a clown without children? Bev was shy, but that wasn't what she was feeling now. No, she knew instinctively that something was wrong with this particular clown. He felt rotten somehow. Like a smell, but only a feeling instead. There was no way for Bev to express these feelings in words because they were beyond a five-year-old's vocabulary.

Bobo the clown reminded Bev of the time she had pulled a quart of milk out of the refrigerator, took a sip, and nearly puked. Marie had explained to her that the milk had turned bad: it was sour, spoiled. Or like the sweet smell of sickness and death hiding under the clean antiseptic smell of the Yakima Hospital where Bev had gone with her family to visit grandpa Dayton, who was dying of lung cancer. Or the time that Teddy Dayton, George's second cousin, had shot a doe and hung it up in their garage to cure. Either Teddy had forgotten about it altogether or he just never got around to butchering it, because when Matthew and Bev had gone into the shed to take a look, and Matthew had poked the carcass with the end of a rake handle, a stream of maggots had spilled out of the decomposing belly in a putrid gush. Both Matthew and Bev had up-chucked their Spaghetti'Os, right there on the garage's dirt floor.

This clown smelled rotten like he had spoiled too, only it wasn't Bev's nose that told her this, it was something deeper. A grownup could have provided her with a few descriptive words: intuition, vibes, ESP. All that Bev knew right now was she was scared, really scared.

"What's the matter little girl? The cat got your tongue? Are you dumb or something? Hmmmm?"

Bev shook her head, her thumb still planted firmly behind her front teeth.

"Well come over here then, you can sit on Bobo's knee. Would you like to hear a funny story? Hmmm?"

Bev wasn't falling for his bull in the least. She started to back cautiously away from him towards the tent flap, gauging the distance carefully, her wide eyes never leaving Bobo for a split second.

"Hey! Where are you going little lady? Bobo won't hurt you. He's got something he wants to show you, something nice." The clown started tugging at his suspenders.

Bev turned and bolted like the wind. George found her in the Lost and Found booth, crying for her mommy and daddy like there was no tomorrow. She never told anyone about the clown, that day or ever, which was a good thing for Bobo, George would have made dog meat out of him in about two seconds flat.

THE SKYTRAIN HUMMED on monotonously, "The next station is Twenty-Second Street."

Bev opened her eyes. There was that voice again. Only one more station to go, she thought, glad to be getting off soon.

They were floating high above suburbia. She could see the Fraser River, look down into the cluttered backyards of New Westminster, and out over the flat valley into Richmond and Surrey. The twin support towers of the Alex Fraser Bridge stood like two sentinels over the south arm of the river.

"**S**HIT!"

Kevin turned the key again. The Camero turned over several times, but did not fire up. Kevin sighed, "No use running down the battery." He got out of the car and grabbed a plastic container of gasoline from under the work bench. He undid the wing nut on the air filter, removed the cover, and poured a small amount of gasoline directly into the carburetor. "That should do it." He replaced the filter cover and returned the gas can to its spot on the shelf.

This time the Camero fired up first try and stayed running. It was sounding pretty good too, the motor purred evenly, and it didn't seem to be miss-firing. Kevin made a couple of final adjustments with a screwdriver and closed the hood.

Alright! Kevin thought as he slipped the shifter into reverse, now it's off to Larry's for some cold brewskies and fifty bucks cash. Not too shabby for only an hours work.

EXCERPT from the journal of Paul Gregory, PhD:

Many of those who undertook a search for the lost mine never returned. Of those who did, some suffered injuries during their quest, whether physical, psychological or both. Here are some examples:

In 1950, Alfred Gaspard, an experienced prospector of some means, decided that in order to overcome the tough terrain and perhaps beat the curse at the same time (if indeed it did exist) he would use an airplane.

Gaspard stocked up his pontoon plane with plenty of provisions and a portable radio, and then landed it on a small lake in the upper Pitt region. From this base of operations, he began a thorough exploration of the surrounding hills and valleys. By prior arrangement, Gaspard checked in at regular intervals on his short wave radio, to keep the outside world informed of his progress and well-being. During one excited report, Gaspard stated that the trail was getting hotter, he was definitely on the right track, and he would probably locate the lost mine within a few days. The next scheduled message never came, and like Volcanic Brown, no trace of Gaspard was ever found.

In 1951, Duncan McPhadden, a sixty-eight year old treasure seeker from New Westminster, fell from a twenty foot cliff. He lay unconscious for over two days before he managed to crawl on his hands and knees to his motorboat. Somehow, McPhadden managed to get his outboard started and navigate the six miles back to his summer cabin, where he was found and taken to the hospital. McPhadden was one of the lucky ones, he survived his ordeal.

In 1960, Lewis Hagbo, a forty-nine year old naval draughtsman from Washington State, decided to spend his vacation searching for Slumach's treasure. His body was found at the bottom of a cliff, cause of death, a heart attack.

In the sixties, Tiny Allen, a handyman at a hotel in Port Moody, spent his summer vacation narrowing the search for the lost mine with information supplied by the New Westminster Daily Columbian's files. After one of his outings, Allen contacted Columbian columnist Alan Jay, an expert on the lost mine mystery. Allen claimed to have found the long lost treasure at last. Allen described to Jay the valley in which the glory hole was located, in almost the exact same words as Jackson had used in his famous letter, including the tent shaped rock which Jackson had broken off on the top to mark the spot. Allen stated that the reason he had not returned with any gold, was because heavy snow and slippery conditions had prevented him from descending into the valley and reaching the creek.

Jay was skeptical, he showed Allen a copy of Jackson's letter, Allen swore that he had never seen it before yet his and Jackson's accounts were nearly identical. Tiny Allen intended to return to the spot the next spring, to claim his booty, but for some reason or another, Allen's return to the mine site was postponed indefinitely. When Jay tried to contact Allen the next year, he was shocked to find out that Tiny Allen was dead, another victim of a heart attack.

Was Allen's story true or just a fantasy made up to gain attention? We will never know for sure.

The deaths and injuries attributed to the lost mine and Slumach's curse, could merely be coincidental. The mystery of Slumach's gold will never be solved conclusively one way or another unless the lost mine is finally found, otherwise it will remain a legend to titillate our curiosity and in many cases, greed.

Nika Memloose . . . Mine memloose.

PART TWO
Preparations

Be Prepared!
 -Boy Scout motto

"After you've packed your pack, check it again! Out there in the bush, there's no room for error, one small mistake can cost you your life. And remember to keep it as light as possible."
 -Simon George, a professional guide

Chapter 8

The beat up VW van bottomed out a few times. The springs were shot, the shocks nonexistent, and the driveway, if you could call it that, narrow, overgrown, and full of pot holes. The van slid around a sharp corner, limbs raking over what was left of the paint job, and then slowed to cross a flimsy looking plank and beam bridge spanning a small creek.

The cabin was set back on a clearing, about half a mile in from the auxiliary highway that flanked the Silver Creek reserve. The logs had never been painted; bark still clung to them here and there in little dried patches. The hand split, cedar barn shakes had curled and cupped, bleached grey by the passing years, and the north side of the roof was covered with a thick layer of dark brown moss. There were two multi-paned windows, one on each side of an intricately carved front door, and a low covered porch ran corner to corner across the front, a place where a man could put his feet up and enjoy a pipe and a brew, maybe contemplate the universe for a while, or just sit and relax in the warm, spring sun. One of the support posts had rotted away, and the porch roof sagged precariously to one side. This gave the place character, like a scene out of a movie set.

Simon George turned off the ignition, grabbed the groceries and the six pack of Birrel, non-alcoholic beer, his liver was in about as good a shape as his van. Dr. Goldberg, an internist in Chilliwack, had told George he wouldn't live another six months if he didn't give up the firewater, that had been over six years ago. George had struggled hard to beat his addition, and had stayed sober ever since. He still went to weekly AA meetings. Sobriety was boring sometimes though, his circle of friends had shrunk for awhile, but gradually he started making new acquaintances, teetotalers like himself, and George couldn't deny feeling a whole lot better.

The van door creaked like the sound track from a B-grade horror movie. It needed a squirt of oil. George stepped out into the sunshine. He grunted from a jolt of pain as he slammed the door shut with his hip, his joints could use a lube job too, the damn arthritis was acting up again. It was one of the shitty things about getting old. "Fuck you, Bessie," he chastised the van like it was the rust bucket's fault. His heels kicked up little puffs of dust. It hadn't rained in over a month, a rarity in the Fraser Valley, meaning it was likely to be a long hot summer.

"Guess I'll have to replace the old porch one of these years," George chuckled, to no one in particular, as he climbed the decrepit stairs which looked like they were about ready to fall down too. He had been saying that now for longer than he cared to remember. George figured he probably wouldn't live long enough to enjoy the new porch, so why bother, let one of the kids fix up the place after he was gone. George—nobody called him Simon except for his mother and she had been dead now for close to forty years—was sixty-eight, tall and slim, with skin that looked like old shoe leather. His shoulder length hair was about fifty-fifty salt and pepper, but his dark brown eyes looked as alert and intelligent as a man half his age. George was dressed in a pair of Levis, a black and red checkered flannel work shirt and his favorite head piece, a grey bowler with a brightly colored band one of his daughters had woven and a spectacular eagle feather stuck on the side. Might as well look the part of the eccentric Injun, George figured. One of his friends had been the late movie star, Chief Dan George, who was no relation. Simon George kind of looked like Chief Dan's twin.

George was the reservation's head mechanic by acclamation. He was by far the best engine man they had. "This Injun can fix your engine," was his motto, "and especially if you're good looking," he would add. Unfortunately, he never seemed to get around to fixing his own vehicle. It was sort of like his porch, if it still worked, why fix it?

When George wasn't tinkering with engines or transmissions, he did a fair bit of hunting and fishing. He knew all the best spots in the valley and surrounding mountains. Occasionally, George would hire himself out as a guide, and take parties of tenderfoots, city slickers usually, up into the dense bush and steep slopes surrounding the valley to the north. Most often, they were hunters or fishermen like him, anxious to bag a three-point buck or catch a ten-pound steelhead, but once in a while, someone would have that hungry gleam in their eye that could only mean one thing, Slumach's gold.

George would always try to discourage treasure seekers from such a fruitless and possibly dangerous undertaking, but in the end, he would give in and agree to go with them. He would rather those naive idiots be out there with him where he could keep an eye on them. Nothing was worse than being inexperienced and unprepared in the wilderness, just a tragedy waiting to unfold. And there was always a sobbing wife with a couple of kids at the funeral.

George pushed open the door, a work of art. Carved red cedar inlays highlighted the yellow cedar planks: a bear, cougar, eagle and raven. John Henry had carved it in '58. It had taken him nearly all winter. He had given it to George as a thank you for fixing his truck.

It was a little cooler in the cabin. The ten inch log diameter construction provided good insulation. George set the groceries and malt on his crowded pantry, and started putting the stuff away. There were hooks for hanging wet rain gear and frying pans above the wood cook stove; and an old Viking refrigerator, tucked in one corner to the right of the sink, was covered with fridge magnets of all sizes and shapes, everything from realtor blurbs to brightly colored animals and flowers. George had collected them over the years. It wasn't a conscious thing, just something that happened, someone would give one to George and he would stick it on the fridge which was getting awfully crowded. Pretty soon George would have to get a bigger appliance or start collecting something different.

There was a loft above the kitchen for sleeping. It was warmer up there in the winter. Before George's wife, Trudy, had died of a stroke, the loft had been used for other things as well. They used to get the boards creaking pretty well; some nights the whole damn cabin used to shake. Those were the good old days: good times, a good woman and good loving. A few of the widows on the reserve had made not so subtle passes at George, but so far he just wasn't interested. He wasn't dried up, he was saving it. Why or for whom, he didn't know.

A cheap, wood-grain laminate table with four mismatched chairs provided a place for eating or playing cards. George was a shark. Once or twice a month, the boys would come over to play gin rummy or poker. He hated to take their money, but somebody had to do it.

An old, black-and-white RCA Victor television was on in the living room, George hadn't bothered to turn it off before he went shopping. It was one of the old console models that took up nearly one whole wall. In front of it, a tattered, burgundy chesterfield, sat on a thick, braided oval rug.

The reservation had installed a water system in the late fifties, and there was a three-piece bathroom in a lean-to addition by the back door, nothing fancy, but totally functional.

George washed his hands in the kitchen sink and peered out the small back window. The backyard was littered with old wrecks, most of them up on blocks, rounds of firewood George had sacrificed for his trade, and used car parts: rear ends, transmissions, rusted motor blocks, dead batteries and a huge pile of worn out tires. There was also a fairly new garage the tribe had built to keep their mechanic happy, with a thick, second growth, coniferous forest towering behind it in a dense wall.

The old outhouse in the corner had never been torn down. George figured it would fall down sooner or later, just like the porch and stairs.

George stopped daydreaming and went back to his groceries. "Funny I should be thinking about the Madsen brothers after all of this time," he mumbled to the walls as if they had ears. It had been eleven years now, but some ghosts don't want to lie down and die.

Charlie and Todd Madsen had come to see George in the spring of 1989. They were young and crazy, looking for an adventure. George figured they had watched too many Star Wars and Raiders of the Lost Arc movies.

They asked George to take them up to the Corbold Creek site, one of the more popular of the many supposed locations of Slumach's lost mine. George declined. He told them it was pointless; there was nothing up there but rock, bush, snow and more rock, and maybe the odd deer, mountain goat, black bear or cougar.

"The only place you're going to find any gold up there is in your mouth," George told them.

The Madsen brothers offered to up his fee, but George told them he had promised his cousin Pete he would pull the motor out of a pickup that week, it needed a new set of rings and a valve grind. The brothers didn't want to wait an extra week, so they decided to go it alone.

Only Charlie Madsen made it out of the bush alive, they brought Todd's body out in an RCMP helicopter. He had accidentally stepped off a hundred foot cliff. The terrain out there was like that, tricky. One minute you're struggling along through thick undergrowth, the four foot salal tangled around your arms and legs, and then suddenly, the forest floor is gone and you're standing on the precipice of a sheer canyon, one step from oblivion.

Todd's death haunted George. He knew it wasn't his fault, yet somehow he couldn't help but feel responsible. He could have put Pete off, told him he'd pull the motor the next week instead. The Madsen kid was only nineteen, it was a real shame. Maybe if George had gone with them, Todd would be celebrating his thirty-second birthday instead of rotting, six feet under Ocean View Cemetery in Burnaby.

"Could have beens don't count," George mumbled as he cracked himself a warm Birrel. He put the other five in the fridge to chill.

SLUMACH – THE LOST MINE

It tasted like beer, well sort of. George sighed. He would love to crack a real beer, but he knew that one would lead to another and another and . . .

Feeling restless, he walked into the living area with the latest newspaper tucked under one arm. The headlines of the Province proclaimed the public's never ending dissatisfaction with taxes and the constitution. And of course, Quebec never stopped talking about separation. I wish they'd just get it over with, George thought, "Au revoir. Good riddance!"

George pulled his reading glasses out of his shirt pocket. "I wonder who that asshole in Ottawa is screwing today." He flipped through the news, scanned the editorial pages, and finally found the comics, the best part of the paper. George was still chuckling over Garfield's latest exploits, bullying poor Odie the dog as usual, when he heard the crunch of gravel on the driveway.

"Wonder who that could be?" he asked the walls again. He peaked out the front window. "A man . . . Oh, and a woman too, she's a real good looker!" George chuckled again, feeling his manhood stir a bit. I'm not dead yet, he thought as he squinted into the bright sunshine, "And he's driving a brand new Bavarian Motor Works, yuppie special. Good sign, they must have some bucks!" George made a mental note to up his usual fee by another fifty dollars a day if they happened to be looking for a guide. He threw down the newspaper and went over to the door. "I wonder what they want?" he asked the air, and then opened the door wide to greet the strangers as they gingerly climbed up his rotten stairs.

THE PICKUP TRUCK moved slowly up the street, pausing at several driveways. It stopped finally, in front of a sprawling rancher with almond colored, aluminum siding and a red tile roof. The huge yard was mowed to perfection, resembling a golf green or lawn bowling court. Several beds of well tended spring flowers dotted the perimeter, crocuses and daffodils.

The dirty, white Dodge just sat with its motor running, watching the house.

"What do you think?" came a whisper.

"Looking good," Kevin replied. "I've had my eye on this baby for some time now, and you don't have to whisper, nobody's gonna hear us!"

"Oh. Sorry."

A three-bay garage stood in front of the trees, its lines matching the decor of the house exactly. It had roll-down, cedar-panel doors, the kind that were certain to have automatic openers, and like the house, white louvered shutters on all of the windows. An open carport had been added on to the side of the garage furthest from the road.

Kevin reached under the seat and pulled out another can of Lucky Lager. He gave the tab a pull. It popped with a hiss and a dribble of white foam ran down onto the crotch of his striped coveralls. "Ah!" Kevin wiped the residue from his moustache. "Now here's the plan." Randy leaned closer like he was going into a huddle at a football game. Kevin was the quarterback.

It sounded good. Randy listened intently to the details. He was feeling a little nervous though, queasy in the stomach. He had never done anything like this before, at least not in broad daylight.

"What if someone sees us?" Randy asked. "Wouldn't it be better if we came back after dark?"

"No! Dummy. The people will be home by then. This is the best time, believe me. If we had a semi trailer, we could clean out the whole damn house. Just remember, act nonchalant, like we own the joint, alright? If anyone happens to see us, just wave at them and smile. They'll think we're supposed to be here. No problem. It works every time." Kevin gulped down the dregs and flattened the beer can between the palms of his hands. "Stay cool, that's the plan my man. Let's get on with it."

Kevin slipped the truck into reverse and backed into the driveway. "Get out and direct me," he hissed as they neared the carport.

Randy scrambled out of the cab, making way too much noise, and nearly fell on his head. He was so nervous now, his hands were shaking uncontrollably. He guided the truck back to the edge of the concrete floor. "Whooa. That's g-good!" Randy stammered and held up his hand. Kevin left the motor idling, then hopped out of the cab to help him. In less then two minutes, they were on their way out of the driveway, towing their prize. It was a real beauty, a sleek eighteen foot, fiberglass hull with an open cabin and a Mercury 150 on the stern that looked like it could really kick ass.

"Hey! Hey! Hey! Yabadabadoo, little buddy, we did it!" Kevin celebrated. They slapped palms. "What did I tell ya, eh?" he continued, "That was a piece of cake!" He gave Randy a playful jab on the shoulder with his big knuckles.

"Piece of cake," Randy agreed as they turned onto King George Highway and headed for Kevin's place in Whalley. He looked in the rearview mirror. "Oh, fuck! There's a pig behind us!"

"Relax, little buddy. Nobody's even reported this tub missing yet. Stay cool." Kevin kept his eye on the rearview mirror. The blue and white R.C.M.P cruiser turned off on Fraser Highway. "See. What did I tell you?" Kevin twirled his moustache happily. "Absolutely nothing to worry about."

"Whew." Randy's heart was still beating fast.

"We'll switch the plate, change the name and ID numbers,

and re-paint the trailer when we get it back to my place."

They looked at each other and laughed. Kevin gave Randy a thumbs-up.

"So what can I do for you folks?" George asked after the formal introductions had been made. They were relaxing on George's front porch, Bev and Paul sitting on two kitchen chairs George had insisted on hauling out for them, while he occupied his favorite old wicker armchair. His guests had both declined the offer of a cold Birrel. "Can't say as I blame you," George had agreed. "It ain't the same without the alcohol." He pronounced it al-kee-hall. George stuck a pinch of Copenhagen under his bottom lip and surveyed his guests inquisitively.

Paul's a city slicker George decided, no doubt there, the mild mannered professor and his pretty young lady friend. She looks Indian though, maybe a quarter or even half-breed; and she don't look as soft as him, nope. She looks like a real wildcat! He felt his manhood stir again. And they're not your typical hunters or treasure seekers, that's obvious. George took a long pull from the Birrel and belched. This just might be interesting.

"We heard that you were the best guide in the valley," Paul began, hoping a compliment might be the correct opening gambit.

"Well, you heard that right," George chuckled, obviously pleased. "Now I say again, what can I do for you?"

He's a sharp old goat, Paul considered. "We want to take a canoe trip . . . up Pitt Lake," he began again, "Probably camp at the head of the lake, do a bit of hiking. I guess we'll stay out for three or four nights."

"So what's the purpose of this little expedition?" George asked. "Recreation?"

He should have been a lawyer, Paul decided, "Mainly recreation, Simon."

"Call me George. Nobody ever called me Simon."

"Okay, George, "Mainly recreation. Also, I'm writing a book about—"

"About Slumach and the lost mine?" George cut him off.

"Well, yes, now that you mention it," Paul replied, feeling a little off balance.

"I see." George looked them over again, his deep brown eyes stripping them naked. Then he smiled and laughed, the ice was broken. "Guess you folks are cool. You don't have that starry eyed look all those dumb treasure seekers have. They always come here pestering me, George, can you help us find the gold, George, we have a copy of Jackson's map, an original yet, George this, George that, get the drift?" George's baritone returned from the falsetto he had used to mimic the gold hunters. "And you ain't reporters either, that's a real big plus in your favor. They're a pain in the ass. Worse than a bunch of vultures picking over a carcass. Bloody nuisance, they are." George knocked back the rest of his malt beverage and belched again. Then he lifted up one side of his buttocks and farted loudly. "Ah . . . Pardon my manners. I feel a man should be comfortable in his own home." He crushed the can in a vice-like grip that could just as easily have broken bones, and threw it into a box with several companions. "Another tin soldier bites the dust!

"Do you have a date for when do you want to start this little adventure of yours?"

"How does Tuesday, the 3rd of July sound?" Paul responded, glancing at his Blackberry. "That's the day after the Canada Day holiday."

"Hmmm . . . Let me see." George scratched the grey stubble

on his chin, he had nothing booked all month, but he didn't want Paul to know that. "I might have to shift a few things around, but, yeah, I reckon that would be fine." George stared straight into Paul's eyes. "And here's the bottom line, I charge two hundred bucks a day plus expenses. And I mean cash in my hand." George tapped his open palm. "No checks. No invoices." His eyes met Paul's. "Also from the time we leave until the time we get back, you can do whatever you want, but you do it my way, understand? 'Cause I am the best God damn guide in this valley and it's my job to get you and your lady friend back here in one piece. Those are my terms, take it or leave it."

"It's a deal," Paul confirmed. They got up and shook hands. Paul pulled out his wallet.

Good sign, thought George. He's quick to the draw with his pocket book. George would have gladly settled for a hundred and fifty bucks a day if Paul had wanted to barter.

Paul peeled off six crisp, fifty dollar bills and handed them to George. "Here, consider this an advance. Use what you need to get supplies, just make sure you keep receipts for those."

"I know the routine, got to give your accountant something to do." George rubbed his thumb and index finger together. "I don't give a shit, just as long as my fee is in cool crisp cash." George smiled, folded the bills and stuffed them into his shirt pocket. "Thank you very much. It's been a pleasure doing business with you, Paul. Be here on the morning of the 3rd, 6 a.m. sharp."

"We will." Paul pulled out a business card and handed it to him. "Give me a call if there's any problem."

"There won't be," George stated. "I don't have a phone, so I can't give you my number, but you can get a hold of me through the band office. Just show up on time on the 3rd. And don't plan on calling anyone on your cell phones while we're out at Pitt Lake, there's diddly squat for reception."

"Okay, George. Nice meeting you." Paul shook George's hand again then started down the steps.

"Bye, Chief!" Bev said. She took his hand and smiled. "Nice meeting you, see you soon."

"Ah, little lady, my heart soars like a hawk!" George replied, stealing a line from a movie by his late friend. Bev smiled again, this time, her whole face lit up. She's gorgeous, George thought, admiring her beauty. "And today would be a good day to die!"

George finished the farewell and gave them a *how* salute as the BMW bounced up the driveway. "City slickers," he muttered. They disappeared in cloud of dust. George pulled the three hundred dollars out of his shirt pocket and smiled.

Chapter 9

"**Home sweet home,**" Kevin announced. The house, an older two bedroom bungalow, was surrounded mostly by industrial parks and warehouses. A sign out front near the driveway, said: FOR SALE/CENTURY 21 UPTOWN REALTY LTD.—COMMERCIALLY ZONED—WILL BUILD TO SUIT. A tall, thick holly hedge prevented a view of the front yard from the street. The place was secluded, a little off the beaten track. Kevin preferred it that way, his business demanded privacy.

"Think they'll sell it on you?" Randy asked as they climbed out of the cab.

"Nah . . . well, maybe eventually, but not for quite a while," Kevin replied. "The Paki wants way too much for it. The house ain't worth a wooden nickel. Only thing anybody would give a hoot about is the land. There's nearly two acres back there, zoned C1-Commercial." He gave a wave towards the rear of the property. "Some day they'll rattle through here with a D9 Cat and throw up a warehouse or maybe another mini-mall."

Kevin walked over to the garage and opened one of the double doors. He undid the trailer hitch. Randy helped him push the boat inside. Kevin closed the doors, folded the hasp shut and replaced the Yale padlock. "Out of sight, out of mind," he noted with satisfaction. "Are you coming in for a cold brew and a puff?"

"Roger, that one!"

In contrast to the worn out appearance on the outside, the interior of Kevin's place was fixed up quite nicely. This was mostly Kevin's doing. He was handy with his hands, and he didn't mind fixing up the joint, as long as the landlord supplied the materials. During the past three years, Kevin had painted the inside from top to bottom, replaced the living room carpet and nearly completely rebuilt the bathroom. Next on the list was the kitchen, unless some rich developer bought the place out from under him first. Randy pulled two cold Lucky Lagers out of the refrigerator, and the two of them retired to the living room to relax.

Here's to being lucky!"

"Aye. Here's to looking up yer assets!"

Kevin had a lot of books. They covered nearly one complete wall. The bookcase was made out of eight cedar planks separated by concrete blocks. Kevin had helped himself to some construction supplies from the new townhouse complex being erected down the street, midnight building materials unlimited. Among the hardcover books, were several volumes on World Wars I and II, a complete set of the Encyclopedia Britannica, some old classics, and a King James Bible—a present from his mother, Cloe. The soft covers ranged from sci-fi, to horror, to mystery. There was also a smattering of "How to Get Rich Quick" theories and some New Age experiences by Shirley MacClaine and others. One whole shelf was dedicated to Kevin's pride and joy, a complete set of Playboys including the first issue featuring Marilyn Monroe. They were in near mint condition too, unlike the torn and stained Hustlers back in Randy's apartment.

Randy didn't like Playboy, but he never mentioned this to Kevin. Randy thought it was boring and the girls were too wholesome. He liked Hustler, now there was a good porn rag! He preferred its spread them wide, beaver shots and hardcore sex scenes over the artsy-fartsy stuff Hugh Hefner published. "Split beaver," he whispered to himself unconsciously.

"What's that?" Kevin asked.

"Oh, nothing." Randy replied, feeling a bit embarrassed by his weird utterance.

Kevin turned on the stereo. "Time for some tunes."

He selected Symphony Number 40 in G minor by Mozart. The opening theme soon filled the room with its restless, haunting refrain. "This is one of my favorites."

The first time that Kevin had ever invited Randy over to his house, Kevin had also said it was time for some tunes. Randy had expected Bryan Adams, or maybe the Boss, or Madonna. When Beethoven's Sixth started coming out of the speakers, the violins announcing the warm, pastoral theme, Randy had looked horrified. His big mistake was to burst out laughing just as the woodwinds joined in the first full orchestral tutti, a statement of the subject in unison and octaves. "What is this shit?" he had asked. "Don't you have any real tunes?"

Kevin had nearly gone through the roof. For a few minutes, Randy didn't think he was going to leave Kevin's house alive. After the yelling stopped, Kevin lectured him for nearly an hour, on the difference between real music, "An art form, for Christ sake!" and the trash the big record companies pumped out endlessly for no mind, low-life losers like Randy. Now, Randy knew better than to make fun of Kevin's music. It wasn't really all that bad either. You got used to it. Randy was actually starting to enjoy some of the classics, although he would never have admitted this to anyone else besides Kevin.

"Yeah, that's nice. Cool," Randy agreed, choosing his words carefully. "Real mellow. I like this one."

"Mozart was a fucking genius! He wrote his last three symphonies in just six weeks. This is one of them."

"Unbelievable!" Randy didn't have a clue how long it took to compose and orchestrate a major work like a symphony, but six weeks for three sounded impressive enough.

"It is when you consider, it took Beethoven over five years to compose his Ninth."

"Oh." Five years to write one tune, seemed a little ridiculous, but Randy didn't mention this as he valued his flesh.

Kevin slipped onto an exercise bench in one corner of the room, and began pumping iron. He started off with sets of ten, and then pushed himself harder with five sets of twenty. That whole area of the house was set up like a gym with the weight lifting bench, piles of weights, dumbbells, a knurling bar, punching bag, heavy bag and a reflex ball. Kevin liked to keep his large, muscular body in tip-top physical condition.

KEVIN MACARTHUR WAS always big. He grew so large in his mother's womb, that, due to his weight, over ten pounds, and the smallness of Cloe Macarthur's pelvic structure, he had to be delivered by Caesarian Section. When Kevin was a toddler, relatives and friends of the family were always amazed when they tried to pick him up. They usually underestimated his weight by fifteen or twenty pounds. "My, that boy is solid!" they would say, and then just shake their heads.

The Macarthur family lived in Surrey, a suburb of Vancouver. John Macarthur, Kevin's father, owned an auto wrecker's yard on

Scott Road. He bought bashed-up cars from the insurance companies and towed away unwanted wrecks from people's yards. Those were the days before I.C.B.C., the provincially owned auto insurance monopoly. John would strip off the choice parts: fuel and water pumps, radiators, transmissions, batteries, chrome, body panels, that sort of thing; and then he'd haul what was left out to the "Graveyard" with his tractor. John's graveyard had three-and-a-half acres of rusting wrecks, row on row, some piled up two or three high. The age of recycling had not arrived yet, so nobody paid a decent price for used steel. Some of John's autos were obtained by less than reputable and possibly illegal means. At least that was the gossip whispered around the Flamingo bar up the road on King George. Apparently John could make a hot car disappear in a hurry. A lot of times, a car was worth more in parts than in one piece, and John could make that happen.

The Macarthur's four bedroom home, a mish mash of add-ons with no discernable style, sat at the front of the junkyard facing the road. The MACARTHUR'S AUTO WRECKING AND USED PARTS office was connected to the family's kitchen by a single door. When the office was deserted, a customer could summon John, Cloe or one of the kids, by pushing a button marked: PRESS FOR SERVICE. It rang a buzzer in the house and honked a horn in the yard. More often than not, Cloe would trot out of the kitchen in her terrycloth housecoat and fluffy purple slippers, a Black Cat dangling from the corner of her mouth, a coffee in one hand, and her hair up in curlers and bobby pins.

"Yeah? What can I do for you?" she would ask in a gruff voice made rougher by years of smoking two packs a day and the Irish Whisky she kept hidden under the kitchen sink. "Whatta ya need today?" Then she would cough, spit up a ball of yellowish brown flem and deposit it into the half full Campbell's soup can on the counter. It was gross, but she had to do something with the crap she coughed up. The customer would state his request and she would answer, "I suppose we can fix you up." If she didn't know whether or not they had a starter for a '61 Plymouth, then she would advise them, "Best you go out back and talk to my 'ubby. 'E's out yonder by that stack of tires." Her duty done, Cloe would plod back into the kitchen for another smoke, and maybe a black coffee spiked with a shot from her stash.

John knew all about Cloe's heavy drinking, but he didn't give a damn one way or another. As long as his meals were edible and served on time, the laundry attended to, the house kept reasonably clean, and the kids kept out of his hair, Cloe could drink herself stupid for all he cared. Once or twice a week, John would mount Cloe and grunt his way to a quick orgasm. After all, wasn't that what a wife was for?

John considered himself to be a reasonable man. He figured he had his priorities straight; everything was pure and simple, period. Every man—and woman, for that matter—had a place. Step outside the bounds of your allotted place, and you were *out of line*. Kevin never forgot the night his father came home to the dinner table, so excited he could hardly contain himself. John had just been accepted into the local chapter of the Ku Klux Klan. They had been recruiting aggressively in Surrey. John had been bringing home their pamphlets for several weeks now, showing the kids page after page of propaganda on white supremacy.

"Yep," John said through a mouthful of mashed potatoes. "It's about time us white folk started doing something 'bout all them Hindus and Chinks. Christ, they're swarming into our country like flies, stealing the food right out of our children's mouths. Damn shame! Mark my words. They're worse than Niggers and Injuns. Pretty soon there'll be no jobs left for us decent, God fearing white folks." John used the word God, figuratively. He never went to church and forbid Cloe to even say Grace at meals. He had no time for that crap. It was all a bunch of hocus pocus, brainwashing at its worst.

Cloe and the kids listened to John ranting like they always did, in total silence. No one talked at the dinner table, except for him, unless it was the bare minimal, "Pass the salt, please."

To say that Kevin grew up neglected would be too harsh a statement. He had his fair share of beatings, that was true, but he always had a pair of shoes on his feet—except in the summer when he and the rest of the kids liked to run barefoot—and he always had three square meals a day, although the endless repetition of porridge for breakfast, pork and beans for lunch, and a rice or macaroni casserole for dinner, grew tiresome at best. Kevin never was one to complain. He was no wimp, no whiner. He accepted his lot in life with barely a second thought; what is, is. What will be, will be. He knew instinctively that his dad was nuts and his mom was a drunk, but what was he supposed to do about it? You don't get to choose your parents.

Kevin did well in school at first. He was a fairly bright kid, but he received no encouragement for his efforts. When he had brought home an excellent report card, Cloe had merely yawned and said, "That's nice, dear," then went on staring out the window at something nonexistent or invisible. His dad had only grunted and asked him to pass a seven sixteenths socket from the tool box. John was busy, Cloe was preoccupied. John was always too busy, Cloe was always too preoccupied. And John didn't think it was a good idea for a boy to get highfalutin ideas about bettering himself. It was best a boy learn a trade and get a job, just as soon as the damn provincial government—interfering commie bastards they were—would allow him to quit school at the age of sixteen.

What did a man need an education for anyway? So you could learn how to screw everybody like those lying parasites who called themselves lawyers? And bureaucrats, they were the worst! Little faggots who got paid big bucks to screw everybody's lives with their fucking red tape, miles and miles of red tape, and millions of pages of rules and regulations and policies. Total crap it was, an endless sea of regulatory bullshit. Try and get something useful done in this world and they drown you in fucking paperwork. It was pathetic, time to start shooting the bastards!

And fucking teachers! Weren't they a joke? Overpaid, sissy crybabies, and still they whined, whined, whined. But they can't even keep the kids under control anymore. "There's absolutely nothing in this world worse that a queer, commie school teacher," John was fond of saying. "Except for maybe two queer, commie school teachers!"

The indifference of Kevin's parents soon had an effect. His marks fell from good, to average, to poor. This was a shame because Kevin had an above average IQ and a sensitivity that could have taken him far if he had only been given half a chance. Instead of exercising his mind, Kevin stuck to activities which brought him praise, even the smallest pat on the back, from his parents. He excelled in shop work, mechanics particularly, and sports. Hockey and baseball were his best. John, who was usually too busy for anything other than car parts and drinking beer with his buddies, even managed to attend a fair number of Kevin's games. The sound of his father's voice cheering him on from the stands, gave Kevin goose bumps. One year, Kevin's hockey team, the Whalley Bombers, won the intercity championship. Kevin scored the winning goal of the final game in overtime, and was voted the most valuable player. John had actually smiled at Kevin afterwards.

"Well done, son," John had slapped Kevin hard on the shoulder, "You did good boy." It was one of the happiest days of Kevin's life. Those few words of praise from his father were more precious then all the gold in the world. John set the trophy up on the mantle, and every time Kevin walked by it, his heart would pound a little bit harder. For once in his life, his father had been proud of him.

When Kevin was sixteen, he was scouted by the Toronto Maple Leafs, but by then, his interests had turned to booze and broads. His skating went downhill. He started smoking. Most of all, he had lost the drive to play hockey. The Leafs cut him from the farm team, Kevin returned from hockey school in Regina, feeling like a complete and total failure. John had merely looked up from under the hood of a Ford Fairlane and said, "I hear they're hiring over at the mill." Kevin got a job the same day.

He started on the cleanup crew, and then quickly got moved to the green-chain. This was where everyone started out in the mill, at the bottom of the bottom. It was the hardest, most monotonous job imaginable. The leather apron and gloves only kept the smallest slivers from lancing your body. After an eight hour shift, you went to bed exhausted and watched the lumber roll by in your sleep. The only way to go was up or out. Otherwise, you spent the rest of your life working the chain. Kevin lasted five months, before he snapped. He picked a fight with one of the charge hands, but Kevin grossly underestimated his opponent, Myles O'Neil was twice golden gloves champ in the RCAF for the bantam weight division. Kevin went home with a broken nose, two black eyes, and some badly bruised ribs, another lesson learned the hard way.

Kevin drifted from job to job. He couldn't handle authority and he didn't like taking orders. Eventually, he started getting in trouble with the law. Small things at first, a minor in possession, disturbing the peace, then he worked his way up to bigger crimes, B & E's, fraud, possession of stolen property and assault causing bodily harm. Kevin did two months in the Haney Correctional Center for wayward boys, then a year in Okalla Prison in Burnaby. Okalla was an adult prison, the big house. A hefty bull queer tried to bend Kevin over in the showers. Kevin broke the guys jaw with one punch. Nobody bothered him after that. He spent most of the six months lifting weights in the prison gym. He also rediscovered a childhood love, reading. The prison library had a good collection of classics, paperbacks and self-improvement books.

After being released, Kevin had to find his own place to live. His father didn't want anything to do with a low-life jail bird. In his father's eyes, Kevin's worst crime was being stupid enough to get caught in the first place.

Kevin set up a modest auto body shop in the garage next to his house. He had met some guys in the can who specialized in auto thefts. They brought their hot scores over to Kevin's place, where he gave them a quick paint job and doctored the serial numbers.

Kevin became very good at making over cars. He bragged that the original owner wouldn't even recognize his own car after. The gang rewarded Kevin well for his effort. It was a nice sideline to a legitimate, if somewhat laid back auto body business. Kevin eventually befriended one of the gang's runners, Randy Smith.

Randy was a bum boy, a gofer really, but Kevin took a liking to the dark-haired, pimply faced kid. Kevin showed Randy the ropes of auto body work, like how to tap out a fender, grind off a rust spot, mask off the glass and chrome for painting, and other equally important tasks like how to grind the serial number off an engine block. Randy was an eager student. The two became friends, Kevin the Hulk and Randy the Weasel.

Chapter 10

"So what do you think of the Chief?" Bev asked. They were on Highway 1, heading back into the city.

"A real character, that's for sure!" Paul answered. "He comes highly recommended though." Paul pulled down the visor. The glare of the late afternoon sun on the windshield was bothering his eyes. "Please hand me those sunglasses." Bev plucked them off of the dashboard and gave them to Paul. "Thanks."

"I've already started packing for the trip."

"That's good." Paul took his right hand off of the steering wheel and placed it on Bev's lap. She wrapped her fingers around his. "Just don't pack too much stuff, there's only going to be so much room in the canoe, and you remember what George said—"

"Aww . . . I can't bring all five of my suitcases?" Bev fluttered her long eyelashes and there was that pout again.

"Nope. A single backpack will have to do."

"That will hold my makeup, but what about my clothes?" Bev teased.

"We're going into the bush, not to Paris," Paul countered.

"Will you still love me even if I look plain and stink?"

Paul gave her thigh a gentle squeeze. "What do you think? And honey, you could never look plain!" Bev smiled back at him and they drove on in silence for a few minutes.

As they neared the Port Mann Bridge, the freeway was paralleled with service roads. There were new developments of warehouses and parking lots galore, and subdivisions of neat row houses that all looked pretty much the same.

"God, if I lived in one of those, I could see myself coming home one night a little sloshed, crawling into bed, and finding myself in the arms of my neighbor's wife," Paul commented.

"Or maybe your neighbor's husband?"

"Eewww!"

"You could have a threesome."

"Seriously, I'll bet it's happened though."

"The threesome?"

"No, silly, the stumbling into the wrong house. This type of suburbia has never appealed to me. Neat little people, in neat little houses, with neat little lawns and——"

"And BMWs!" laughed Bev.

"Hey! I like my car. It's the one indulgence of yuppiedom I allow myself."

"Oh? And what do you call a four bedroom house in Point Grey that's worth over half a million dollars? A hovel? You might not like those neat little houses, Paul, but they're all a lot of people can afford. In fact, most people can't even afford that." Bev smiled and ran her hand down the front of Paul's Cashmere sweater. "Face it, Paul. You're as yuppie as they get."

"Oh yeah? Well in the sixties, I had hair down to my ass and everyone called me a hippie. I lived in an old house in Kits with four or five other heads. We furnished it in early Hippie: low couches and chairs with no legs, big fluffy cushions, bamboo and beaded curtains, and of course, glow in the dark posters galore. Our coffee table was a big old wire spindle, compliments of BC Hydro. There was usually some incense burning on it, and maybe a package of Zig Zag papers and a bag of Acapulco Gold. In my bedroom there was just a mattress on the floor with a sleeping bag thrown over top."

"And lots of free love?"

"Well, yeah, it kind of went with the times. We had the odd Mazola party. And the VD clinic on Fourth Avenue used to be a fairly busy place. Back then, the worst thing you had to worry about was a shot of penicillin in your butt, not like now with AIDS. More like a bullet in the head."

"You ever get a dose?"

"No, but I got crabs once."

"Yuck."

"Yeah, they itched like crazy, they burrow right into the skin around your pubes."

It made Bev itchy just thinking about it. She changed the subject. "Did you do a lot of drugs?"

"Oh... My fair share I guess."

"Ever get busted?"

"No, well, fortunately not. A lot of my friends did though. I was lucky, I guess. I used to grow a fair crop in the attic."

"Did you sell it?"

"Nah. Just grew enough for my own personal use and gave a lot of it away to my friends. In those days, it was a pretty serious rap, even for simple possession. This one girl I hung out with got six months in jail for possession of one measly little joint."

"You ever do LSD?"

"Yeah." Paul stared straight ahead and didn't elaborate.

"What was it like?"

Paul looked directly into her eyes and said, "Pretty scary stuff," then turned away.

Bev could tell he didn't want to talk about it, so she changed the subject again.

"You were a radical?"

Paul laughed at that. "I guess you could have called me that. I used to go to the odd protest rally. Tricky Dicky ruled the White House, Watergate still being a few years in the future, and the war in 'Nam was still raging on. It was good for the US economy. Napalm and Agent Orange were selling like hotcakes. The big munitions and chemical companies were laughing all the way to the bank. And the post World War baby boom provided plenty of able bodied young men for fodder. Uncle Sam knew how to keep the kids off the streets. Some people were not so eager to be better off dead than red though. I had lots of buddies who were draft dodgers from the States . . . Anyway, I'm rambling."

"That's okay. This is interesting, the alter ego of the mild mannered professor."

"There was one big rally organized by the Brotherhood for Peace. These days with gender neutrality and all, it probably would have been called People for Peace or something like that, but back then the word brotherhood was still cool. They were mostly peace loving guys that didn't want their smiling faces in Life Magazine along with the other dead war heroes. A medal doesn't do you a heck of lot of good when you're lying stiff, tits up in a coffin, under the Star Spangled Banner while they're blowing Taps. Anyway, the Brotherhood took out a full-page ad in the Georgia Straight inviting everyone to this big demonstration at the Peace Arch in White Rock, a rather appropriate setting.

"I went down in my old beater van, a rusted out VW something like the one the Chief's got. There were signs and banners everywhere. Slogans like, STOP THE WAR NOW! and GIVE PEACE A CHANCE. A couple of fairly successful local rock bands donated their services. That was when rock musicians were still a part of the scene, not like now, when rock stars do beer commercials and spend more time juggling their stock portfolios and talking to their accounts than they do playing their guitars.

"Anyway, it was a good time, until the good citizens of White Rock and Blaine started complaining about all of the noise. They weren't exactly thrilled, having all these long haired degenerates in their town, blowing weed and corrupting the morals of their young daughters."

"I bet you did your fair share of corrupting the girls," Bev teased. Paul just smiled and raised an eyebrow. "What happened?"

"Well, finally, the police showed up in full riot gear, overkill as usual. There was some pushing and shoving, but all in all, it broke up fairly peacefully. Not like Kent State. Most of us would rather go home, put on some tunes and smoke another joint then get our heads beaten in with a Billy club or get shot. After what happened in Ohio, the movement was a little gun shy, if you'll excuse the pun. Me and Lori, my main squeeze at the time, just went home, got ripped and balled our brains out."

"Lori? What was she like?" Bev asked, feeling a tiny pinch of jealousy.

"Lori? She had long red hair and big puppy dog blue eyes."

"Was she good in the sack?"

"Hey! A gentleman doesn't kiss and tell," Paul said and smiled, his eyebrow twitching ever so slightly.

Bev had her answer. "That good, huh? So what happened to her?"

"That summer, we all went to Long Beach on Vancouver Island. Camped out at Wreck Bay, they call it Florencia Bay these days. It was quite the community—it's all part of Pacific Rim National Park now—but in the sixties, there were maybe three or four hundred people living on the beach. Some of them even built permanent cabins up on the cliffs, but most of us just camped out in tents or built driftwood lean-tos that would last until the winter high tide. Nobody bothered to wear clothes unless they were cold. Sort of like Wreck Beach now. I met people from all over the world there, New York, London, Texas. It was an interesting place in interesting times.

"Anyway, Lori met these four guys from Oregon and went back to their tent to smoke a joint. Next thing, I could here her howling all the way up the beach while they took turns. Lori was a real screamer when she was getting laid. She ended up spending the night with the Oregonians, while I got to lie there with a bruised ego and listen to her get gang banged. Not much fun. We had a big fight the next morning. I split. Never saw her again. End of story. No loss." Paul paused to adjust his sunglasses. "Enough of the past. All of this talking has made me thirsty. Would you like to stop at the French Quarter Pub in Coquitlam for a cold beer?"

"Hey, that sounds good to me."

Paul turned off the freeway at the Burnette Avenue exit.

"Hi, kitty."

"Merroww," replied the scruffy looking orange and white tabby. He strolled from the shade of the oak tree, crossed the sidewalk, and rubbed himself against one of Randy's legs.

"You're a friendly old fellah, aren't ya?" Randy bent down and scratched the tom behind the ears. The cat immediately began to purr loudly. "Like that, do you?" The cat rubbed against Randy's legs again in acknowledgment. Randy picked the cat up and patted his back. The fur was matted and there were scars on his ears, nose and head; an old scrapper. "Wanna go for a ride?" Randy stroked him under the chin. "Maybe I'll even treat you to a nice bowl of milk."

"Errmeow!" the tom responded happily.

Randy walked over to his car, carrying the cat. He tucked it under one arm and opened the door. Then he plopped the cat on the front seat next to him, and quickly closed the door, careful not to let it slam, he didn't want to startle the poor kitty. The cat sniffed around the seat and dash, curious of the new surroundings. Randy drove out to Richmond. The tom seemed to be a good rider. He didn't freak out and go crazy like some cats do. Randy headed east on River Road and turned up a gravel drive leading to an overgrown, deserted homestead, one of the few abandoned properties left on the delta. The cat put his paw up to the passenger window and started to scratch at the armrest. "Hey, cut that out!" Randy ordered and grabbed the cat by the scruff of the neck. The tom went limp. "That's better," Randy said, his tone softening. "Wanna see your new home?"

"Err..." the cat replied timidly. Randy opened the door and carried the cat across the field.

There, near the remains of a caved-in barn, stood a small rabbit hutch. It was closed in on all sides by plywood, except for an open front covered with rusted chicken wire. The plywood was bleached white from exposure and the layers of veneer were delaminating. The floor of the hutch was covered with dead grasses. On it sat a big bowl of milk.

"See, what did I tell you?" Randy exclaimed. He set the cat down inside the hutch, closed the door, and then pushed the corroded barrel bolt back into the locked position. "There you go old guy!" The cat attacked the bowl of milk eagerly, thankful for the meal.

Randy stepped back and pulled out a box of wooden matches. He struck one and threw it into the tinder dry hay that he had piled up underneath the hutch. The wind blew it out. Randy struck another match, and then cupped his hands around the blossoming flame. This time it didn't blow out. Randy tossed the burning stick with a quick flick of his wrist. It caught the hay on fire with a quick poof and it began to crackle. Randy stepped back several paces to watch.

The cat didn't notice the smoke immediately. It was still preoccupied with the bowl of milk, but as the flames reached the wood at the bottom of the hutch, the old tom realized that something was wrong. The cat began to examine the walls of his prison, back and forth, faster and faster, desperately looking for an exit. The flames were already leaping up the sides. The cat panicked and began to howl. His claws pulled frantically at the chicken wire, but there was no escape. The flames highlighted the naked fear in the tom's huge green eyes.

Randy stood dead still, hardly blinking. His eyes were glazed over and he was breathing heavy. The howling stopped just before the hutch collapsed into a ball of flames. Randy loved the smell, it gave him goose bumps. He stood and stared at the fire until it was just a flat blanket of white powder and glowing embers, and then he returned to his car and drove back into the city.

Randy relived the burning over and over in his mind, the screams, and the smell. Only this time it wasn't a cat, it was the young hooker he'd fucked a few weeks ago. She was stark naked in the hutch, screaming and begging for help as the flames licked higher and higher, finally consuming her completely. He was out of breath, his pulse racing wildly, when he got back to his apartment.

Randy began to masturbate as soon as he stepped in the door.

Chapter 11

"**Take a look** at these," called Bev. Paul walked over to where she was examining some navy blue, Arctic down sleeping bags. "They're on sale, thirty percent off."

"Okay by me, as long as we can zip two of them together." Paul gave her a wink. "It's liable to be mighty cold up in them there hills. The body heat from a dog has saved many a trapper."

"Then why don't you bring a Saint Bernard?" Bev replied, rubbing her hip against his seductively.

"Cause I'd much rather curl up with you." Paul put his arm around her waist and pulled her close to him.

"But seriously, what do you think?"

"Well, they're light, they seem to be well stitched, and the price is certainly right."

"Then let's take them."

"Sure." Paul put two of the sleeping bags into the cart.

The Army and Navy surplus store had a large selection of camping gear. Bev went through the list George had given them, adding to the cart a heavy duty flashlight with spare batteries, a gas lamp, tin mess kits, a small plastic water jug, and a first aid kit.

"That should about do'er," Paul said when the last item was secured in the basket.

The Chief had warned them against bringing along anything but the bare necessities. "You want to keep your pack as light as possible," he had explained to them, "It can be very rough going in those steep hills."

Paul paid for the purchase with his VISA card, the checkout girl stuffed them into some large plastic bags, and then they took the elevator up to the rooftop parking lot. Paul pushed the buggy between the long rows of vehicles. When they came to Paul's BMW, they put their purchases into the trunk and drove down the ramp into Gastown. "What would you like to do now?" Paul asked. He glanced at his watch. "We've done all of our shopping and it's still only two-thirty.

Bev considered it for a moment. "Hey! I'd really like to see the new movie that's playing at the IMAX theatre. It's a double feature."

"That sounds good to me. I haven't been to the IMAX since Expo."

"Then why don't we park around here somewhere and walk the rest of the way. Parking at Canada Place can be a real bitch."

"I'll say. And after the movie, I'll take you to the Old Spaghetti Factory for dinner."

"Great!"

Within minutes, the couple was walking on the promenade along the outside of Canada Place, past the giant sails that form the roof of the convention center and out the quay into the harbor. A glass faced elevator at the end, took them up to the second level.

"The decor in here sucks," Bev commented as they walked through the lobby. Workmen were putting the final touches to what had obviously been a major renovation. "Can you believe that?" Bev wrinkled up her nose, "Lime green, pink and black, Yuck! I wonder what the designer was stoned on."

"Kinda reminds me of those tacky old McPukes before they renovated them and tried to make them classy."

"Yeah, but you still get a greasy hamburger in a Styrofoam box, not my idea of class."

"Mine either." They walked along the corridor towards the theater entrance.

"Some of these places have money to burn."

The IMAX movies were breathtaking and dynamic. The 3D effects and surround sound had the audience swooning. The fast paced action on the huge curved screen jumbled their equilibrium.

"Whoa!" Paul said when the lights came back on. "That was almost as bad as riding on a roller coaster."

"You're not kidding!" agreed Bev. "When that old crop duster went in for a dive, I thought I was going to toss my cookies."

They walked back into Gas Town, and headed down Water Street towards the Old Spaghetti Factory.

"BEEP," WENT THE checkout till as the cashier scanned in the last item. She was a pleasant looking woman with a big smile to match. Her name tag said: HELLO! MY NAME IS KARIN, and underneath in smaller print, THANK YOU FOR SHOPPING AT SAVE ON FOODS.

"That'll be two hundred and eleven, sixty-three, sir," Karin stated politely, then waited patiently while Kevin pulled out a check book and check cashing card. Randy was busy stuffing the groceries into paper bags, OUR BAGGERS ARE THE BEST IN THE BUSINESS, OUR CUSTOMERS, the sign read above his head.

Kevin handed Karin the completed check and card. She quickly punched the information into the computerized register for an authorization. After a few seconds, the machine accepted the purchase and spit out a receipt. Karin quickly checked the signature on the check against the signature on the card. Kevin was among other things, a pretty good forger. "Thank you very much, Mr. Anderson. Have a nice day!"

"You too." Kevin grinned. He helped Randy load the last of the bags onto the shopping cart. The store's doors opened automatically. Randy pushed the cart out into the parking lot. There was a toy horse by the door, one of those ones kids can plug in a quarter, and then ride on for a few minutes. Randy didn't like the way its plastic eyes followed him. Its nostrils seemed to be flared wide like it was angry, watching him. Randy felt an irrational stab of fear like he wanted to run for his life. He was happy to get outside.

"Boy, am I glad to get out of there," and away from the scary horse, "What a zoo!"

"Yeah," Kevin agreed, and smiled. "It was sure nice of Mr. Anderson to buy us our grub." Kevin had lifted a briefcase full of goodies out of the front seat of an Audi 5000 earlier that day; the door hadn't even been locked. Some people are so accommodating it made being a crook easy.

"He's a fine chap indeed!" Randy concurred. He started plunking the bags of groceries into the back of Kevin's pickup.

"You stay here and guard the grub," Kevin commanded. "We wouldn't want somebody to steal it, would we? I'm going over to the liquor store, too bad they don't take checks!" They both laughed. "We can spend most of what I've got left from my unemployment check on booze, the only other thing we need is gas for the boat, and we can get that compliments of Mr. Anderson's Petro-Can card."

"Right on, partner! Go for the gusto."

Kevin gave him the thumbs-up then walked across the parking lot of the strip mall into the B.C. Government Liquor Store.

It was busy, but not as bad as the supermarket had been. Kevin grabbed an empty cart. They were smaller than the supermarket ones. He started down an aisle marked: RUM and BRANDY. He selected a forty of Bacardi Amber and a twenty-six ounce bottle of Napoleon Brandy. From the next aisle, he grabbed a bottle of Crown Royal whisky. Might as well have a little of the good stuff, Kevin considered, and this started him thinking about his mother Cloe. She used to love her whisky, big time.

WHEN KEVIN WAS twelve, he got sent home from school one day because he had beaten the crap out of a boy who had laughed at him in class. Kevin hated to be laughed at; people who laughed at him, had a death wish. The principal gave Kevin a three-day suspension and threatened him with expulsion if he didn't learn to control his temper and fists.

Kevin walked home brooding. It wasn't fair, sometimes it seemed like he couldn't win for losing. His dad had taught him to stick up for himself, "Don't take no shit from nobody, son," but reality always seemed to work differently. The more you stuck up for yourself, the more you got beaten down again.

As he walked up to his house, feeling dejected and forlorn, Kevin noticed that his father's tow truck was gone. Then he remembered that it was Wednesday, the day his father worked in town. John had a contract with the Surrey RCMP to service their police cruisers. Every Wednesday, John gave one of their vehicles the once over, changed the oil, pumped up the grease nipples, adjusted the carburetor. Afterwards, John usually hung around with the off duty cops, slurping down rye and sevens in the maintenance garage. They all knew about John's sometimes questionable business practices, but they ignored it. He was an ace mechanic and he kept their squad cars running great.

When Kevin grabbed the door knob, it was locked, then he noticed that the WE'RE OPEN sign had been flipped over to SORRY, CLOSED. This surprised Kevin. His mother didn't often go out on weekdays, especially on Wednesdays, when John expected her to hold down the fort while he was working in town. She usually went out to do laundry or grocery shopping on the weekend.

Kevin went around to the back door. It was locked too. He lifted the woolly brown welcome mat and fetched the spare key.

When he unlocked the door, Kevin heard music. It wasn't the usual country and western Cloe played all day long on the AM radio in the kitchen. He heard the voices as he entered the living room. At first, he was puzzled, but then it dawned on him, his mother was home after all. Classical music was coming out of the console stereo in the living room. Kevin knew his mother had a few "long hair" records. She would play them for the children sometimes when John wasn't around. He had no patience for "that highfalutin crap!"

Kevin poked his head in the kitchen. Nope. Nobody there. When he got to the hallway, he realized that it was only one voice he was hearing after all, Cloe's droning on and on. Pretty weird. Chatter from Cloe's lips was not a common occurrence, at least not in Kevin's recollection. As he walked down the hall, his curiosity intensified. The door to the master bedroom was open just a crack. Kevin peeked in.

The first thing he saw was his mother kneeling in front of the bed, her back facing him. Now he could hear what she was saying. Cloe was praying.

"O God, Thou hast graciously fed my soul with the Bread of life, and made me verily indeed to eat and drink of the Body and Blood of my crucified Savior. I humbly thank Thee for the precious Gifts of Thy love; and beseech Thee that, through the merits and power of that holy Sacrifice which I have hereby commemorated, my soul shall be filled with the Divine Life of my ascendant Lord, and that, abiding in Him, I may bear fruit to Thy glory; through the same Jesus Christ our Lord." Cloe prayed softly, in her rough voice.

"Lord I pray for my children, for you to bless them and keep them safe, and for my husband John that he may someday find his way to your Grace . . ."

Kevin could hardly believe it, his mother, praying? He didn't even know that his mother was religious. They never went to church as a family and never said grace at dinner. His dad had no patience for religion, said it was "just opium for the masses, son. When you're dead, you're dead. End of story," but John wasn't finished, "Ain't no pearly gates up there with St. Peter standing in front to welcome you to Heaven boy, or no sitting around fer all eternity strummin' on a harp either, God that would be boring!. Nope," then John would snap his fingers, "Just lights out, and a lot of nothing, forever. That's what we all got to look forward to."

Kevin turned away and tiptoed out of the house as quietly as possible. His mother had a secret, and that was fine with him.

THEY WERE STILL shopping for booze. Kevin headed for

the wine section and selected two bottles of California Champagne and a Gala Keg of cheap white wine. Next time, it'll be Dom, he figured, but for now, we just need some beer.

With three flats of Foster's cans tucked away on the tray under the main basket of the cart, Kevin headed for the checkout.

The cashier was a burly guy with a hair-lip. He gave Kevin the up and down, then rang in the purchases. The transaction was conducted without a single word spoken. Kevin pocketed his change and pushed the cart towards the exit door. The cashier stood there staring at Kevin's back. Kevin could see the guy's reflection in the store front. What a gimp, Kevin thought, who are they going to hire next, retards in wheelchairs?

An old, bearded fellow, wearing a guitar on a leather strap, opened the door. Kevin grunted a quick acknowledgment but didn't bother to make a donation to the open guitar case. *They're nothing but bums, anyway,* Kevin thought, *they should give us all a break and get an honest paying job.*

With the liquid supplies accounted for, Kevin had a bit over eighty dollars left from his first unemployment check. Two hundred bucks a week, just to sit on my ass, he considered, "Not too shabby."

"Wow! Party time," Randy exclaimed when he saw the over loaded cart.

"Hey, hey, hey, little buddy! Jus' remember this trip's business before pleasure," Kevin reminded him. "I don't want you falling down drunk when we're out there looking for the mine."

"Aw, no problem, Kev." Randy held up his hands in a gesture of agreement and surrender.

"Just the same, we're going to ration this firewater carefully," Kevin told him. "Except for these suckers." He pointed to the champagne. "There's one for each of us when we find the gold!"

"Too much!"

"Yep, we'll have a victory celebration right on top of the hat rock."

"I've never tasted champagne," Randy admitted.

"Hey, hey, hey! Someday we're gonna bath in this shit." Kevin held up the two bottles, "But now, let's boogie! Destiny awaits us."

They got into the truck and headed for Kevin's house. "You might as well crash on my couch tonight," Kevin suggested, "We need to get a really early start in the morning."

Randy nodded his reply and stuck the Boss into the cassette deck.

Chapter 12

THE TELEVISION ILLUMINATED the darkened living room in a ghostly glow of flickering tentacles. The dry, almost mechanical voice of the CBC eleven o'clock anchor, droned on the speakers, the flat monotone telling of a plane crash in Brussels: "Two hundred and twelve passengers and crew were on board. There were no survivors," A killer tornado in Kansas: "It swept through a townhouse complex early this morning, leaving in its wake a trail of death and destruction," And a mass murder: "An unidentified man entered the hotel at about noon. He opened fire with a semiautomatic. Three people were killed and seven were wounded. Two of them remain in critical condition tonight."

During the tornado lead, the on-the-scene correspondent allowed just the right amount of sympathy to color his voice as he interviewed the survivors, "Mrs. Dominee, we understand that you lost your husband and two young children in this morning's tragedy. We're very sorry, you have our deepest condolences. Now can you tell our viewers just what you were doing when your house exploded? . . . Speak up, Mrs. Dominee, we can't hear you!" The woman burst into tears and turned from the camera. Her sobbing faded and cut to a commercial break for Geritol.

"Why do you always watch the news?" Bev asked. It's so depressing."

She had her head on Paul's lap. They were on the couch at his house at Point Grey.

"Now tell us, Miss Sanchez, how did it feel?" The news was back. Another on-the-scene announcer was pushing his microphone almost up the nose of a survivor of the shooting. The woman was lying on a stretcher, obviously in shock or heavily sedated. She moaned something. "Huh? We can't hear you, Miss Sanchez. "Can you tell us how it feels to be shot?"

Paul yawned. "I guess I like to keep up with what's going on in the world." He took another sip of Chevis Regal, his usual nightcap. The woman on the screen moaned something incomprehensible as an answer.

"Can you believe that guy?" Bev commented, "How cruel and insensitive! If I were her, I'd shove that mike right up his asshole!"

"And now for the weather..."

"He's just doing his job," Paul suggested.

They sat there in silence for a while, watching the diagrams, maps, and satellite photos that said, without a doubt, it would be sunny with highs in the mid twenties Celsius. That usually meant it was going to rain. The weather commentator was a real ham, and he conducted his report like a comedian doing a monologue.

"What was your ex-wife like?" Bev asked, a little reluctant to bring up the subject, but curious just the same, it was new ground for them, as Paul had never talked much about Carol.

PAUL GREGORY WAS born in London, England. He immigrated to Canada with his parents, right after second year of grade school. The Gregory family moved to Montreal for a brief stay, before deciding that the winters were too harsh and perhaps it would be nicer to live on the West Coast. Stuart Gregory, Paul's father, everyone called him Skip, applied for a job as a draughtsman with an engineering firm in Vancouver: McCalley, McClain and Robertson. He flew out to the coast for an interview and was hired on the spot. Skip spent the next three days searching for suitable accommodations and ended up buying a nice clean two-bedroom rancher on Gilbert Street in Richmond for $8,900. The same house today would sell for over four hundred thousand.

In those days, Lulu Island was still very much a farming area, but the inevitable sprawl from Vancouver was gradually converting it into a bedroom community. Skip returned to Montreal to pack and make arrangements for the move.

The Gregory family settled into their new lives quickly. In the early sixties, Richmond was a small, but vibrant and growing community. It did not take the family long to develop new friendships with their neighbors and colleagues.

Skip did very well at his new job. The post war economy was booming, soon he was promoted to the sales department. The promotion carried with it a few perks, a commission split on top of his monthly salary, a company car and a modest expense account.

Paul grew up an only child in a secure, comfortable, but sometimes a little too sheltered environment. Stella Gregory had had some complications during Paul's birth and could not have any more children. She and Skip had toyed with the idea of adopting another child, the Korean War had left plenty of orphans to go around, but they never pursued the idea seriously. Paul didn't seem to mind the absence of siblings. He was a pleasant, if not somewhat serious child, who could amuse himself for hours with a few makeshift props and his always overactive imagination. Paul loved to read. He devoured adventure books like a hungry beast. <u>Tom Sawyer</u> and <u>Treasure Island</u> were two of his favorites.

Paul did very well in school. He skipped the third grade and would have also skipped the fifth if his parents had not intervened, and held him back. They didn't want Paul to get too far ahead of his own age group. Paul seemed destined for an academic career, "university material," his teachers called him. Paul made some lifelong friends during his school years: Marty Vanderkoff, who would become a millionaire developer in the seventies; Colin Sears, who would become a commercial fisherman and eventually own his own boat; Ginder Singh, who would become a lawyer and then a judge on the Supreme Court of British Columbia; and Billy Taylor, who would die ever so tragically on their grad night.

Paul also met his future bride in high school, Carol Bakker, a somewhat dour girl who wasn't terribly well liked by her classmates. They thought of her as spoiled and rather stuck up. Their dislike probably stemmed more from jealousy than anything else as Carol's parents were very well off. Paul didn't give a hoot what anyone else thought, he always tended to see things a little differently than the average Joe, and he must have seen something in Carol that no one else did.

Paul graduated from high school on the honor roll, and went to work in a warehouse for a year to save up money for university. His parents were very supportive. They told Paul they would help him out as much as they could, but the Gregory clan had limited financial resources, as Skip had had to take an early retirement because of a bad back. Then Paul attended the University of British Columbia as an undergraduate, working every summer to earn the next year's tuition. He married Carol Bakker the summer before his final year, and went on to graduate top of his class with honors.

Paul applied to several graduate programs before being accepted to McGill with a full scholarship. He completed his master's degree and immediately started working on his doctorate in anthropology which he completed in a record two and a half years.

When Paul returned to his alma mater, UBC, in 1978, he accepted a position as an assistant professor on a two-year, trial contract. The faculty and staff liked Paul's easy going but extremely thorough style. The university renewed his contract and eventually appointed him to a full fledged professorship. Paul became their leading authority on the Salish and Haida Indians. His writings and opinions were sought by scholars from all over the world.

While Paul's academic life was soaring to new heights, his personal life was in a shambles. Carol and he fought constantly for several years, then finally separated and divorced.

THE NEWS AND weather was over, now came the endless scores, replays, and statistics of the sports rap-up. Paul picked up the remote control and clicked the TV to another station. Sports had never interested him very much. He found an old western starring the Duke.

"The first word that comes to mind, when I think of Carol, is tenacious," Paul spoke finally, answering Bev's inquiry, "the second, beautiful, and the third, a first class bitch, but not necessarily in that order. That about sums her up. She could be sweet on the surface, but sour as a lemon underneath."

Bev rolled over in his lap, her straight black hair caressing his fingertips like fine silk. Her big brown eyes seemed to yearn for him to continue.

"I met Carol when I was seventeen. We were both going to Richmond High. Her dad was a partner in the law-firm: Bakker, Thomas and Associates, and as Queen's Counsel Harold Bakker was the senior partner, he had megabucks.

"The other kids didn't like Carol much. She always had nicer clothes than everybody else. When she turned sixteen, her dad bought her a car, one of those first little Japanese imports, a Honda or something. And Carol had that spoiled, pout-look about her too, like nothing was quite good enough for her. I guess she inherited it from her mother. "Nancy, my ex-mother-in-law was a class-A witch. I hated her almost as much as she hated me, but that's another story.

"The first time I met Carol, I wanted her. I guess it was kind of love at first sight, or maybe I should say lust. I can't really explain why, she definitely wasn't my type. It just happened.

"Carol had medium length, kind of blondish hair, grey-blue eyes, and a tight little mouth that looked too small for her face. Her chin had a slight dimple that always reminded me of Kirk Douglas." Bev laughed at this. "She wore expensive clothes; her father always bought her nothing but the best, yet she seemed to have the knack for picking out combinations that looked smart, but simple. Carol didn't go in for those flashy, gaudy fashions you see on some rich kids. She was more practical." Paul smiled, "And she had a tight, little ass that drove me crazy." Bev gave him a jab in the ribs. "Oouuu . . . Cut that out!" Paul cried. They rolled around on the couch for a minute before he was able to continue.

"Carol had a real sourness to her. Sometimes talking to her was like sucking on a lemon. I don't know if it came from insecurity, I know for a fact that she was that, or from a deep rooted fear of people in general, maybe it was just in her genes, but whatever the cause, Carol was definitely not a very social person. She preferred quiet one-on-one times, a dinner for two, a movie or long walks. She hated parties with a passion. I began to get the feeling that my friends weren't welcome around us any more, that maybe Carol felt that they weren't good enough for us, something like that.

"After graduation, we split up. I did my own thing for a couple of years."

"Sowed some wild oats?"

"A few."

"Just a few?"

"Well, uh, I was going to UBC at the time, living in Kits, and for awhile it was like the old cliché, I changed my girl friend more often than I changed my socks. Then I got into the hippie thing, acid rock, pot, free love, peace man, like wow—"

"That's when you were banging Lori?"

"Er, yeah. You know that story. I think me and half of the male population of the province were banging Lori, but anyway, Carol and I finally got back together and when we eventually got married, things got better for awhile. Carol seemed to come out of her shell, and I thought everything was going to work out. I had just finished my third year here at UBC, and Carol was starting an RN internship at Grace Hospital. We were both extremely busy, but very happy, at least I thought so anyway.

"Then the nagging started. It was little things at first. Carol didn't like the smell of my pipe, and she wanted me to quit smoking it in the house. The house was always a mess because I wasn't pulling my weight with the chores. I didn't notice it when she got her hair done or wore a new dress. This quickly progressed to, you don't say you love me anymore, you don't bring me flowers anymore, and we never talk anymore, blah, blah, blah.

Basically, she was screaming, pay attention to me! The more demanding Carol became, the further I wanted to back away.

"Things went down the tubes quickly then. I felt trapped, claustrophobic. Carol was an energy suck, and she was smothering me, sucking the life force out of my body like those space vampires in Mind Parasites. She accused me of having affairs with other women, which wasn't true, at least not then. Then she became suspicious of everyone, I couldn't so much as even talk to another woman without Carol flying into a rage. I tried to get her to seek counseling, the lady was paranoid, but she wouldn't hear of it. She said that I was the one who needed my head examined. It got to the point where we couldn't go out together without fighting, so we started going out alone.

"Our infrequent sex life became our nonexistent sex life. Carol always had a headache or some other excuse and to tell you the truth, I didn't really care. Who wants to make love to an ice queen? After awhile, she stopped making excuses altogether and I started sleeping in the guest room. That's when I started drinking fairly heavily. And I had a couple of affairs, one night stands. Heck, I was lonely. I wasn't getting it at home and I was getting accused of doing it anyway. What's the difference? Finally something just snapped. I'd had enough. I packed up my stuff and left. And that's about all there is to tell." Paul sighed and finished the last of his scotch. "I'm just glad we never had kids. Really glad!

"Carol's remarried now; I hope she's happy. I pity her new husband. They're living somewhere in Toronto. Last I heard they have two children."

"Thanks for opening up, Doc." The thought of having Paul's children some day made Bev feel kind of warm all over. She grabbed his neck with both arms and pulled his lips to hers. "Time for bed," she whispered.

"Yep. Tomorrow's the big day, the beginning of our little adventure, and we've got a very early start. The Chief is expecting us at six and it takes at least a couple of hours to get out there."

"What time should I set the alarm for?" Bev asked.

"3:30."

"Whoa, that's early. I guess we'll have to go right to sleep then."

"Guess so." Paul clicked off the TV and carried her to his bed. It was another hour before they slept.

INTERLUDE

January 16, 1891

My days are past, my purposes are broken off, even the thoughts of my heart. They change the night into day: the light is short because of darkness. If I wait, the grave is mine house: I have made my bed in the darkness. I have said to corruption, Thou art my father: to the worm, Thou art my mother and my sister.

And where is now my hope? As for my hope, who shall see it? They shall go down to the bars of the pitt, when our rest together is in the dust.

-Book of Job, Chapter 17, Verses: 11-16

FATHER MORGAN CLOSED the Bible. Job was the book that he nearly always turned to in times of tragedy or depression. It wasn't his favorite, that was John, nor was it the powerful prophecy of Revelation, but it was comforting somehow to know that his troubles and problems were minuscule compared to the terrible burdens cast upon the unfortunate man from Uz. A wager between God and Satan, and poor Job's life gets chucked into the shit-house:

"Let's test your faith, you poor bugger. Do you believe? Do you have faith? Do you trust me? Sure you do, we'll just tighten the thumb screws and lay on the lashes. Is there hope? You bet!

Roll the dice, cut the cards, aces wild . . ."

Father Morgan set the Book on a side table and tugged a gold chain. His pocket watch fell out of a vest pocket: 10:45, nearly time for bed.

His cot looked small and lonely in the corner. It reminded him of his life, small and lonely. The loneliness made him feel guilty though. He was married to God and through God alone would find fulfillment in life. Still, the loneliness was real enough.

FATHER MORGAN HAD been in love once, had almost gotten married. He had been very young then, just nineteen, living near the small village of Glenavy about a days carriage ride west of Belfast near the Lough Neagh.

Life was hard for a Catholic family in Ireland. His father Thomas Morgan had been a peasant farmer. He died when William was only a skinny five year old. The blight had struck in September of 1845. After the potatoes turned black, the Morgan family starved. Only William and his mother Shelly survived the great famine. They would have perished too, had Shelly not found part-time employment at the manor of Lord Arthur Church.

It seemed like a miracle. One moment they were starving and the next, they were sipping hot soup on the rear steps of the servant's wing.

"Would you like a biscuit?"

William nodded and snatched one from the plate. He jammed the warm dough into his mouth so quickly he nearly choked.

"My name is Nelda MacClarey."

"Illiam," William sputtered, his mouth still full of dough. "Illiam Organ."

"Pleased to meet you, Illiam Organ."

William turned red and swallowed twice in quick succession. "William Morgan," he finally managed meekly.

"Pleased to meet you, William Morgan." Nelda smiled grandly and shook his hand. William felt like it was all a dream.

Shelly Morgan secured a permanent position at the manor and the quality of their lives improved greatly. They shared a small room on the first floor servant's quarters, with a view of the yellow pastures and dark blue lough beyond.

Nelda and William became fast friends. She taught him the alphabet, numbers, and finally how to read and write. He taught her knots and how to tie down a bent sapling to make a snare. They made a pact the year William turned ten—Nelda was two years older—as soon as William was of age, they would marry.

The years past by quickly, William and Nelda never forgot the promise they had made each other and sealed with an awkward kiss.

The wedding was set for three weeks after William's nineteenth birthday. Shelly had saved enough money over the years to buy a bolt of fine material to tailor William a wedding suit. He was relieved when it was finished. He had spent what seemed like hours on end, standing still while Shelly pinned and tucked, trying to get the fit just right. Her handsome son was going to look absolutely splendid on his wedding day.

Late in the morning, just a week before the wedding, Nelda complained to her mother Tess of a headache. Tess sent her back to her room to rest. When Tess checked in two hours later, to bring Nelda a cup of tea, the girl was as cold as a stone. The cause of death was unknown, there being no medical examiner at Glenavy. These things happened. Death was no stranger to Ireland.

At the wake, William drank himself into a stupor, finally

passing out after he'd thrown up all over his new suit for the third time. The next day, he wished that he too had died.

After Nelda's funeral, a very depressed William left home and headed for Belfast. He felt like a broken man. There was no work to be found in the city. William spent his days hanging around the taverns, and he got into drunken brawls with anyone who crossed him. The coins in the bag Shelly had slipped him the day he'd left were almost gone. William spent the last of it becoming a man. God had robbed him of his wedding night with the woman he loved, there was no one left to save his innocence for.

William handed the coins to the stern faced Madame, and then one of the whores led him up to her room.

Darlene O'Day was a rather plump woman in her early thirties, with a pleasant round face. She removed her robe and then helped William undress. He was so nervous; it was obvious that he was a virgin. Darlene reached down and guided his erect penis into her vagina. William moaned out loud. In a few minutes, it was over. He quickly got dressed and left the whorehouse without saying a word. He felt relieved and awful at the same time.

The deed done, William went straight from the whorehouse to the monastery, where he became a novice to the priesthood.

After his final vows, Father Morgan immigrated to Canada. It was in 1867, the year of confederation. He was immediately sent out west to the young colony of British Columbia to take over a small parish in New Westminster, the capital.

IT TOOK THREE matches to get the lamp on his desk going. Are my hands trembling that much, he wondered. From the bottom drawer came a fifth of Canadian whisky and a shot glass. Father Morgan poured three fingers and knocked it back in one go.

"Ahhh..." The warmth flooded his throat and quickly spread down his shoulders into his chest. He coughed. A warm shiver ran down his spine. "Yuhhhzzz." He shook his head. The tingling subsided into a dull buzz. Nothing like a whisky rush.

The pencil drawer yielded a small, black bound book edged in silver leaf. "Time to update the Book of the Dead," he sighed.

Father Morgan thumbed through the pages until he came to the last entry: *Timmy Johnson (consumption)*. He opened his ink bottle, dipped in the quill, and began to write in the precise, measured strokes of someone well versed in calligraphy.

Charlie Slumach (Indian).
Born:?
Died: January 16, 1891.
(Hanged for the murder of Louis Bee.)

"May you rest in peace, Amen."

Father Morgan closed the book and returned it to the drawer. He felt like pouring another whisky, but resisted the temptation.

He extinguished the desk lamp and crossed the darkness to his cot. He couldn't sleep. He tried to pray but fragmented images kept swirling around in his mind: Nelda, standing in the sunshine, handing him a hot biscuit, the round-faced whore in Belfast, what was her name? ... Darlene! And Slumach, dangling on the noose—hands and feet twitching grotesquely like a rag doll on a string— and finally a raven sitting on a white picket fence, its cold dark eyes looking right through him like he didn't even exist.

"Father, forgive me for I have sinned."

PART THREE
The Transformer

Men fear death as children fear to go into the dark;
And as that natural fear in children is increased with tales,
So is the other.
    -Francis Bacon, *Of Death*

And I looked, and behold a pale horse:
And his name that sat on him was Death,
And Hell followed with him.
    -*Revelations*, Chapter 6, Verse 8

O great spirit
What darkness awaits
Those who walk so blindly
Into thy talons?
    -Simon George, from an unpublished poem

Chapter 13

July 3, 2007

EXCERPT from the journal of Paul Gregory, PhD:

Day One-
The one word that comes to mind when describing my first impression of Pitt Lake is *eerie*.

That feeling started to gnaw at the pit of my stomach as soon as we left the Wild Duck Inn, where we had a quick pint for the road, George settled for a tomato juice, and then picked up the last of our 'supplies' at the cold beer and wine, two cases of ice cold Kokanee beer. Then we all piled into the rusty V.W. van, Bev scrunched up on the passenger seat beside me, and Simon George driving like a madman. Thus began our little adventure!

I have to wonder or should I say marvel, at what keeps George's rusty bucket of bolts moving; the motor coughs and sputters constantly, the brakes squeal like a cat in heat, and the body is so rusted out, I could see the pavement rolling by under my Adidas.

We crossed the bridge into Pitt Meadows and headed off the

highway, down Dewdney Trunk Road, finally turning north on Harris Road. In the distance, we could see Sheridan Hill, one of the supposed locations of the Lost Mine, a rocky, wooded bluff rising above the surrounding farmland, and beyond that the rugged Coastal Mountains loomed like a sheer blue-green fortress. They seemed to be very far away.

As we passed around the base of Sheridan Hill, close to the spot where Slumach shot Louis Bee, I realized that appearances can be deceiving; the mountains were much closer than it had seemed. The land on either side of Neaves Road is marshy grassland, cross-hatched by a maze of dykes and drainage ditches. Most of this land was reclaimed from swamps by turn of the century Dutch settlers. White-washed farmhouses and brightly painted barns dot the fields, along with herds of black-and-white Holstein cattle. A row of tall poplar trees lines one side of the road, I suppose planted there as a wind break.

Nearer the lake, the mountains tower over each side of the flatlands, closing like a funnel at the head of the Pitt River.

The air here is drastically different too, thicker, more humid, it seems to tingle with static electricity as if at any moment a violent summer storm will erupt, filling the valley with thunder and lightning. The road ends at the boat launch on the southern end of the lake. Cars and trucks, most of them with empty boat trailers attached, are parked up both sides of the road for several hundred yards. George dropped Bev and I off with all of the gear, then backed down the road to find a parking space. I'm now sitting here on a log that blocks the service road, scribbling away in this journal. Bev went over to the concession near the wharf to grab us each a burger and some fries, energy food for the long paddle up to the head of the lake. As soon as George gets back, we'll make arrangements for the canoe rentals, one for Bev and I, and one for

George and the supplies. Then we'll have to wait an hour or so for the tide to change.

Pitt Lake is one of the few tidal lakes in the world, averaging a four or five foot rise and fall. We want to catch it when it's on the rise, so we can take advantage of the strong back currents.

And George had been right; our cell phones got zero bars as we approached the lake so we decided to stash them in the van.

THE WHITE DODGE truck rounded a curve in the narrow pavement, barely wide enough for two cars to pass, and slowed to a crawl.

"Look at all the cars!" Randy pointed to the empty boat trailers, cars and pickups that lined each side of the road.

Kevin cased the parking situation and shrugged. "Yeah, everybody and their dog are on the lake today. We'll have to launch Saddy, unload the supplies, then come back up here and find a place to park."

The boat launch was still out of sight. The dykes on either side of the road, drained large flat fields covered in tall grasses. They looked more like swamps than farmland. Birds seemed to be everywhere, ducks, geese, cranes and the familiar scavengers, crows and gulls. A large crow flew right up in front of the truck, and cawed loudly, landing on one of the poles that brought power and telephone to the foot of Pitt Lake. Its black eyes followed the truck up the road, watching intently.

There seemed to be no break in the parade of parked vehicles. "We'll have to walk at least a mile!" Randy groaned.

Kevin glared at him through his shades. The one thing about Randy that Kevin didn't like was the whining. Kevin didn't like wimps or crybabies. Like his father, Kevin was not a very tolerant man. "Quit your whining!" he growled. "A mile is nothing compared with how many miles we're going to have to hike once we get up in those mountains. So are you with me or not? If you're gonna wimp out on me, I'd rather it be now than later. I'm on a mission!"

"Don't worry! I'm with you all the way." Randy took a long drag on his cigarette and flicked the butt out of the open window. "I won't let you down."

"You better not," Kevin replied icily. "If you jam out on me out there in the bush, I'll just leave you behind for bear bait."

Randy looked straight ahead and didn't say a word.

When they finally arrived at the boat launch, there was another truck loading a boat, so Kevin had to pull over to the side and wait his turn. A pretty young woman walked in front of their truck.

"Wow, I like that!" Randy commented, as she headed down the dirt path leading to the boat rentals, wooden wharves and concession. He rolled down his window and let out a loud whistle. "Hey, beautiful! Where are you going?"

The woman in grey sweats, turned her head briefly, and kept right on walking. Her long black hair glistened in the late morning sunlight.

"Want some company?" Randy persisted. The woman ignored him again, and went into L & J's, a one story, whitewashed lean-to that served burgers, fries and any other high cholesterol junk food that can be cooked in a deep fryer or on a grill. A large red Coca Cola sign hung above the front door and a bulletin board on the outside wall was hidden behind posters and business cards advertising cabins for sale or rent, fishing charters, items for sale, local entertainment and other services. Through the dirty glass storefront, Randy could see the woman walk up to the counter. A fat, red haired guy with a white chef's hat was flipping burgers while a grey haired woman jotted down orders on a pad. There were a few people ahead of her, so the woman leaned against the back of a plastic chair with L & J's stenciled on it in black paint. Her hips swayed to the rhythm of unheard music, probably a jukebox or radio playing inside.

"What a fine piece that is." Randy licked his lips. "I'd give my right arm to spend a night with her!"

"Pretty broads are a dime a dozen, little buddy," Kevin replied with a yawn. He pushed in the clutch and pulled the long stick shift back into reverse. The gears protested briefly until he found the right notch. "And don't swear away your bodily parts so cheaply. Once we find the gold, you can have a different woman," Kevin pointed in the direction of L & J's, "just as pretty as her, any night of the week!"

Randy's eyes grew bigger and he smiled. "That's right."

"Unhuh, now could you possibly concentrate that bean brain of yours on something else for a few minutes? It's our turn to use the boat launch."

"Aye, aye, Captain!"

Kevin eased out the clutch and prepared to back the trailer down to the river. The launch was fairly narrow with logs on either side to protect the grass, pedestrians and bystanders. From the pavement at the end of the road, the drive was hard packed gravel with a few potholes, but the forty or so feet of the actual launch itself were concrete. On one side, a green and yellow sign warned boaters about the danger of spreading Milfoil Weed.

The Pitt River at this point was a deep green color, and it appeared to drop off fairly quickly. On the far side, two canoes were just entering the mouth of Widgeon Creek which joined the Pitt River just south of the lake, their four paddles cutting the water in perfect unison, sending ripples into the current. Just north of the creek, was a bluff of low laying cliffs covered in moss, arbutus trees and small shrubs, a favorite spot for picnickers and hikers, and finally, the huge sandbars that had formed at the junction of the river with Pitt Lake itself. Several speedboats raced up and down the deep channel that cut to the southeast of the sandbars, large waves in the foamy wake bouncing back and forth off the sides of the narrow channel, creating a complex pattern of ridges and troughs. Some waves reinforced each other and piled up even higher, while others cancelled each other out, leaving a momentary area of calm.

Kevin cut the steering wheel too hard and the trailer began to jackknife, heading towards one of the logs.

"Whoa! Straighten her out." Randy warned.

"I'm not blind!" Kevin yelled. "Quit being a back seat driver!"

"Okay, okay." Just then, a man with short hair and a sandy beard got up from the log where he had been sitting, and started giving Kevin directions via hand signs. He spun his finger clockwise, showing Kevin which way to turn the steering wheel.

Kevin grabbed the rearview mirror and adjusted it violently, nearly tearing it off of the windshield. "Who's this fuck-head? Does he think that I don't know how to drive or what?" Kevin's face flushed red under his tan. Randy couldn't see his eyes behind the shades, but he knew they were burning like laser beams.

"I'll go teach the guy some manners," Randy volunteered. He set his beer down on the floor of the cab, opened the door and hopped down onto the gravel.

"Howdy," the man said. "Nice day for a cruise."

"What the fuck you doing, asshole?" was Randy's reply, "Can't you mind your own business?" Randy approached the man with both fists clenched.

"Hey! What's the problem?" the man asked, "I was just trying to help, nothing to get sore about."

Up close to Randy, the man looked like one of those queers that hung out on Davis Street in Vancouver. Every hair on his head and beard were immaculately in place, and he was dressed in a bright red jogging suit, with a black leather fanny bag on his right hip. His running shoes were as white as the day they came out of the shoe box. A queer yuppie, no doubt, Randy figured.

"What's that?" Randy gestured towards the fanny bag with contempt, "I thought only girls carried purses." Randy approached the man and flicked him on the shoulder with the backs of his fingers. "So are you a faggot? Huh?" The man backed up a step, but didn't reply. "I said, are you a faggot?"

"Look, I don't want any trouble," the man said flatly, his eyes fixed firmly on Randy's.

"Yeah? Well trouble's my business." Randy started to move closer, but hesitated. There was something about the way the man was standing that made him wary. Also the tone of the man's voice didn't indicate that he was even the least bit afraid and worst of all, the look in the man's eyes seemed to dare Randy to go for it. Being a coward at heart, Randy let it go. He jabbed his finger towards the man and screamed a few last obscenities, mostly for Kevin's benefit, and then turned around and climbed back into the pickup. "I sure told that little faggot off!" Randy bragged, as Kevin backed the boat down into the water. "He won't fuck with us again."

Kevin looked at Randy, but didn't say a word. What a wimp, he thought. If Kevin had handled it, the guy would have been on his way to the hospital, instead of sitting back there so smugly on a log, writing in some book. But then, Kevin had much more important matters on his mind. "Let's get this puppy launched."

Chapter 14

THE LAKE WAS a little choppy, a strong breeze coming from the northwest. Bev and Paul's green, fourteen foot canoe was in front, Bev giggling at their lack of co-ordination at keeping the thing going straight, with Simon George bringing up the rear, his red, eighteen foot pack canoe cutting the water gracefully with his long, smooth strokes.

"We're going crooked again!" laughed Bev.

"Shit. Let me paddle on your side for awhile."

"You've got to get a rhythm going," interjected George from behind them. "If you try too hard, you'll end up going around in circles!" City slickers, he thought. "Caress the water with your paddle, don't attack it."

After an hour or so, Bev and Paul stopped working against each other and got a rhythm going. They managed to keep their canoe going in more or less a straight line. The sun came out, and Bev peeled off her UBC sweatshirt and jogging pants, revealing a rather skimpy two piece bikini. The lead canoe started wandering again.

"Keep your mind on the oar, boy," George chuckled.

"There'll be plenty of time for that later."

Paul blushed.

"Which oar are you talking about, Chief?" quipped Bev with a sly grin.

"If I were twenty years younger, I'd be happy show you!" George returned.

"Oh, I bet you're a dirty old man!" Bev reprimanded him. "And I also bet you used to be a real gigolo too!"

"I warmed hearts all the way from Alaska to Oregon. And what do you mean used to? Just cause there's a little snow on the teepee doesn't mean there's no fire in the wigwam."

"How far have we come?" Paul asked, changing the subject.

"About five or six miles," George answered. "We got about another ten or so before we reach the head of the lake."

Ten more miles, thought Paul miserably. He was in pretty good physical condition, jogging mornings, and regular work outs at the handball courts in the Faculty building at UBC, but right now, his arms felt like rubber bands.

"Any chance we could stop for a little lunch?" Bev yelled back. "I've got a box of fried chicken and a whole container full of potato salad that's going to spoil." Bev pulled up her oar and laid it across the bow. "It'll go good with the beer, oops! Sorry, Chief."

"That's okay. Chicken and potato salad will suit me just fine. We can stop in about an hour. I know a nice spot on the other side of Little Goose Island. It's about the halfway mark." George brought his canoe up beside theirs.

Another hour? Paul thought.

"And you guys take it easy on the beer," George continued, "It makes you tired, and we've still got a whole mess of paddling to do if we want to make camp before nightfall."

THE SOUND WAS faint at first. Bev turned around and squinted south. A speed boat was approaching them on a collision course, the roar of its motor growing louder by the second. He's going to turn away any second now, Bev thought, but he's sure cutting it close—

"Look out!" Bev yelled. The speed boat missed the lead canoe by inches. Bev lost her paddle as the wake nearly flipped them.

"Hang on!" Paul screamed against the roar of the large outboard motor, the pitch of its whine falling as it raced away. Bev just managed to catch the oak trim on the bow cover. The ends of her hair touched the surface of the water and floated there.

Paul hacked at the waves desperately with his paddle, trying to re-establish their centre of gravity.

"You okay?" George called across. Concern lined his face as he closed on their starboard side. "Those bastards should be reported!" He hovered beside them like a honey bee inspecting a blossom. "You all right there, Sunshine?"

"I'm okay, Chief." Bev smiled weakly and gave a thumbs-up, we're okay. She cleared the water from her hair with a flick, and recovered her paddle, the wake kept it close to the canoe. "I'd like to have their balls, and not for a good time either!" She set the paddle down across the sides of the canoe and re-adjusted the straps on her bikini; one of her breasts had popped out in the commotion. George watched her with a poker face.

"Either one of you catch the I.D. number on that sucker?"

Both Bev and Paul shook their heads.

"Name? Anything?"

"No," Paul replied for both of them, "But I think that it was the same two idiots that were hassling me back at the boat launch."

"Sure about that?"

"Positive."

"Well, if their truck is still parked there when we get back, make sure one of us gets the license plate number. We'll report those morons to the Mounties."

"The guy driving was laughing when they went by," Bev added.

"Well he won't be laughing for long." A single ray of sunshine bounced off the gold cap on George's front tooth, sparkling like the ripples on the surface of the lake. He whispered a single word in Chinook.

"What was that, Chief?"

"Nothing, Sunshine. Let's move out!" George paddled with strong, even strokes and moved his canoe into the lead position.

Bev and Paul soon forgot the near miss as they struggled to keep up.

"**D**ID YOU SEE the look on their faces?" Randy was still laughing. "Should we go back around for another pass?"

"Nah, you proved your point. Besides, the way you drive this rig, you're liable to wipe us out too."

"Ha! I scared that bitch right out of her bikini. Nice tits!" Randy whistled.

"Quit thinking with your dick and get us to the head of the lake. This is a business trip, remember?"

"Yeah, yeah, yeah." Randy nosed the boat out into the open water. "Pass me a beer."

Kevin gave him a stern look.

"Please."

"That's better." Kevin reached back and fumbled with the

white cooler.

It was just a speck above them. Randy watched it dive, thinking that it was a hawk or maybe an eagle. As it approached the boat, he was startled by the size. It was huge. It would probably crush the boat. Its feathers were black as coal, and it wasn't a hawk or an eagle, it was a giant raven, the size of a small plane. But that was impossible, Randy thought, and the eyes! The eyes were on fire, molten pools of hate and hunger. The talons spread open and the huge beak opened in anticipation.

Randy slammed the lever to STOP. The oily bilge rolled over the fiberglass ribs and spilled into the bow section as the boat tried to stand on its end.

"Whoa!" Kevin was thrown forward with the momentum. The beer slipped out of his hand and fell into the bilge as he walloped his head hard on the clear acrylic windshield. "Owww!!"

Randy sat staring at the horizon, white knuckles wrapped tightly around the steering wheel. "Holy Mother!" He blew out a quick breath and shivered, "What the fuck was that?" The bird had disappeared.

"What?" Kevin spat back angrily, rubbing his temple where a bruise had begun to form, a big purple-red blotch.

He winced, and then glared back at Randy, looking like he was ready to bite his head off. "What the fuck was what?"

"That bird! That—" Randy choked off the rest of his description as the full impact of what he had seen caught up with him. Some things are better left alone, unsaid, taboo period. "Nothing man, sorry. I, ah, I thought I saw a deadhead. I, I, didn't want to rip the bottom out of Saddy here."

Kevin shook his head. His temple had begun to throb. "I heard you say, bird."

"Did," Randy mumbled. His legs trembled and his blood pressure felt high enough to blow an artery. The lies came easy. "A bird was sitting on a damn deadhead. Lucky too, otherwise, I wouldn't have noticed the sucker above the waterline. The waves were just lapping over the top of it, must have been at least two feet in diameter. We were lucky!"

"How come I didn't see any fucking deadhead? Huh? Am I blind or something?"

"No," Randy cringed. "I'm sorry." Kevin looked angry enough to blow a gasket.

Just then the two canoes slipped between Little Goose Island and the point. Randy watched them disappear, and then gave them a one fingered salute. Later, bitch, he swore to himself.

"Let's get moving," Kevin growled. "And I'm driving! You're a fucking maniac!" Kevin and Randy traded places and Kevin slipped the boat back into gear. "Crack me another beer," Kevin commanded, "I hardly got a sip out of the last one." Kevin stomped the empty can angrily with his boot.

The sharp wedge of the bow cut the water briskly. Combs of frothy spray curled over the fiberglass hull, beading in silver ringlets on the windshield that had inflicted Kevin's headache just minutes before. The 150 Mercury purred like a kitten in a fish cannery.

"Wish there was a wiper on this baby. Hard to see where we're going," Kevin complained, craning his neck sideways to peek around the windshield. He rubbed the sore spot on his right temple. "Wouldn't want us running into another deadhead, would we?"

"Ah, Kev. I said I was sorry, man." Randy popped the lid off of the Styrofoam cooler and pulled out a frosty can of Foster's. "Here ya go, partner. This one's on the house!"

Kevin grabbed the can, his huge fist closing around it like a vice. There was a brief pop as he cracked the tab. "Ahhhh! The golden throat charmer," he mimicked the T.V. ad. Another long pull on the can brought back some of Kevin's humor. He wiggled the tab in his fingers until it broke off of the can, and dropped it into the dark green water. "There you go little fishes. Some nice food for you!" he chuckled, feeling a lot better. The headache was almost gone.

Randy thought about the aluminum strip switch-backing in the water like a dry leaf falling on a calm day. In his mind, he could see a fish chomping on it. It gave him a little shiver. He could picture the frantic back and forth dance of the head, the circles of bright red blood spreading from the mouth and gills, followed by the slow agony of death.

D<small>EATH HAD ALWAYS</small> fascinated Randy. It was exciting: the ultimate horror movie, the last rush before the big sleep. Better than drugs, better than booze, almost better than a night in the sack with Norma Jean—Randy worshipped Marilyn Monroe, he had posters of her all over his bedroom walls, the fact that she had died about the same time he was even born, made no difference. Sex and death were intertwined, were they not?

When he was young, Randy invented a game, something to pass away the endless hours in the closet at Aunty Velma's. It was an escape from the shroud of darkness that clung to his deepest fears and secret dreams, the stale antiseptic smell of wool suits, mothballs and age. The suits had belonged to Randy's grandfather, a man that Randy had heard much about, but never met. Herbert Curry had passed away from stomach cancer several years before Randy was born. Aunty Velma had inherited the house, being the only single child left of the three daughters, and most likely to remain that way. But she had never given away Herbert's clothes. Velma had simply hung them all neatly on hangers, folded them in boxes, and stored them in the closet of the room he had died in, destined to become Randy's bedroom many years later.

Velma had had a rocky love-hate relationship with her father. She knew that the cancer, those long months of pain and rotting decay until Herbert resembled a skeleton with dry skin stretched over bones, had been God's punishment for Herbert's many sins: the cigars, the whisky, and the other women. Her mother Carolyn, bless her soul, had never known about the other women, but Velma knew all about them. Like the time she had seen him sitting at the back of a trolley bus necking with a stranger, some little harlot, his fingers feeling up her skirt with wicked intentions. Herbert had been too busy to notice her, and Velma had pretended not to know him, but she had observed his evil wickedness first hand. The final confrontation, the split between daughter and father that was never mended, occurred when her mother had been away in Saskatoon, visiting her sick sister.

Velma came home early from school that day. The curse was bad that month. The school nurse had told her to go home, drink a hot cup of tea and lay down for a couple of hours. Hopefully the painful cramps would go away.

Velma opened the front door of the house, with her insides feeling like she had swallowed a whole pack of razor blades. As she passed the dining room, she heard a giggling noise coming from the kitchen. Velma could see two distorted shapes moving together through the obscure glass of the French door. She opened the door.

There was father, his trousers around his ankles, fornicating with a skinny, blonde woman on the kitchen counter. The slut's long fingernails had clawed long, red streaks down the length of Herbert's hairy back. The woman heard the door creak and looked towards Velma. The woman immediately stopped moaning. Her eyes grew wide and her mouth fell open. Herbert rolled over to see what was causing the annoying interruption. His eyes caught Velma's for several seconds before she broke off the staring match and went running upstairs to her room, slamming the door and locking it behind her. (Not a word was ever spoken between them about the sordid incident, but it hung in the air like the blade of a guillotine waiting to fall.) Velma had a new power over him. Both of them knew that she could bring the sword of truth down on him at any time, destroy him, and squash him under her foot like an insignificant bug. Velma found God in the deep hatred she felt for her father. It drew her closer to Him and His word, and gave her strength to ward off the evil stirrings that had now begun to come too often to her own loins. Velma would not give in to temptation. Lust would not consume her, like it did her father. But life went on.

Velma took care of her father after Carolyn—bless her sweet soul—died of a sudden heart attack in 1964. Velma cooked her father's meals, cleaned the house and did his laundry. She was the perfect daughter. And after Herbert took sick, she nursed him through the long battle with cancer, clearing away the trays of uneaten food from his bedside table, giving him pills, "opium," the doctor said, and changing the yellow, sweat stained sheets. The smell bothered her at first, but she got used to it, the smell of death.

When Herbert went into his final death throes, helpless, gurgling, his eyes bulging in their sockets, demanding pity, Velma had simply said, "Soon you can chase your little hussies in hell, father." Herbert had gurgled louder, trying to speak. "Save thy speech for thy maker old man. I will not forgive you." With that, Velma left the room and got ready to go shopping. When she returned several hours later, Herbert was just a corpse.

"Holy, holy, holy," she whispered like a mantra while she put away the groceries. Then she went to fetch Doctor Watkins.

Velma kept her father's clothes as a reminder, a symbol of the evil that can befall you if you disobey God's sacred commandments. But young Randy, all alone in the dark closet for hours on end, knew nothing of his grandfather's sins. All he was aware of was the dark and the awful smell. Herbert's clothes had aged like Aunty Velma's heart, old, rotten and musky. As Randy sat there, clutching the wet crotch of his knickers with one hand, the other thumb planted firmly in his mouth, and the snot running done his upper lip in a thick, clear stream, he made up a little game to pass the time.

The game that Randy invented wasn't like the innocent ones he used to play with his mom and dad before Jack's death. Like the time they took the ferry and drove up to Kelowna, and then camped on the lake where the big monster, Ogopogo lived. All the way up the Hope-Princeton Highway, the family had played "I spy with my little eye" and sang happy songs. Those games were fun.

No, the game Randy played, those dark afternoons in the closet, was much different. It had a central theme with variations.

Randy would picture an animal, any species would do, a dog, cat, rabbit, guinea pig, and then he would dissect it slowly in his mind, exploring every part of its anatomy, layer by layer, piece by piece, using a scalpel sharper than the knife his mother used to cut up pickles and cheese or carve a roast beef. And Randy always pictured the butchering of his subjects in a clean, antiseptic way, like Ben Casey conducting brain surgery on the boob tube: scalpel, sponge, let's cut out that nasty tumor, Doc!

One day, Randy took his game out of the closet. His "coming out" happened by chance when he found a large bullfrog by the Swamp, a patch of marshy water near the Pacific National Exhibition grounds. Randy picked the frog up and stroked its warts. It felt kind of slimy in his hand, the way frogs do. "Hi, there," Randy greeted Mr. Frog with the toothless grin of a ten-year old. "Would you like to play a game, huh?" The frog didn't reply, but Randy's grip tightened, the frog now looking more like a wiener ready to be skinned.

Randy set up the execution with the efficiency of a Nazi S.S. Captain. Two three-quarter inch alder saplings were bent over and pegged to the ground with twine, looking like a crossbow waiting for a bolt to shoot. Randy lowered Mr. Frog to the ground and held him there on his back with one finger. With his free hand, Randy attached two butcher string nooses to the frog's rear legs. Randy pulled out his penknife, pronounced a sentence of death, and then asked Mr. Frog if he had any last words. Mr. Frog chose to remain silent, so Randy counted backwards from ten and cut the alders loose from the stake. The two saplings sprung up in a flash, tearing the frog's rear legs from its body. Mr. Frog didn't die instantly, but tried to crawl away on two front legs. Randy finished him off with a sharp stick.

Snakes proved to be even better playmates than frogs. Randy discovered this one drab September day when he found a good sized gardener out behind Aunty Velma's tool shed. "Hi, Mr. Snake. Who'd you eat today?" Randy had seen the pythons on Tarzan eat grownups for a snack. He picked up the snake by the tail. "You wanna play a game with me?" Randy began to spin it. "Round and round the mulberry bush, the monkey chased the weasel." Randy spun the snake around faster and faster. "Pop goes the weasel!" Randy piped in a crackly soprano. Then he dropped the reptile on the ground and watched it try to wriggle away in a dazed state. At that very moment, Randy spotted the red, five gallon container of mixed gas sitting beside Aunty Velma's lawn mower. He could see Mr. Edison's light bulb come on in his mind, the way it did in cartoons. Soon Mr. Snake was sizzling like a steak on a barbecue.

"Neat-o," Randy gasped softly as he watched with bright eyes. Death by fire became his favorite modus operandi.

THE BOAT THUMPED over a wave. The jolt brought Randy back to the present. He surveyed their progress. The terrain all looked the same to him. "So how far to the end of the lake?" he asked. They had just passed the bluffs at the point where Pitt Lake veers to the northwest.

"Just a few more miles. Hey! See that cave up there?" Kevin pointed at the cliff. Randy squinted at the shore, trying to make out where and what he was pointing at. "We should check it out on the way back, might find something interesting." Kevin pulled out a couple of cigarettes and lit them. He handed one to Randy. "We should hit the mouth of the upper Pitt in about fifteen minutes or so. You want to take over the helm for a while?"

"Sure. No problem."

"No more deadheads?"

"No. Gee, I said I was sorry."

"Well, take it easy, okay." Randy traded places with Kevin, who stretched back on the padded vinyl passenger seat.

"Ahhh . . . This is the life." The monotonous drone of the engine soon had Kevin's head nodding in time with the cross waves.

Chapter 15

"**This is it**, folks," George informed Bev and Paul. They paddled towards a white beach of mixed sand and pebbles. A few large rocks and boulders broke the surface of the water close in by the shore. Above the high water mark—a pickup stick pile of grey driftwood logs—stood a line of second-growth hemlocks, their gnarled branches twisted by the strong winds that often swept up the lake in the late afternoon, lifting up the waters and pounding the shore with two or three foot high whitecaps. Today was no exception.

"Pull your canoe in over there," George directed, pointing to a break in the beach where a small creek emptied its cold glacial waters. He had to shout to be heard above the roar of the waves. "Careful! And keep your stern facing windward. If one of those suckers catches you broadside, it will flip you!"

Bev cupped her hands. "Okay, Chief," she screamed back. Paul corrected their course and followed George's canoe in towards shore. The last three miles had been a battle. The current and wind had both worked against them, and it had made for a bumpy and sometimes nerve racking ride. Their arms ached from hours of hard paddling.

When they finally reached the calmer waters of the creek, they relaxed, letting their tired muscles rest. Paul and George both leaped out of their canoes at the same time and pulled the wet hulls up onto the coarse sand.

"Yipes! This water is freezing!" Paul exclaimed, his teeth chattering. But then Bev disembarked without getting so much as one drop of water on her white sneakers. "This way, your majesty." Paul gave her a mocking bow, "Queen Beverly, the First."

They unloaded the supplies, as much as they could carry in one trip, then George showed them a trail that cut through the dense foliage. It ended in a meadow, about a hundred yards from the edge of the lake. George had camped there since he was a boy, so had his father and probably his grandfather and great-grandfather. It was the site of an old Katsie satellite village, used only in the summer. In the winter, food was scarce and the icy lake too dangerous to navigate safely in a canoe. The colder months had always been spent at the main village near Port Hammond.

The rocky meadow was covered by soft moss and short dried grasses. There was a circle of sand on one side big enough to pitch three or four tents and a large stone fire pit in the center. The three of them quickly began setting up camp, trying to beat the lengthening shadows of the approaching dusk. Bev and Paul set up their blue, canvas pup tent, and laid out their sleeping bags, zipping them together to form a double sized bed.

George had his tent erected in no time at all. He had had years of practice. Paul raised his eyebrows at its ratty appearance, the canvas covered in multi-colored patches.

"Are you sure that thing will keep out the water, Chief?"

"Yep. You just worry about yourself and the little lady. This Injun can take care of himself jus' fine thanks." George threw up a makeshift lean-to with a blue, plastic tarp and some poles. They needed some place to store their grub and other supplies in. When everything was in place, he built a roaring fire while Bev and Paul foraged the area, trying to scrounge up enough firewood to last them the evening.

"This tastes fantastic!" Paul exclaimed, as he took a sip of steaming hot chocolate. "Mmmm..." It was the Real McCoy, not one of those instant, stir and mix concoctions that come in little one serving packages or a can. Bev had heated up a whole can of real condensed milk, added a generous heaping of powered chocolate, and then added boiling water. She served it with a sprinkle of cinnamon, and didn't forget to add a few miniature marshmallows. They bobbed around the surface of the foamy liquid like buoys in a harbor.

"Ugh! This heapin' good medicine, Sunshine," George complimented her. He continued the conversation with a series of sign language, gestures and guttural grunts that soon had Bev and Paul doubled over with laughter. Then George jumped to his feet and started dancing around the fire, Indian style.

"Hope that's not a war dance!" said Paul, as Bev got up and joined George in the farce. After a few times around the fire, Bev grabbed Paul and pulled him to his feet. They all danced until they were exhausted.

"Got to have a sense of humor about these things," George philosophized as they collapsed onto their seats, a couple of log benches. "It gives the tourists something to write home about." George scratched his crotch. The dancing had made his balls itchy. "Any of that hot chocolate left, Sunshine?" Bev poured the last of it into his mug.

"Actually, my people still keep up the traditional dances. In fact, some of them take it very seriously. It's a form of socializing, worship and celebration all wrapped up in one.

"It begins when the medicine man leaves the longhouse wearing his sacred robes, the head of a grizzly and the fur and paws of a cougar. He wears a leather pouch around his neck. In it is strong magic. In one hand, he carries a rattle drum, in the other, an eagle feather. Two young maidens lock arms with him and slowly escort him around the reserve. This takes about an hour. When they return to the longhouse, the fires are lit and the drums begin.

"The chants start slowly, the men singing in unison. Then the drums pick up tempo as the dancers enter. They too are in costume. Their steps speak the story of the great Khaals, a supernatural being who through his deeds became known to my people as the Transformer. Khaals could transport himself to any place instantly with a mere thought, and he had the power to change matter at will, be it flesh or stone. He could turn a stone into a fish or a bear into a rock."

"He was one of your Gods?" Paul interjected. He was supposed to be the expert on the subject.

"No. Well, not in the way that a Christian would think of God. Khaals was not the Supreme Spirit who created the sun and the moon and all the tribes of man. Khaals was more of a servant sent here by the Supreme One to sort out the good from the bad. He often appeared in the form of a raven." George yawned. He told a few more tales of Salish mythology, then said abruptly, "Time for this old sack of bones to hit the hay. See you in the morning." He got up and headed for his tent.

"Night, Chief!" Bev and Paul replied in unison.

Paul put his arm around Bev and nibbled on her ear. "I think it's about time we hit the sack too," he whispered.

"I hope you don't plan on going right to sleep," she replied.

Paul shook his head. Bev smiled and took his hand, guiding him to their tent.

AT **THE MOUTH** of the upper Pitt River, about three quarters of a mile from where George, Paul and Bev slept, another small campfire burned between two pup tents. Kevin Macarthur sat with his back against a log, trying to read <u>Gaijin</u> by a propone camp light. Randy Smith sat on a cedar round closer to the fire, roasting marshmallows with a stick and sipping a beer. They had chosen to camp on a flat, sandy spot near the edge of the river, the tents pitched on one of the few grassy areas available. Dense forest surrounded the camp on all three sides, but they had found several well used trails going in different directions. An exploration of the trails was on the agenda for the morning.

"Damn mosquitoes." Randy slapped at the insects. He felt like they were eating him alive. "How come I can't see them?"

Kevin laughed. "They don't call them no-see-ums for nothing. They're tiny, biting flies actually. The light of the fire attracts them." He reached into his pack and pulled out a bottle. "Here, rub some of this on your arms and face."

"Thanks." Randy rubbed the repellant on his exposed skin, and then tossed the bottle back to Kevin who snapped it out of the air with two fingers. "Nice catch." Randy inspected both of his arms carefully. "Seems to be working already."

"You betcha. It's good stuff." Kevin went back to his reading.

Randy pulled out a deck of cards and tried to play a game of Solitaire, but he wasn't into it. He still felt wound up from the day's activities, and he couldn't get the girl in the canoe out of his mind, and the fact that the faggot he had nearly made mince-meat out of, was with her, probably her lover—the lucky bastard—and who knows, maybe he's even doing her right now. Randy threw the deck down in disgust. "What's the book about?" he asked Kevin, hoping to strike up a conversation, anything to get his mind off of the beautiful bitch.

"It's the sequel to Shogun. Remember the movie?"

"Oh, yeah. I liked the part where the samari chops off the guys head 'cause he didn't bow proper. Then he chops him up into little pieces. Cool." Randy hand cut the air with an imaginary samari sword. "Eeeeaaaaiiii!"

Kevin shook his head at Randy's antics. "It also ties in Taipan and Noble House. James Clavel was a fucking genius!" Kevin turned back to his book.

Randy figured it would be pushing his luck to interrupt Kevin again, so he decided to hit the sack. Maybe if I jerk off, I'll feel better, he considered. "Good night, Kev. See you in the morning."

"G'night. I'll wake you up about 5:30, so we can get an early start. How's eggs, bacon and pancakes sound, with real maple syrup?"

"Sounds great! You know I'm easy, easy as a three-dollar hooker."

"Yeah, and I'll lend you two bucks. Now go to bed, you hoser!"

Randy removed his jacket, climbed into his tent feet first and quickly zipped up the zipper on the mosquito netting. The little suckers could find something or someone else to eat tonight. Randy pulled off his shirt, socks and jeans, and then climbed into his sleeping bag.

The sand was soft and with a bit of grass, it made a reasonably comfortable mattress. Randy thought about the girl in the canoe again and got an instant erection. He stroked himself as quietly as possible, not wanting Kevin to hear. He pictured her undoing her bikini, imagined her gorgeous body as it was slowly revealed to him. "Mmmmm . . ." Just as Randy was about to orgasm, his Mother's face intruded on the fantasy. She was scowling at him like he was being a very naughty boy. His penis went soft in his hand. "Shit," he whispered. Randy tried for ten more minutes, but couldn't get another erection. All he could imagine now was his mother's face, that look of disapproval, the angry scorn. "Damn." Randy was sweaty from exertion. He lay there in the dark, feeling cold and frustrated, listening to Kevin snoring away in the other tent. It seemed like forever before he finally drifted off to sleep.

Chapter 16

THE DREAM IS very familiar. Paul has had it since he was a child. The funny thing is that each time he has the dream, it is always the same and yet totally different, a paradox. Like variations on a theme, a mad J.S. Bach or Ludwig Van Beethoven improvising elaborate sculptures of melody and rhythm over a thread bare theme: da da da dee dum, da da da DA! The style and the plot were always the same, but the characters, settings and circumstances changed with each reoccurrence. The dreams were based on some unknown template deep in the shadows of Paul's mind. Paul knew one thing only: the dreams came from his more primitive, reptile brain, the seat of his emotions. The template of Paul's nightmares was fear, pure and simple, raw naked fear: fear of the unknown, fear of death, fear of living, fear of pain, and fear of fear itself. Sure, some shrink might ask him how he felt about his mother and father, the Freud thing, or did he have feelings of inadequacy sexually, but Paul knew better; that psycho analyst stuff had nothing to do with this. This dream was different. It was like a package left on your doorstep with a bomb inside. Ticking. Waiting to explode and blow your guts all over the sidewalk. Some things are better left alone. Undisturbed. Like turning over a big rock or rotten log and seeing the blind crawly things that live in the damp dark soil. The human mind is like that. Open it up and who knows what hidden thoughts or alien feelings might come wriggling out. Like a microscope can open a window to a whole new world of the microcosm, a dream can open the door to the scariest thing in the universe: one's naked, inner self.

The dream had become so familiar by now that Paul recognized it almost instantly. He would be dreaming along normally, but the second *that* dream started, he would know it, and try to wake himself up fast.

A typical version of the dream might go like this—

Paul is alone in an old abandoned house. There is no furniture, just rotten floor boards and tons of dust. The ceilings are decorated with cobwebs and the windows are so dirty that you can't see outside, the sills littered with dead flies. They were buzzing in his head, but how could dead flies make any noise?

There is a staircase. Paul ascends it slowly, the aging stair treads groaning in protest. At the top of the stairs there is a door. It is closed. It is an old fashioned raised panel door made out of dark wood with a tarnished brass door knob, Paul reaches for the knob. The buzzing is much louder. At first the doorknob seems to be locked, but it is only stiff from lack of use. It finally turns in his hand. Paul pushes the door inward slowly, the hinges creaking loudly. The buzzing is so loud he covers his eyes, but it doesn't help. The awful noise makes his skin crawl and causes the hair on the back of his neck to stand up. Paul finally looks into the room and screams. But he sees nothing but blackness.

Then Paul is falling into a deep black pit. He is trying to claw his way back to consciousness. He does not know what he saw in the room. Something bad. Something evil. But from the moment he looked into the room, everything is blank. All he knows is that he is terrified. The buzzing has stopped, but his head is filled with weird ringing noises and his scalp tingles. Finally he wakes up in his bed, shaking, and his skin clammy, covered in cold sweat.

The room is pitched dark. Paul reaches over to his bedside lamp. Click. But the light does not come on. He gets out of bed and stumbles across the room to the main light switch. Click. The overhead light is not working either. Maybe the power is out or—

The terror returns as Paul realizes that he is still in that awful dream. Again he sees the blackness and screams, again he is falling down that dark bottomless pit, yelling and thrashing until he wakes up in his bed, shaking.

But is he awake? Sometimes, the cycle continues for two or three times before an exhausted and frightened Paul Gregory reached for the light switch and the room is finally filled with light.

IT **IS A** cool, overcast morning. Wisps of mist hang on the trees, giving them the look of an enchanted forest, a fairy tale about to happen. Randy is out alone, looking for the lost mine. He reaches the top of a sharp ridge and there it is, the hat rock gleaming in the sun, a giant gold nugget. "I'm rich! I'm rich!" he screams, throwing his black Stetson high into the air.

The hat does a double somersault and turns into a raven which flies off screeching an echo, "I'm rich! I'm rich!" When Randy turns back towards his treasure, it is gone.

In its place is the girl from the canoe. She is laying on a dog hair blanket, totally naked, her bronze skin glistening under a layer of bear oil. Her long, black hair spills onto the grass, silhouetting her face like the petals of a dark flower. Randy has never seen anything so beautiful, so sexy. Writhing, moaning, her hips gyrating seductively. It seems as if every cell in her body is vibrating pure passion. She beckons to him softly with a finger, "Come closer . . . Closer."

Spellbound, Randy moves towards her.

"Closer, Randy. I know you want me."

Like the song of a Siren, her call is irresistible. Randy continues forward trace-like, unbuckling his jeans, letting them fall down around his knees with his under shorts.

The girl reaches up with both arms and pulls him down on top of her. Her skin feels incredibly smooth, soft and warm. Randy cups her breasts with both hands and kisses her. Her tongue is hot in his mouth. "Oh, baby!" Randy gasps. He can feel the heat coming from her body in waves. Her hand reaches down to guide his manhood into her. Randy moans in anticipation. This is it, his ultimate love, such sweet, sweet ecstasy.

The moment he enters her, the girl smiles triumphantly and turns into a long rattlesnake. The sharp fangs tear savagely at the flesh of his penis, sending a bolt of hot pain up his spine. His mouth opens in a scream, but it gets lost in his throat. The snake releases its venom and slithers off into the tall grasses, hissing.

Randy is dying. He knows it. The numbness is creeping up his torso. Soon it will reach his heart. Death is only minutes away.

"I'm rich! I'm Rich!" the raven mocks from high in a tree.

"Shut the fuck up!" Randy screams back, clutching his swollen member with both hands. "She was so beautiful!" he sobs.

Everything is fading, losing its color. Soon all that he can see are a pair of eyes glowing in the darkness. Am I in hell yet, Randy wonders? Nothing exists except for those eyes, but whose eyes? The raven's? No. There is something awfully familiar about these eyes, too familiar. They are— They are! "Oh, noOOO!!! No, Mommy!" Randy cries. "Please!"

THE LIGHT IN the bathroom came on with a sudden click. Randy was sitting on the john at Aunty Velma's house, masturbating. His clothes were piled neatly on the hamper beside the tub. A couple of weeks earlier, his friend Sid Holman had given a demonstration, and showed him the white stuff that came out to make babies. Randy was trying hard to duplicate this feat, but without success; Sid was fourteen, nearly two years older.

There was no lock on the bathroom door, Aunty Velma had it removed, but Randy thought his mother was sleeping.

"You little pervert! How dare you!" Elaine Smith smacked her son hard across the side of the head and sent him sprawling between the tub and toilet. "You want me to cut it off? Huh? I will!"

Elaine dragged Randy by the hair, down the hallway and into the kitchen. With her free hand, she grabbed the chrome pull on the silverware drawer. The whole drawer pulled out of the cabinet and crashed loudly onto the floor, spilling its contents in a heap.

Elaine selected a large butcher knife.

"You see this?" She pinched his shriveled penis and held the butcher knife about an inch above its base. "You want to lose it? Huh?"

"No, Mommy. Please!"

"If I ever catch you doing that disgusting thing again, I'll cut it off! I swear! You hear me?"

"No, no, Mommy. Please!" Randy shrieked. "Please don't cut off my pickle! I'll be good. Honest. I won't touch it anymore. I Promise!"

Randy looked up at his mother. Her face was wild, distorted. There was no sanity left in her glazed brown eyes.

"Go up to your room right now! Get in the closet and don't come out until I tell you to. Tell Jesus you're sorry, and pray for forgiveness."

"O,Okay, M-M-Mommy," Randy sputtered, wiping the snot on his sleeve. "I'll be good!"

"Get out of my sight! You disgust me."

Randy dragged his sorry butt upstairs to the closet. It seemed even darker and scarier than usual.

"PAUL . . . PAUL." Bev snuggled closer to Paul and gave his shoulder a gentle shake.

"Huh?" Paul replied groggily. "What?"

"You were yelling in your sleep."

"I was?"

"Yes. It woke me up."

"Oh."

"Was it a bad dream?"

"I dunno. Guess it was." Paul lifted his head up and looked around, obviously disorientated. "I have them sometimes."

Bev kissed him on the cheek. "Try and go back to sleep."

"Okay." Paul rolled back over on his side. Bev put her arm around his chest and pressed her body against his back.

"I love you," she whispered in his ear.

RANDY WOKE UP slowly. Someone was jabbing him hard on the legs. "Owww," he groaned. "Please don't, Mommy. I won't p-play—"

"I ain't your mommy. What the fuck is wrong with you?" Kevin snarled. "You scared the living shit out of me, screaming like a bloody banshee."

"Sorry, man. It . . . I guess it was just a bad dream. A nightmare, that's all."

Kevin grunted something unintelligible and went back to his tent. Randy was still trembling from head to foot, his sleeping bag soaked with sweat. It was a long time before sleep came again.

Chapter 17

July 4, 2007

Excerpt from the journal of Paul Gregory, PhD:

Day Two-

I didn't sleep very well last night. I had an awful dream. It was about the day Billy Taylor died.

It's kind of strange, but I don't think that I've thought of Billy in ages. It's funny how unpleasant things slip your mind for years, and then come back to haunt you when you least expect it. It's natural, I guess, some reflex of our subconscious, trying to forget the really bad things that happen to us.

It was supposed to be one of the best nights of our lives. Carol and I were both on the Grad Committee. We spent that afternoon, helping to decorate the school gymnasium for the ceremony.

Billy was there too, in all his glory. I remember him standing on top of a tall step ladder we borrowed from the janitor, fastening crepe-paper streamers to the metal trusses supporting the gym roof. And he was goofing off as usual, pretending to moon the girls below. I remember them laughing, and calling him a scuz bucket.

"Hey, down yonder, there's a full moon shining tonight!" Billy stuck out his ass and did an Elvis double-hip grind.

"Oh, you scuz bucket, Billy," the girls chirped back, loving every minute of the attention.

Billy just grinned and blew them all a kiss. "Thank you. Thank you. Yer a lovely audience! We've got a really big SHOE for you tonight." He had the world by the balls. Silver spoon—dad was a doctor—good looks and enough smarts to be a very successful con artist if that was his inclination. Billy Boy was a guy on a mission. To our parents, he was always suspect, a James Dean style radical, which meant troublemaker; but to us, Billy was just cool. None of us really had a clue what made him tick. He was a Rubik's Cube, a Chinese wood puzzle, like trying to play pickup sticks with an overcooked plate of spaghetti, hard to define. With him anything might happen.

Billy loved Mission Impossible—

"Your mission, gentlemen, should you decide to accept it, is to get Mrs. Simmons"— our geography teacher—"to have a triple orgasm while reciting the fifty state capitals in reverse alphabetical order. Your brains will now self-destruct in twenty seconds!"

And the Twilight Zone—

"You have entered a dimension beyond time and space . . . You will all report to Principal Baker's office for praise and candy. Your report card will have more A's than Alabama. Your parents won't make you clean up your room for a whole year!" Billy loved attention. From the time I met him in first grade, Billy was always the class clown. He drove the teachers batty with his endless pranks and practical jokes. And these were the days before corporal punishment was banned from schools. Billy got the strap more times than any other kid I knew. Sometimes his hands looked like raw pate. The Principal, Mr. Patterson, was a really mean man, sadistic. I'm sure he enjoyed the Gestapo routine. "First ve vill pull out the fingernails, then ve vill get down to zee more serious business."

One time, Billy put an open Playboy centerfold and an upwrapped condom in the desk drawer of our guidance teacher. She was a very old prude who thought sex could be controlled with diagrams of reproduction, films depicting the horrors of venereal disease, and lectures on the joys of celibacy. She had obviously never set foot in the boy's locker room. Mr. Patterson strapped him really good that time; Billy couldn't make a fist for a week. A prissy little goody-two-shoes named Susan Phillips had finked. She'd seen him put something in Mrs. Moore's desk just before class that morning.

Another time Billy snuck into the girls' changing room while they were out having gym. Next thing we knew, there were a couple of dozen bras and panties flying from the school flagpole. Yep, Billy knew the inside of the detention hall better than anyone else in school. And his grades were always questionable, yet somehow he managed to squeak by and pass.

We were the class of 1975, a good year! When the decorations were all in place, the chairs laid out for us on stage and our parents on the gym floor, we all went home to have dinner and don our spiffiest duds.

I guess everyone remembers their graduation ceremony in their own way. For me, the whole thing seemed kind of surreal, seeing us all for the first time in a strange, new light: the young men in suits and ties, carnations in the button holes, fresh haircuts all slicked back, and the young ladies in long gowns with corsages—pretty posh—and there were my parents sitting in the third row, a stupid grin on their faces just like everyone else in the audience; they all looked kind of contented like they had just taken a big dump and really enjoyed the experience. I had this awful premonition that I was going to trip and fall going down the stairs from the stage. The horror of making a fool out of myself in front of the whole town made me break out into a cold sweat—"Hey, did you see young Gregory during the Grand March? Fell right on his ass and split his pants wide open. What a fool!"—when it was my turn to go up and get my diploma, I thought I was going to die of sheer nervousness. Fortunately I got the important paperwork and made it down the stairs without falling flat on my face. The girl I was escorting, or should I say, was escorting me—Diana Forton, I think her name was—told me to lighten up. I was stiff as a board or a corpse after rigor mortis set in. But have you ever tried to walk with two left feet?

After the valedictory and all the speeches, which seemed to drag on forever, we assembled on the dance floor for the first waltz. I'm sure mom's feet were sore for a day or two after. In my generation, we didn't usually come within a few feet of our dance partner, just bobbed around, and flailed our arms, grooving to the back beat. Needless to say, I'm still a klutz on the dance floor.

We only hung around with our parents for the minimum amount of time required by edict. We were all dying to get to the real grad, a rip roaring party we had been planning for weeks.

Out near the nature park on Westminster Highway, there were several acres of scrub land that didn't seem to be used for anything much. There were a couple of dirt access roads, a gravel pit near the middle where you could park a few dozen cars and have a bonfire. I don't know who owned the land. It might have been a railway right of way, there were some rusted tracks running through it, or maybe it belonged to B.C. Hydro, who as you shall see, also used it for their own purposes.

I picked up Carol at her place about ten o'clock. She looked great in a wool knit sweater and a pair of stretchy jump pants. I fantasized about how easy it would be to slip my hands down the back of those pants. Love that easy access!

We drove to the party in my dad's 1960 Studebaker. It was his baby. He handed me the keys with a stern warning, "Don't drink, if you're driving, and don't drive if you're drinking, and I'm sure there'll be a fair bit of that tonight. Take an old pillow and some blankets and sleep it off in the back if you have to," he said. "And don't do anything I wouldn't do!"

"I won't, Dad!" I replied. For once in a long time, I agreed with him. I thought the pillow and blankets were a great idea, more comfy for Carol and me to make out on in the backseat later. I had only had sex once before, and I was definitely looking forward to a repeat performance.

I lost my innocence to a girl named Susan Prescott. She was what you might describe as easy. Looking back, I guess that was a kind way to describe Slippery Sue, as all the boys liked to call her. The other girls just called her a slut. They hated her because she had slept with most of their boyfriends at one time or another. Sue's married now, but hasn't changed much from what I hear. I don't envy her husband, poor guy.

Losing my virginity wasn't such a big deal, at least not as big a deal as I had dreamed it would be. Carol and I were both at a party at Tim Holiday's—his parents were out of town for the weekend and it was a real house wrecker—but Carol had to leave early; her father always insisted she be home by midnight.

After I walked Carol home, I decided to return to the party. After all, the night was young and I still had nearly half a pint of Wood's Navy Rum left. I couldn't let it go to waste now, could I?

I wandered around the kitchen, squeezing through the crush of babbling bodies and finally made my way into the living room. There was a small vacant space on the couch, so I sat down beside Sue and struck up a conversation. Sue wasn't the brightest star in the universe, more like one of those really dim ones you can just see with the Hubble telescope, and I don't remember what we talked about, probably not much. The Beatles were telling us that "all you need is love," and Sue agreed. Before the song was over, she was all over me. We started necking. One thing quickly led to another, and we ended up in one of the bedrooms where Sue deflowered me.

Billy was grinning at me from the kitchen, when Sue and I emerged half an hour later, both looking more than a little disheveled. He never told anyone though, and I was glad for it. He was a real bud, ol' Billy. Carol never knew that I had cheated on her.

The grad party was in full swing by the time Carol and I arrived. The bonfire was huge and white hot. Red Neuville's dad owned a Texaco station on Three Road. His dad had donated a whole pickup load of used tires. Someone found a stack of rotten railway ties abandoned near the gravel pit, and some of the guys were hauling them over to the fire. Every time they plopped one on the blaze, a huge shower of sparks would fly up, landing just about everywhere. A big spark landed on Carol's sweater, but I managed to put it out before it did any real damage. Trevor Carlson got his hair badly singed when he ran in too close to heave a tire on the fire, but he didn't care, he was well into the bottle of Canadian Club his father had given him as a graduation present.

A couple of guys had brought acoustic guitars along, and it wasn't too long before we all got into a sing song—

"Cause she's a honky-tonk woman. Give me, give me, give me, the honky-tonk blues..."

I don't know who said it first, but someone shouted, "Hey, look up there! Billy is up to his tricks."

Billy had climbed up onto one of BC Hydro's steel transmission towers. He was waving down at the party from one of the cross beams at about the forty foot mark.

"Com'on down from there before you break you neck, Billy Boy!" I shouted.

Either Billy didn't take me seriously or he didn't hear, because he immediately started climbing higher. I started to get worried. Billy was in no condition to be climbing around that high up. "Hey, Billy, be careful!" I yelled, afraid he was going to fall any second. He was walking out onto the second cross beam, and he looked like he was losing it, waving back and forth. My stomach felt like it was in my throat. Then Billy threw up his arms for better balance.

The one brief instant that followed will stay burned into my memory for as long as I live: the brilliant, blue flash of the arc jumping down from the wire to Billy's fingertips, Billy's hair and jean jacket exploding into flames. He didn't even scream. In fact, he didn't make a sound. The doctor who did the post mortem stated that Billy must have died instantly, but I could have sworn that I saw him beating at the flames like he was trying to put them out. Maybe it was a reflexive action, muscle spasms or something. I don't know. We were all in shock. Everything was happening in slow motion.

Billy's body seemed to hang there, the scene frozen like somebody had pressed the pause button. Then it teetered and plummeted the sixty or seventy feet to the gravel. The sick thud it made when it hit the ground, bones snapping like match sticks, was the worst sound that I've ever heard. Even now, I can hear it play over and over in my mind: "thud, crunch . . . thud, crunch."

I ran over to Billy, thinking in my panicked and somewhat drunken state, that there might be something I could do to help him, which was ridiculous. He had just been electrocuted—later we learned that it was a three-hundred-thousand volt main line, enough juice to run an entire city—and that he had fallen at least sixty feet. The only person who could have helped Billy at this point was Jesus, and He hadn't put in a personal appearance on this planet in a long, long time.

Billy's face was charred black, except for his eyeballs which looked like two poached eggs, and his white teeth grinned through shrunken black lips. His hair was burnt right off, including his eyebrows, and his sooty clothing was still smoking. There was a sick, sweet smell of cooked meat in the air.

All of the girls were crying by now, except for Sally Henderson. She just stood there wide-eyed, mumbling, "No. No. No." Sally had been Billy's sweetheart. They had even talked of getting married someday, but no one had taken that too seriously. Billy hadn't seemed like the marrying kind.

I was crying too. Carol had taken one look at Billy, and then had run over to some bushes, holding her mouth. I could hear her puking. Most of the guys were just standing around with their mouths half open, too shocked to speak, let alone move.

We buried Billy at Mountain View Cemetery in Vancouver. The entire graduating class of Richmond High went to the funeral. As I watched them lower the casket into the dark hole, I remember thinking that this is only a joke, that's all. Ha, ha, ha. Just another one of Billy's endless gags. Any second now, the lid on that coffin will pop open, and out will jump Billy with a big grin, and he'll yell, "Boo!" But that didn't happen.

Chapter 18

KEVIN PICKED UP a small stick and stirred the embers of the previous night's fire. The coals were still hot underneath the grey ashes on top, and pretty soon the flames licked up the unburnt wood he added. It was 5:10 a.m. Kevin filled up a black cast-iron kettle with lake water, and suspended it over the fire pit.

"Hey, Randy! It's time to get up little buddy." A loud groan came from the yellow pup tent. "Coffee's on."

Another groan, followed by a mumbled, "What time is it?"

"Just after five."

Kevin got out a large frying pan, laid in some strips of bacon and cracked four eggs. The aroma of the food, mixed with the brisk morning air, made his stomach gurgle with anticipation. "Mmmm...Sure smells good. Hey, Randy. Chow's almost done. Up and at 'em."

"Aww, man. Can't I sleep for another hour?"

"Nope. We got us some treasure to find and the sooner we start looking, the sooner we're going to find it. Early bird gets the worm." Kevin dished some food out onto a plate and poured himself a large mug of coffee. "Come and eat before it gets cold."

Randy crawled out of the pup tent in his underwear.

"Brrr . . . It's freezing out here."

"What do you mean? It's beautiful out! Are you allergic to the fresh air or what?" Kevin gobbled down a mouthful of scrambled egg. "Mmm, mmm. Nothing tastes as good as when it's cooked outdoors." Kevin poured Randy a cup of black coffee. "Here you go." Kevin handed him the cup, then dished out another plate of breakfast. Randy set it down on the log beside him. He was still getting dressed.

"What was all that screaming about last night?" Kevin asked.

"Hey, I'm sorry about that. It was just a real mother of a bad dream."

"No more rich foods for you before bedtime."

"Yes, dad!" Randy pulled on some jeans, a sweater, and then laced his boots on a makeshift log bench close to the fire.

"Wow! This is good," he finally acknowledged when he dug into his breakfast. He hadn't realized how hungry he was. "So, where 'bouts are we gonna start looking for the gold?"

Kevin finished chewing a mouthful, considering their options, and then answered. "I think we should spend today checking out those trails." He pointed to the north and east. "We'll try the inland one first, two hours up then two hours back, and then we'll explore the one that seems to run off parallel with the river."

"Then what?" Randy asked. His plate was almost empty.

"Well, if anything looks promising, we can break camp tomorrow morning and head up into the bush, if not, we'll take the boat up river to Corbold Creek. Jackson's find was supposedly somewhere in the general area between here and the creek, while Volcanic Brown's last camp was quite a ways due east of that on the Stave Glacier." Kevin grabbed the kettle and poured them each another coffee. "So, what do you think?"

"You're the boss," Randy affirmed.

Kevin gulped down the rest of his coffee. "Then let's get this show on the road."

They packed some provisions for the hike. Kevin slung an old British .303 over his shoulder. It had a scope and a clip. It was his favorite rifle, one of the few things his father had given him besides grief. A spare clip dangled from his belt, next to his bowie knife. Randy carried a large caliber semi-automatic that would have looked more at home with a SWAT team. They both had canteens, and a small pack held provisions, lunch and a first aid kit. Kevin volunteered to carry the pack for the first shift, with the understanding that they would switch every half hour or so.

It was a beautiful morning. Only a few puffs of cumulus clouds dotted the blue sky. It was still a bit cool, the sun had just made its appearance over the mountains, but you could tell that it was going to warm up and possibly be a real scorcher by noon. It was a great day to be out in the woods on a hike. The trail was easy going at first. It had obviously been established for a long time—a bare strip about three to four feet wide with only moss and short grasses—although the salal and brambles on either side looked almost impenetrable. Kevin suspected that deer and elk used the path regularly to access the river.

As they got further inland, the trail became steeper, with the odd rise that needed to be scaled on all fours. Second-growth fir and cedar trees lined the way here, shorter and more sparsely spaced, their limbs gnarled and misshapen—a rocky side hill with little top soil and exposure to high winds was not a hospitable place—gradually species more adaptable to the higher altitudes became prevalent. Kevin and Randy stopped for lunch under an arbor of pines that provided shade and a mossy place to sit amongst the coarse glacial till that littered the hillside.

Kevin started to sing, "I can see for miles and miles." The Who song had been a chart buster when Kevin was a teenager. The view was incredible. They could see for miles . . . miles and miles, right across the lake to the snow-capped coastal mountains that separated Pitt Lake from Howe Sound. To the south, they could see beyond the point to where the lake bent sharply to the southwest. Part of Little Goose Island was visible, the rest hidden behind the outcropping of rock that housed the cave they had observed on the boat trip up the lake. Far below, they could see a red canoe heading south along the shoreline. The tiny beings paddling in it looked smaller than ants. Kevin imagined himself as a giant, picking up one of the nearby boulders, and hurling it down onto the canoe, squashing the occupants like a couple of insignificant bugs. A minute later, the canoe pulled in closer to the shore, out of sight.

"Ain't this the life, little buddy!" Kevin exclaimed, after they had finished their lunch and stretched out on the moss for a short siesta. "No hustle, no bustle. No telephone or rush hour traffic. No headaches. Just peace and the blue sky."

"Ain't that the truth," Randy replied, feeling full and a bit horny. He imagined the girl from the canoe dancing in the sunlight. And there she was, looking so real, Randy felt like he could have pulled her right out of the air. Life would be perfect, if only she were his. A sudden flash of his mother's face, twisted in rage like some mythological gargoyle, spoiled the illusion. Damn her anyway, Randy fumed, the old hag!

A wasp flew by and landed on Kevin's cheek. At first he froze. It looked like his heart had stopped, not even the hairs on his arms moved. Then he screamed. It was one of those low guttural utterances that might wake up the dead. As he rolled to the right, swatting madly at his face, the wasp flew off indignantly, perhaps seeking more friendly territory.

"Hey, Kevin! What's the matter?" Randy was concerned, Kevin had never looked so vulnerable. "You okay?"

"Yeah," Kevin sighed, the sudden sweat beading on his forehead. "I'm alright. I just can't stand those little suckers. I sat on one of their nests when I was a kid... hate the fuckers. They, they—"

Randy was puzzled, he had never seen fear like that in Kevin's eyes before.

GEORGE AND PAUL decided to take a paddle down the lake. They planned to hug the eastern shore. George knew a good spot. He was going to teach Paul how to catch a Dolly Varden, Indian style of course. They loaded up the canoe with George's tackle box, a couple of lightweight casting rods, and some live earthworms in an empty Libby's bean can. Bev helped them carry everything down to the lake.

George was sporting a straw coolie hat. "Ahso!" he kept saying to both of them, his eyes half closed and squinting, a cross between Ho Chi Min and Geronimo, "Eeeeeeiii!!"

Paul was wearing a dark green cap that said, TRIUMPH and below that, Atom Smashers!—UBC's scientific research center called Triumph had one of the largest particle beam accelerators in the world.

Both George and Paul were wearing Floater Jackets designed by a professor at the University of Victoria. Their main innovation was protection against hyperthermia: inside the jacket were neoprene pullout sections that wrapped around the groin. The sleeves were also made of this material. The professor had used results from experiments conducted by Nazi Germany on Russian prisoners of war during World War II. The Germans had taken healthy prisoners and thrown them into pools of icy water. Then careful measurements were taken to document the loss of body heat and the inevitable death that followed. The Germans were hoping to discover ways to prolong the life expectancy of their downed pilots in the English Channel and North Sea.

The Floater Jacket was a big success, which shows that some good can come out of anything, no matter how sinister or nasty. In icy waters, the average person will last for no more than twenty minutes, but with the added protection of a Floater Jacket, the same person can survive for up to three hours.

Paul had his Cannon 35 mm. with zoom lens hanging around his neck, and a miniature digital tape recorder in his vest pocket, in case he wanted to document the voyage. They were taking the larger red pack canoe. Paul had suggested the smaller one as it was faster and easier to paddle, but George had shaken his head and explained that the flat bottom on the eighteen foot canoe was a lot more stable; it made a better casting platform.

Before they left, George took Bev up to the camp and showed her his Winchester rifle and where he kept the .30.30 cartridges. "Just in case a cranky old bear comes by," he said.

Bev assured him that she would have no problem loading and firing the gun—when she was younger, she had gone out to the garbage dump on the reserve with her brothers on many occasions to shoot rats, and had soon become the best shot of the three of them—and if need be, "I won't hesitate to use it."

"Good," George replied. "But if you have any trouble, Sunshine, you just fire a shot into the air and we'll come back up the lake in that canoe like one of them drag boats." His hand zoomed across an imaginary body of water.

"Okay, Chief."

"Time to push off." He gave Bev a pat on the shoulder.

Paul gave her a bear hug and a wet one on the lips, "Bye, sweetie."

"I'll bring him back in two hours," George promised. He dragged the canoe into knee deep water and let Paul climb in first.

"Bye guys. Catch a big one!" Bev waved and watched them paddle away until they rounded the first point and disappeared from view.

All of a sudden the lake looked deserted. It must have looked like that to the first settlers. Bev washed the remnants of scrambled egg out of the frying pan with some sandy gravel, and then went to work on the stew pot, tin mugs and cutlery. She hummed a floating, non-descript tune while she worked, the haunting melody weaving through the implied harmonies of the silence like the threads of a pastoral tapestry. The dish soap left little rings of foam around the larger rocks that poked up near the shore.

When the dishes were more or less spotless, Bev rinsed them, shook off the excess water and wrapped them in a large dish towel. She carried the bundle back to camp, walking slowly with great care. Her bare feet were still a little tender. Some of the rocks on the beach had sharp jagged edges, and there were the odd patch of prickles and stinging nettles. When Bev was a kid, she and her brothers used to run around the reserve barefoot until the bottoms of their feet were like shoe leather. "Guess I'm turning into a sissy," she giggled to herself. "Soon I'll be Mrs. Paul Gregory, live in a big white house and have nothing to do all day but file my nails and watch the soaps." And of course, she would have a couple of polite, well behaved children to round out the domestic bliss. No hyper, snot-nosed little brats allowed. "Yuck!"

she said out loud, breaking the spell. "How boring!"

Bev put the camp in order. She hung the sleeping bags on a line to air, sorted their provisions and put everything away. Then she put on her thongs, her feet had had enough toughening up for one day, and headed back down to the lake with two large plastic containers. She filled them both with lake water, the air bubbles chug-a-lugging merrily in the light breeze. Bev replaced the lids on the containers and struggled back to camp. They were a lot heavier on the return trip.

Bev put one container in the cooler, for drinking; the other was for washing and cooking. She wiped down the Coleman camp stove. "Now what?" Bev mused. The chores were all done. She wiped her hands on the sides of her jean cutoffs. "It'll be an hour or so before the boys are back."

Bev decided to take a short walk up the main trail. It was too nice of a day to waste sitting around the camp. The trail was wide and clearly marked; there was no danger of getting lost.

She pulled off her halter top and shorts. The breeze felt deliciously cool on her naked skin. She stood there for a few minutes feeling totally free and alive. She would love to have wandered through the woods in her birthday suit, but Bev knew better. Be prepared! The old Boy Scout Guide motto. She donned a pair of long pants, a button up cotton shirt, which she tied at the waist, and a pair of black leather hiking boots. "Always look after your feet, child!" her father had told her time and time again. "Take care of your feet and they'll take care of you." Bev fixed her hair into two long braids and secured them with elastic bands from her purse.

Paul always teased Bev about how messy and full of junk her purse was. One night, they had returned to Bev's apartment from a night on the town, and Bev had had to dump the entire contents of her purse onto the carpeted hallway just to find her apartment keys.

"What do you expect?" she had quipped at the time. "You got me all drunked up just so you could take me home and take advantage of my inebriated state. How the fuck am I supposed to find my keys in this condition?" Paul had just laughed and helped her into the apartment.

KEVIN AND RANDY spent another two hours exploring various inland trails which wove in and out of the trees, around the hills at the mouth of the Pitt River valley, and then gradually climbed the steeper slopes of the mountains in the east. At the higher levels, the trails disintegrated into over-grown footpaths of loose shale covered with reddish moss and other sparse vegetation.

Nothing looked very promising. They hadn't found anything remotely resembling a creek at the bottom of a steep gorge. No sign of a tent shaped rock either. Exhausted and discouraged, Kevin and Randy realized that finding Slumach's gold wasn't going to be as easy as they had originally thought.

"Christ, Kevin, my feet are killing me!" Randy exclaimed. His new leather boots had not been broken in properly and his feet were getting blisters.

"Quit whining!" said Kevin, but his feet and legs were starting to ache too. "Let's call it a day. We're still about an hour out from camp."

"Okay by me." Randy cringed at the thought of another sixty minutes of walking.

"Yeah. Let's head 'er back," Kevin confirmed, "We can get up early again tomorrow and check out that other trail that follows the river straight up the valley."

"Okay." Randy didn't like the idea of getting up early again either, but he didn't say anything. He didn't want to give Kevin any reason to yell at him again.

THE HOOK AND weight sailed through the air in a sweeping arc. It entered the glassy water with a gentle plop. George let it sink for a moment, then began reeling it in slowly click by click, just fast enough to keep it from snagging on a clump of weeds or a rock on the bottom. Paul watched George make another cast, and then let his own hook fly. The line tangled around the end of the rod and the hook landed about ten feet from the canoe with a feeble splash.

"Careful!" George commented, suppressing a chuckle. "You're gonna hook your hat if you don't let your finger off the line just a tad bit quicker."

Paul struggled with the tangles in his tackle.

"Watch me!" George landed another one about two feet from his last cast. It looked easy enough. Paul tried again, and this time he managed a shaky, but passable, thirty-footer.

AT ONE TIME, Paul had been a pretty fair fisherman, but that had been years ago. During the summer breaks when Paul was a kid, he would often round up the gang—Billy Taylor, Marty Vanderkoff, and sometimes Stu Adams, Colin Sears or Ginder Singh—and the boys would head down to the docks at Steveston to do a little fishing. It was a fair walk, about three miles from the Vanderkoff's farm.

In those days, Steveston was an old whaling-fishing village

that looked pretty much the same as it had at the turn of the century. But even at this time, the growing bedroom community of Richmond was creeping closer and closer, urban sprawl. The flat level farmland was easy and cheap to build on, you just dug a trench, laid down some two by ten planks, mixed up a few yards of concrete, and presto, you had a foundation. There was no bulldozing or blasting of bedrock, so the developers loved it. The fact that it was some of the best farmland on the earth was not an issue in the early sixties, land was cheap and there was lots of it available.

The boys would walk down Steveston Highway to Number One Road, and then head south to Moncton Street, the main drag. There were a couple of fresh fish-and-chip shops—the smell always made the boys' tummies grumble—a barber, post office, and a second-hand store.

The Steveston Hardware and Tackle store did a booming business. Its shelves and racks were cluttered with everything that you could possibly need to build or outfit a commercial fishing boat. On Third Street there was a bookstore and an ice cream parlor, kitty corner to the Steveston Hotel. If the boys had anything left from their allowance or paper route, they'd stop in at the parlor for a triple scoop cone on their way home. The glass-fronted freezers held every flavor imaginable: vanilla, chocolate, strawberry, peach, Neapolitan, licorice—Paul's favorite—and many more.

To get to the docks, the boys would walk the length of the wooden causeway then down the ramps, which could be steep at low tide, and onto the wharfs. There they would cast into the muddy water of the Fraser River for bullheads and dogfish. One time Billy caught a spring salmon. He bragged about it for weeks afterwards, until finally the other boys pretended to puke if he even so much as mentioned it.

They all dreamed of catching a legendary sturgeon, which could grow up to six or eight feet long and weigh in at nearly a ton. The boys didn't worry about how they would land such a monster, with their homemade rods and tiny net, details such as this were unimportant in daydreams. Often the boys would strike up a friendship with one of the old fishermen, and spend the afternoon on his boat, watching him drink straight rye whiskey and listening to tales of giant waves, shipwrecks, and the tough heroic men that sailed one of the most dangerous coastlines in the world. If the fisherman was in a really good mood, the boys might go home with some fresh prawns, halibut or even some live crabs in season.

"Say, chief," Paul interrupted the brief silence. "I thought we were going to fish Indian style?"

"We are," George replied.

"Huh? I don't get it."

"I'm an Indian and we're fishing ain't we?" George's brown eyes twinkled in the sunlight reflected from the water.

"Yeah? So." Paul wasn't convinced. "Are you putting me on?"

George sighed, shook his head, and pulled a bone rattle from his bag. It was covered in braided leather and beads. It looked almost like a baby's toy.

"Aiya, aiya, eiii!!!" George chanted as he shook the rattle on the off beats. The look on Paul's face was difficult to describe, a cross between astonishment and total disbelief. When George set the rattle down in his lap and made his cast, he was still chanting away.

It was a picture perfect cast. Just as the hook hit the water,

George's rod bent and started jumping like crazy. George stopped chanting and began to play the catch with the smooth finesse of an expert fisherman, letting out slack when the fish wanted to run or dive, reeling it in with the rod upright when the fish stopped fighting or paused to rest.

"There it is!" Paul pointed excitedly as the fish jumped out of the water about twenty feet in front of them.

"See," George beamed as Paul reached down with the net and pulled in a beautiful two pound rainbow trout. "That's how you fish Indian style!"

"Wow! That was incredible," Paul exclaimed. His logical mind didn't want to believe what he had just witnessed.

"All in a days work," George muttered nonchalantly as he gutted his prize with his razor sharp bowie knife. What Paul hadn't seen, was George sneaking the little pink ball of fresh salmon roe out of his tackle box and squishing it onto the silver spinner just before his lucky cast.

"No, really, how'd you do that?" Paul persisted.

George shrugged. "Can't give away all of the trade secrets now, can we?" This guy watches too much TV, he thought to himself. The bone rattle was just a toy. George had carved it for his granddaughter Brenda, who was expecting her firstborn in September.

Chapter 19

A STEW WAS bubbling on the fire. Kevin stirred it carefully and then pulled a loaf of bread out of a cooler. He cut it into thick slices and buttered them liberally with fresh butter from a plastic container.

"Smells delicious," Randy observed, as the smoky aroma drifted his way. He was hungry from the long day of hiking.

"Yep," Kevin replied proudly, "It's my own special recipe." He was a pretty good chef; he had worked for a while in a prison kitchen, then for several months as an assistant cook at a steak and lobster place in Langley. "Beats Injun food."

"What's that?"

"Fried baloney and boiled macaroni!" Kevin roared at his joke and at Randy's gullibility.

"Huh?"

Randy didn't get it. Oh, well, nothing new; Randy was no Einstein. "Let's eat!" Kevin dished out two heaping plates of stew and grabbed a container from the cooler. He gave it a shake. "I like mine with this." He sprinkled a generous portion of parmesan cheese all over his plate. "Want some?"

"No thanks," Randy replied. He hated parmesan, thought it smelled and tasted like moldy cheese.

"To each his own." Kevin smiled. "One man's poison is another man's caviar."

Randy had never tasted caviar. Just the thought revolted him. Raw fish eggs!

They ate their meal in silence, too famished to bother with small talk. They washed the food down with cool cans of Fosters. Kevin had stuck them in the lake; it wasn't ice cold, but it sure beat lukewarm beer.

"So how are we a-a doing?" Randy stammered when their plates were empty. "I mean, do you think we'll find the gold?"

"Aw, I don't know, little buddy. It's kind of early to tell. I think we're on the right track though, I can feel it in my bones." Kevin brewed up a pot of coffee and fixed them a night cap, adding a couple of generous shots of brandy into each mug.

"Maybe we should have just robbed a bank," Randy sighed, "It would have been a lot easier."

"Nah, bank jobs are for losers," said Kevin. He lit up a small cigar, "Ya hit a bank and what do you get?" he puffed to get it going, "Maybe a grand or two. That's all. And they got cameras and alarms. You can end up doin' big time for little gain." He lay back against a log and got comfortable, a drink in one hand and a smoke in the other. "Not like the good old days, the James brothers . . ." He put down his coffee, made the shape of a gun with his right hand and pointed it at Randy. "Stick 'em up! Your money or your life, sir."

Randy held up his hands in mock fright. "Oh, please don't shoot me. I have a wife and four little children."

"All the more reason to put you out of your misery. Bam, bam, pow!" They both laughed. "Then during the depression, bank robbery became a real profession, you had Bonnie and Clyde and Baby Face Nelson; and then locally of course, we had Billy Miner, the train robber."

"Billy Miner?"

Kevin gave Randy a look of incredibility. "What? You never heard of Billy Miner?"

"No."

"Where ya been, boy?" Kevin asked. "Billy Miner was a local folk hero, a legend really. They called him the gentleman train robber on account of how he was so polite to the Pinkerton men while he was sticking them up." He chuckled. "He was the one who came up with the phrase, hands up!

"Billy was originally from Kentucky, but he was in his sixties when he robbed a CPR train right here in Mission. That was in 1904. It was Canada's first train robbery. There's a pub in Haney now, called the Billy Miner. Hell, there's even one in Fort Worth, Texas called the Billy Miner Saloon, and I've been to that one too. Billy got around. He was wanted in seven states and in Canada. They called him the Grey Fox. He used to wear a long overcoat and a wide brimmed black hat. He was a train robber, opium smuggler and con man; all in all, my kind of guy.

"About a year after he robbed the train in Mission, the Royal Northwest Mounted Police caught Billy and two accomplices robbing another one near Kamloops. There was a bit of a shoot-out—which was unusual, most of Billy's capers were non-violent—and Shorty Dunn, one of Billy's gang, was slightly wounded in the gun fight. Billy was sent to the old BC Penitentiary in New Westminster, but within a year, he escaped and made it back to the States where he continued his fine work. All together, Billy spent about thirty-six of his seventy-one years behind bars, and finally died in 1913, in a jail in Milledgeville,

Georgia."

"Wow," was all Randy could say.

Kevin fixed them each another special coffee, spiking them hard this time with the bottle. "Last drink of the night. We've got to get an early start." He handed Randy back his mug.

"Thanks." Randy took a sip of the steaming liquid. No mistaking the brandy this time.

Kevin lit up a fat joint, took a few puffs and handed it to Randy. "How about Mesachie Sam?" he asked, as he blew out a cloud of smoke. "Bet you've never heard of him either."

Randy shook his head. Kevin told him several more stories.

When Randy crawled into bed later, his mind was spinning with the THC, caffeine, brandy and images of train robberies, gun fights and gold bullion. Once again, Kevin had amazed him with his knowledge.

"**CATCH ANYTHING?**" Bev asked when Paul and George pulled up to the beach in the canoe. They had been gone about an hour longer than expected.

Paul just grinned and held up three good sized trout on a stick. "Dinner."

George climbed out of the canoe behind him and pulled it up onto the pebbles. "Sorry, we're late, Sunshine. Once I showed the boy wonder here how to fish Injun style, he didn't want to quit!"

"It was pretty cool," Paul said, and grinned again. "This guy really knows how to catch fish!"

"All in a day's work. All in a day's work," George mumbled twice as he hauled the gear out of canoe. He whistled all the way up to the camp. Bev recognized the tune: Over the Rainbow.

Bev fried the trout with a little butter and lemon, then served them with rice and mashed turnips.

"Mmm . . . This is delicious!" Paul told her. He had never eaten fish that tasted so good.

"Damn good grits, girl," George added with a wink.

"Glad you boys appreciate me slaving over a hot stove." Bev's eyes sparkled as she laughed. "Even if it's only a campfire."

God, she's beautiful, both Paul and George thought at the same time.

"I did the cooking, you boys get to do the dishes," Bev commanded.

"Yes, Ma'am," they both responded. Bev sat there, relaxed and enjoyed a cup of hot cocoa while they hauled the dirty dishes down to the lake for cleaning.

"You got yourself a fine woman there," George said to Paul as they scrubbed the pots and plates. "You're a lucky man."

"You got that right, Chief."

"She's got a lot of spirit. You can see it dance in her eyes." George sighed. "My Trudy used to have spirit like that. She was an unbroken mare and I was just a proud young stallion. Never did figure out who broke who, but I suspect that it wasn't her that gave up her freedom." George smiled at the memories, and then shook his head sadly. "Miss her something fierce sometimes." He turned towards Paul, his eyes misted slightly. "You take care of Sunshine, Paul. She's more precious than all the gold in the world."

The two men locked eyes. "I will, Chief. You have my word."

"Good." They shook hands.

"What took you boys so long," Bev asked, when they returned with the dishes. "Were you waiting for the dishes to clean themselves?" They both nodded their heads like two little kids. "The lake's not a dishwasher; you don't just throw in some soap and turn it on."

"No, dear!" said Paul with a serious look. "We scrubbed those pots and pans until we could see our handsome reflections in the bottom."

"Let me see."

"The pans or my handsome face?

"Both. Come over here." She beckoned with her finger. "Closer."

George just grinned, set down an armload of dishes and went over to his tent. I'll leave the love birds alone for awhile, he decided; I recon the ground will be shaking tonight, probably about a five on the Richter scale. Sometimes there was just no getting away from being lonesome.

Chapter 20

PAUL WAS LOST. He had climbed out of the tent for a quick pee but he couldn't have gone more than thirty feet. After he'd watered the underbrush and given his cock a quick shake, he had been unable to find his way back to the tent. Now the forest surrounded him in a dark, unfamiliar blanket. Pale shadows in the moonlight looked up at him with hostile faces from knee-high ferns, their branches rustling dryly as they met his bare legs, scraping and scratching. Paul was definitely not having a good time. He smashed his knee into a windfall. "Oww . . . fuck! That hurt." He grabbed his leg with both hands and hopped on one foot until the hot flash of pain subsided.

Up to this point he had been too proud to call for help. He wanted to avoid the embarrassment of being found by George and Bev, bare balls to the breeze, all because he had gotten lost while taking a piss. But now the cool night air was bringing goose bumps to his arms and legs. It made his nipples hard; he started to shiver. "Brrr . . ." His balls felt like they were trying to shrink up inside his groin and hide. His knee still throbbed in a dull ache. Dignity and vanity no longer seemed all that important.

"Bev! George!" Paul yelled.

"Bev, Bev . . . George, George . . ." the mountains replied.

"Can you hear me?"

". . . hear me? . . . here me?"

No answer followed the echo. Paul started to feel the panic take root in the pit of his stomach. "Welcome to the Twilight Zone," a familiar voice came on in the jukebox of his mind. "You have just entered a new dimension of space and time, the outer limits of your imagination..."

Paul felt a major anxiety attack coming on. Where was his Paxil when he needed it?

"You're home, Paul," a choir of angels whispered softly behind him.

This time, Paul screamed as loud as he could, "Bev, George . . . Help!"

"Help! George, Bev. Help! George, Bev. Help!" the echo reversed his cry.

He succumbed to the panic and started running blindly though the bush, tripping and falling, bumping into trees and stumps. Then the ground vanished and he was falling into a black void.

Paul was still mumbling, "George, Bev, help," when he woke up thrashing like a madman. By some miracle, Bev was still sound asleep next to him. Her body felt hot against his cold sweat. "Just another bad dream," Paul sighed, "Second night in a row." He could still feel the dull ache in his knee. "Whew. I'm glad that's over." Paul slid his arm across Bev's side and pulled her closer. He felt safer just knowing she was beside him. It was with great annoyance that he realized that he did indeed need to take a piss. For awhile, he tried to ignore it, hoping the urge would go away, but it only got worse, a dull ache. With a sigh of resignation, Paul slid out of the warmth of the sleeping bag. It was damn chilly. He pulled on his buckskin jacket and boots, not bothering to lace them. He fumbled with the mosquito netting, finally got the zipper down, and crawled out of the tent.

Paul stood there and took a long pee. Relief! It was a clear night. He got a little star gazing in. There was the Big Dipper. He followed a line up to the North Star. The air was so clear up here in the mountains, it seemed like you could see forever.

"Sort of gives you something to think about, eh, son?" came a voice out of the darkness.

"Wha—?" Paul jumped back, startled. He turned quickly towards the source of the intrusion. His heart was beating fast.

"Not there, dummy. Over here."

Paul turned again and came face to face with a bald-headed priest. He was dressed in the traditional collar and robes, wore wire-rimmed glasses and his thick black oxford shoes floated about a foot off of the ground. He also glowed in the dark, giving off a kind of a greenish hue. "Well, what are you doing, standing there with your chin halfway to the ground? I haven't got all night you know, I'm a busy soul."

"What . . . I mean, who are you?"

"Oh, come now, son. You know who I am. Think!"

Paul looked more puzzled than ever.

The priest sighed, "William Morgan, at your service."

"Oh . . . ah, pardon me, Father. Paul Gregory." Paul stuck out his hand, but the apparition didn't appear to notice.

"Yes, yes. I know all about you, Paul, everything. I know where you go, where you've been, the essence of every thought, feeling, and deed of your short life." The father wrinkled up his nose and frowned. "I even know the dark side of you."

"But—"

"Don't sweat it, son. There's a dark side to every man, woman and child on this planet. It's part of what makes us human.

"Oh."

"And I'm not here to judge you. That's not my job. We'll leave that one for someone much more qualified." The priest pointed up at the stars. "I just came down from Heaven to have a chat with you, maybe give you a little advice, that's all. It seems to me that you've got yourself between a rock and a hard place."

"What do you mean by that?" Paul asked.

"Well let's just say that you've opened a door that should never have been opened—call it a Pandora's Box, if you like. You know what that is, don't you?"

"Yes. But I don't understand."

"What I am trying to say, son, is that none of this is real, it's all an illusion, a dream within a dream within a dream."

"But what about you, Father? Are you real?"

The priest sighed again, "I was once, a long time ago. As you know, I was there when they hanged Slumach, the poor old bugger. But he wasn't the first man that I saw hanged and certainly wasn't the last. It was pretty much a run of the mill affair as far as executions go.

"John Slumach—some people liked to call him Charlie—was just a harmless old man, and Lois Bee, the man he killed, was a crazy hot head with a big chip on his shoulder the size of that mountain over there." Father Morgan gestured at the shadowy black outline of the mountain that towered to the east. "The killing was a clear case of self-defense, but the Daily Columbian reporter condemned Slumach with his biased, one-sided account of the incident. Slumach lived in fear of Lois Bee, who threatened and harassed him constantly. The day of the killing, Bee attacked

SLUMACH – THE LOST MINE

Slumach with a fish club. In the ensuing struggle, Slumach shot Bee dead.

"It was typical white man's justice: a white man's court, white man's laws, a white man judge and an all white jury. There was no need for a trial. It was a sham, just some Friday morning entertainment for the locals. They were greasing up the noose long before Slumach was even captured. During the many months he spent in jail awaiting his trial and execution, Slumach was often beaten and whipped, a practice that unfortunately, was common with Indian prisoners. In those days, they were treated like a sub-human species. We tried to put the fear of God into them."

"But what about the gold . . . the lost mine?"

"Gold? Ha! Poppycock. You wouldn't know real gold from a donkey's ass. The only real treasure exists in your heart, son. Remember that! And as for that silly curse, the only reason so many people got into trouble up here and died can be summed up in just one word: greed. If you spend your life lusting for gold, all you're going to end up with in the end is knee deep in horseshit."

Paul still looked puzzled. There was nothing to say in response.

"Mark my words. When you stray from the old straight and narrow, Satan will throw every misery your way that you can think of and some you couldn't even imagine. They don't call him the devil for nothing!" Father Morgan stifled a yawn. It seemed like he was getting bored. "Enough preaching, I'm supposed to be retired now."

"But—"

"I don't know what else to tell you, son. You know all of the answers already. All you have to do is to look for them. Seek and ye shall find. I got that right from the horse's mouth." Paul cast a nervous glance skyward. "Don't worry, son. It's just a figure of speech. God's got a sense of humor too, he created us didn't he?" Father Morgan reached into his pocket and pulled out a halo. "These things are required dress up there," he said and plopped it on his head. "Sort of like your white shirt and black tie at a cocktail party." He started to float away. "Well, it was nice chatting with you, Paul. And good luck, it's been a slice."

"But—"

"Maybe we'll see each other again someday, but then again..." Father Morgan shrugged. "As Santa says, you better be good!" The apparition cracked a toothy grin and floated up and away, melting into the stars.

Paul waved at the Milky Way, and then started back towards the tent. But where was it? It shouldn't have been more than twenty or thirty feet from where he urinated. He retraced his steps, then zigzagged back and forth figuring he must have just missed it. No sign of the tent or the camp. Pale shadows in the moonlight looked up at him with hostile faces from knee high ferns, their branches rustling dryly as they met his bare legs, scraping and scratching.

"Bev! George!" Paul yelled.

"Bev, Bev . . . George, George . . ." the mountains replied.

"Can you hear me?"

". . . hear me? . . . hear me?" No answer followed the echo.

This time, Paul screamed as loud as he could, "Bev, George. Help!"

"Help! George, Bev. Help! George, Bev. Help!" the echo reversed his cry.

Paul panicked and started running blindly though the bush; just like in the dream, he was tripping and falling, bumping into trees and stumps. He smashed his knee into a windfall.

"Oww! . . . Fuck! That hurt." He grabbed his leg with both

hands and hopped on one foot until the hot flash of pain subsided. This was no dream. And he was hopelessly lost. Paul considered his options, deciding to sit tight and stay where he was until daylight.

CHAPTER **21**

Day Three-
July 5, 2007

CLANG, CLANG, CLANG... "Good morning. Up and at 'em. Rise and shine." Kevin was banging a spoon on the bottom of a pot right outside of Randy's tent.

"Uhhhh?... Alright," Randy groaned; it was still dark out, the sun wasn't even up yet. "I'm coming." He crawled out of the warm cocoon of the sleeping bag. It was cold out for July, even in the mountains. He grabbed some extra thick sox from his knapsack, partly for the warmth and partly because of the blisters from yesterday's endless hike. He hoped the wool would provide some padding for his poor aching feet.

Kevin had breakfast cooking. Randy crawled out of the pup tent on all fours. When he got to his feet, he sort of staggered over to a bush. His bladder was so full, it hurt. "Ahhhh!" Randy zipped himself up and walked over to the fire. Kevin handed him a hot mug of coffee. It tasted like Heaven itself, rich coffee with a healthy dose of cream and sugar, which was nice of Kevin as he took his black. "Thanks. That sure hits the spot!"

"Yep. Nothing much better than a good cup of campfire

coffee. So how are you feeling this morning, little buddy?" Kevin asked, "Did you sleep okay?"

"Pretty sore," Randy admitted, "but I slept like a log."

"No more nightmares?"

"Nope."

"That's good. I even managed to get some sleep myself, not like the other night when you were screaming like a bloody banshee." Randy averted Kevin's eyes and stared at the ground kind of sheepishly. Kevin scooped some ham and scrambled eggs onto a couple of plates. He had already made a stack of pancakes. Kevin definitely liked his food.

"**P**AUL?" BEV WOKE up alone in the dark. The other half of the double Arctic sleeping bag was damp cold. It had been unoccupied for some time. "Paul?" she called a little louder. There was still no answer. Bev unzipped the side of the bag and pulled on her bra and panties. The night was dead. The silence rang in her ears; it was so quiet it almost hurt. She struggled into her Levis and a black heavy knit turtleneck sweater. Dressing in a small tent in a hurry wasn't easy.

Bev lifted the flap of the pup tent and shone the flashlight into the void; nothing but dark trees floating on a shallow grey mist. Her hands were shaking badly from the cold and the growing fear. "Paul, are you out there?" Only silence answered. One of the laces on her hiking boots broke as she was tying them up. "Damn." That always happens when you're in a hurry. Bev snapped up her parka and crept across the clearing to Simon George's tent.

"George . . . George. Wake up!"

"Mmmmm." The old guide stirred slightly moaning in his

slumber.

"George, it's me, Bev."

"Huyh?"

"It's Bev. Paul's gone. I've called for him, but he doesn't answer."

"Oh." George replied, waking up somewhat. "Maybe he went out to water a tree."

"No. You don't understand. He's been gone for a long time, and—"

"Hmmm?"

"And without his pants, they're still in the tent. His boots and coat are gone. But—

"Oh, George," Bev cried. "Something has happened to him. I . . . I just know it!"

"Calm down, Sunshine," George replied, fully awake now. "It's okay. I'm sure that he's all right, but I'll go out and have a look for him," just in case. He didn't like the sound of it, but didn't want to worry Bev needlessly. Only a crazy man or someone in heaping big trouble would go out with bare legs and his balls flapping in the breeze on such a cool night in the mountains.

George got up—he was still fully dressed under his blankets—grabbed his rifle and disappeared into the darkness. About twenty minutes later, Bev heard the snapping of twigs and rustle of bushes that announced his return.

"Any sign of him?" Bev asked anxiously as George emerged from the darkness.

George shrugged and shook his head. "No sign."

"What are we going to do?" Bev asked, bursting into tears.

"Nothing more that we can do right now. We'll just have to sit tight until dawn. Then hopefully I can pick up his trail."

"I'm coming with you!"

"Nope. You'd just slow me down. You're going to stay put here at the camp.

"But—"

"No buts. The last thing that I need is to have both of you lost."

"Shit. I feel so fucking helpless."

"Well, if we're going to sit up for a while," George said, changing the subject. "We might as well be comfortable." George quickly built a campfire and they spent the rest of the night huddled beside it, Bev's head resting on George's shoulder. They sipped hot pioneer coffee while George told her many colorful tales of life before the white man. He half hoped it would take Bev's mind off of Paul.

"Your father was a Yakima?"

"Yeah." Bev nodded.

"I used to have a good friend from Yakima. Back, oh, I guess I met him 'bout the end of the second war, white man's war that is. I did some trapping with him up north in the Cariboo. His name was Charlie Dan. He's dead now; wrapped his pickup around a tree in the spring of '66. I went down for the funeral." George poked the coals of the campfire with a stick. A shower of sparks floated skyward as the flames started up again on an unburnt log. "Perhaps your father might have known him."

"Maybe."

Before the sun was even up, George prepared for the search. He filled a small backpack with condensed food, a blanket, rolling tobacco, a flashlight, a rope, extra ammunition, and lots of matches in a waterproof container. On his belt he carried a razor-sharp hunting knife in a leather sheath. When he was ready, George picked up his rifle and pointed his finger at Bev. "Now you stay put, Sunshine. Promise me."

"I promise," Bev replied sullenly.

"Good. Before you know it, I'll be back with Paul," or his corpse, George thought darkly. Bev gave George a long hug and a kiss on the cheek. Her big brown eyes were still clouded with tears.

"Hurry back!"

"I'll be back as quick as a hungry coon in a hen house." With that George headed out from the camp, whistling to the trees as if they had ears.

"Brrr." Bev went back to her and Paul's tent. She didn't think she could sleep, but she crawled back into her sleeping bag anyway to snuggle there until the sun came up.

Chapter 22

GEORGE BEGAN HIS search by slowly walking the circumference of the camp. He was listening more than anything; it was too dark yet to see very much. He was hoping to get a feel for what had happened here, piece together the story, what had gone down with Paul. George shined his flashlight on the ground. The ferns were wet. Smelled like fresh urine. George surmised that it hadn't been very long since Paul was standing here taking a leak, so which way did he go? George pulled out a can of Copenhagen and put a plug under his lip. He chewed for a minute staring into the blackness of the surrounding forest; considering the options and the odds.

George decided to begin searching on the trail that paralleled the beach. When it got to the Pitt River, it veered almost due north to the Alvin Fish Hatchery, where it branched: the Iceworm Creek Trail followed the river up into the mountains past the Stave Glacier and then cut east to Glacier Lake, while the Sloquet Creek Trail, was more or less a straight line northeast, across the Stave River, coming out at Port Douglas on the north end of Harrison Lake. These trails were well established; the natives had used them for hundreds of years. After the invasion of the white man, the trails were also used by them for prospecting and trapping.

The sky in the east was getting lighter; the sun would be up soon. George walked at a steady pace, keeping a sharp tracker's eye out for any sign of Paul. As he approached the end of the lake, he could see smoke in the distance, rising above the trees, a campfire. Somebody was there. George slowed his pace and hugged the inland side of the trail, skirting the trees and bushes. Better to be cautious until he knew who it was.

As he approached the camp, George left the trail and walked into the woods. His feet never made a sound. He circled one side of the stranger's camp, and moved in for a closer look.

There were two men sitting beside a fire. It looked peaceful enough. They were eating a morning meal and sipping what appeared to be coffee from tin cups. One big guy and one smaller. They looked vaguely familiar. George wondered if they might be the two morons who had almost run down Paul and Bev with their speedboat. There was no sign of any weapons, he observed, that was a good sign but who knew what kind of firepower might be hidden from sight.

George made his way noiselessly back to the trail and went down towards the beach. Sure enough, there was the boat. It was the morons after all.

"I guess I better go have a talk with them," George whispered to the rippling waters. He didn't really want to have anything to do with these two, they were definitely troublemakers, but they might have seen Paul. And right now any information would be valuable. I better be careful how I approach them though, George considered, not wanting to get himself shot. He quietly padded back up to the main trail, and then walked towards their camp, intentionally making some noise so as not to startle them.

RANDY STOPPED CHEWING his eggs. His jaw dropped and his eyes grew wider. "Holy, fuck," he sputtered through his breakfast. "An Injun." Kevin spun around for a look, the adrenalin kicking in. Sure enough, an old Indian man was walking towards camp, and he was armed. Kevin recognized a Winchester .30.30 rifle, the gun that won the west; old technology, but still popular and deadly.

Good morning," the Indian spoke first with just a hint of a smile. He was still about fifty feet away, wearing a heavy, red and black-checkered work shirt with a padded, dark green hunter's vest, and a crazy looking bowler hat with a feather on one side. He carried his rifle casually with the barrel pointing down, but Kevin knew it would only take a second to raise it and fire.

"I'm gonna get my gun," Randy whispered to Kevin, and then started to get up.

"Sit down and don't move," Kevin whispered back. It was a command, an order. Randy looked uncertain, but he did what he was told. "Good morning," Kevin said, as the Indian approached them.

"Sorry to intrude on your breakfast."

"No problem. Would you like some coffee?" Kevin offered.

"I appreciate the hospitality. But I'm on urgent business." The Indian stopped about twenty feet from the fire pit.

He wants to keep us both in his angle of fire, Kevin figured. "What's so urgent?"

"Either of you see anybody come by here? Or hear anything out of the ordinary last night or this morning?"

"No. Why do you ask?" Kevin stirred the coals of the fire

with a stick, but kept his eyes fixed firmly on the rifle.

"A man has gone missing, he might be lost: a white guy, about forty, with brown curly hair and a beard. He was wearing a dark brown, buckskin coat with long tassels." George didn't bother to add, "And only a pair of boots."

"Hmmm... No. I can't help you out there, old timer," Kevin replied, feeling more relaxed now that he knew what the intrusion was all about.

"How about you?" the Indian turned to Randy. "You see or hear anything?"

Randy shook his head and scowled. "I didn't see nothin'."

The Indian stood there for a minute, his eyes switching back and forth between the two of them. Randy felt naked under the scrutiny.

"Guess I'll let you get back to your breakfast. Sorry, to bother you." The Indian tipped his hat with his free hand.

"No problem," Kevin replied. "Good luck."

"Thanks." The Indian turned and walked away from their camp heading north along the river.

"Jesus Christ," Randy exclaimed, after the Indian disappeared from sight, "We're lucky he didn't shoot us and then scalp us!" He combed his fingers through his hair as if he was glad to still have it.

"Don't be silly," Kevin chuckled at Randy's naiveté. "He wasn't going to hurt us." Kevin scraped his plate clean into the fire. "Didn't you recognize him? He was with the couple you nearly ran over, riding shotgun in the second canoe."

"Oh." Randy cleaned his plate too.

"I guess that asshole with the good-looking girlfriend went and got himself lost." Kevin laughed.

"Oh!" Randy liked that idea. He laughed too. The faggot was lost and the old Indian was out looking for him, so that meant that the girl from the canoe was all by her lonesome, alone and vulnerable. I wonder if she wants a little company, Randy fantasized, I wouldn't mind keeping her warm tonight.

"Let's get this show on the road," Kevin broke the spell. "We'll never find that gold just sitting around on our butts."

They quickly packed some lunch and assembled their gear for the day. They both felt a little more secure once they were armed. Randy left the safety off his rifle and stuck an extra clip into his vest pocket, just in case.

KEVIN AND RANDY began their day of treasure seeking, heading north, following the footsteps of the old Indian. The trail was wide. It was easy going. They followed the banks of the river as it snaked a course up the valley toward the snow peaked mountains in the distance. The sun was finally coming up in the east. The glare was bright. Kevin pulled his sunglasses out of a pocket and put them on. Randy followed suit. Now they looked like the Blues Brothers. Life is a comedy.

"This is the route that Volcanic Brown took on his last trip," explained Kevin as they walked along. "It was August in 1931, somewhere along here, he ran into another prospector named Swanson, who was coming out of the woods. The two of them traded stories for a while, and then Swanson gave Volcanic some beans and rice from his pack; he was heading back to civilization and wouldn't need it. Volcanic thanked him for the extra provisions and Swanson wished Volcanic the best of luck prospecting. That was the last time anyone ever saw Volcanic Brown."

"Did he find the mine?" Randy asked hopefully.

"No one knows for sure," Kevin continued. "Volcanic did have a copy of Jackson's letter with him. And Jackson's big find was supposed to have been somewhere in that general area." Kevin swept his hand across the mountains to the north. "When Volcanic never showed up at his normal rendezvous in the fall, the RCMP sent out a search party, but they never found his body. It probably got buried in the ice fields somewhere, but they did find his last camp up near the Stave Glacier—that's about fifteen miles due north of here—and a jar with eleven ounces of raw gold and quartz that Volcanic must have pounded out of a vein with his rock hammer.

"Wow," Randy liked the sound of that. Gold!

"It might have been from the Lost Mine or maybe Volcanic found another mother lode. No one knows for sure."

"So are we going up there?" Randy asked.

"Up where?"

"To Volcanic's last camp."

Kevin smiled; Randy could be so clueless sometimes. "Not today, little buddy. That would take several days of very hard travel. We'll start with some easier terrain to get our feet wet, before we try anything too adventurous."

Randy wondered what yesterday's ordeal had been if today was just to get their feet wet. He still had blisters on his feet, only they had popped and that made them hurt even worse. Finding lost treasure was a lot of work. He hoped they found it pretty soon. He didn't know if he was cut out for this Survivor TV show crap.

Shortly after eight, Kevin decided that they should explore a smaller trail that forked off to the east. He had one of his feelings. "Something tells me we should go that way."

"Okay by me," Randy sighed. "You're the leader."

The grade got steeper in a hurry. They were soon huffing and puffing. They could see back across the whole Pitt River valley. The peaks on the other side were almost a mirror image of the ones in front of them. The trail narrowed abruptly as it wrapped around the top of a large gully. There was a huge eagle's nest there in a treetop. It looked almost close enough to touch, but it was empty.

The trail narrowed even more and they had to proceed in single file with Kevin in the lead. Randy looked down, felt the sickening pull of vertigo, and quickly looked up again. It was a long vertical drop to the bottom of the gully. He decided that it was wiser to keep his eyes focused straight ahead at Kevin's back. They were almost to the other side, when Kevin stopped.

"What's up?" Randy asked.

Kevin didn't answer. Instead, he started swatting at empty air and frantically brushing his clothes with the back of his fingers.

"What's the matter?" Randy asked again, getting concerned.

"BEES!!!" Kevin finally shrieked. "Oh, God! Help me!" The clay crumbled and one of his boots slid off the ledge.

"Look out!" Randy shouted. He didn't see any bees. "You're gonna fall!" Too late. Everything went into slow motion.

KEVIN HAD BEEN inching along the ledge, careful to keep his feet on solid ground, the edge looked really unstable. He was almost home free; he could see the end of the gully about twelve feet further ahead. Just then, his peripheral vision caught something move out of the corner of his right eye. He turned and his eyes opened wide. They were swarming right out of the very earth, hundreds and hundreds of wasps crawling out of the brown clay. And they were attacking him, biting and stinging mercilessly.

Kevin felt the panic wash over him like a tidal wave. "BEES!!!" he shrieked. "Oh, God! Help me!" Then he was falling. Everything went black.

RANDY WATCHED HELPLESSLY as Kevin toppled off of the ledge. His body bounced against some rocks on the way down and then landed with a crunch on a shale slide that fanned out onto the forest floor at the bottom.

Kevin wasn't moving, not one iota. Is he dead? Randy thought with horror. It had to be at least fifty or sixty feet to where Kevin was laying. "Now what am I supposed to do?" Randy sobbed. He looked around frantically for an easier way down. There was none visible. Then he remembered the tree with the eagle's nest. Randy eased his way back to the start of the gully. He took off his pack and rifle, and set them on the ground.

The branches of huge old cedar looked pretty sturdy. Randy grabbed one with both hands, tested it with his weight, and then swung in towards the trunk. His feet slipped on the bark until he finally found a toehold on one of the lower branches. He grabbed the trunk and held on for dear life. Now what? It had been years since Randy had climbed a tree, and never one anywhere near as big as this old sentinel. It's just like climbing down a ladder, he thought, one arm and then one leg after another. Slowly he made his way down the tree. The last branch ended about ten feet above the base of the trunk. Randy grabbed onto the branch with both hands and lowered himself until he was just dangling there. Then he closed his eyes and dropped the last few feet to the ground. The impact gave him a good jolt, but he didn't break anything.

Randy quickly walked up the loose shale to where Kevin was lying in a heap.

"Kevin." Randy put his ear up to Kevin's chest. There was a heart beat. Kevin was still alive, barely. Randy knew next to nothing about first aid. He did know that you weren't supposed to move the victim. Keep him warm, he remembered. Randy took off his coat and draped it over Kevin's shoulders. "There you go, big guy. Everything's going to be alright." There wasn't much more that he could do for Kevin. "Don't worry, Kev. I'm going to go and get help. You hang in there! Okay?"

Randy looked back at the tree. There wasn't much hope of going back up the way he came down. He surveyed his surroundings. There seemed to be an overgrown path going off to the northwest, everywhere else the gully was too steep to climb or the forest looked more or less impenetrable. Randy was out of options. He started following the deer trail, hoping it would hook up with the main trail sooner or later.

Chapter 23

It was past dawn. The sparrows were starting their morning choir practice, and the sun peeped in softly through the mosquito netting that covered the front of the pup tent. Bev yawned and opened her eyes. She felt warm and cozy, so peaceful. The birds' song was cheerful, full of joy. Oh, good, Paul's back, she thought lazily as she felt a cool body cuddle up against her back, I wonder where he went last night, I was worried sick about him. Bev rolled over to give Paul a kiss and screamed.

"Good morning, honey," said the clown. "I had a wonderful time last night, didn't you? It was even better than I imagined it would be." The grin was so wide it seemed to split his face in half. "You're a fine piece of tail, Bevie girl, premium grade A American pootang. I haven't had that much fun since I was a teenager!" A purple, snake-like tongue slithered from his mouth, across twelve inches of pillow, and touched the end of Bev's nose. It was colder than cold, approaching absolute zero, it numbed her nose instantly. Just then, something hard and slimy brushed her thigh.

Bev was pounding her pillow with both fists when she woke up screaming, alone. Paul wasn't beside her. He's still gone, she thought sadly, lost in the forest. The clown was gone too, thank God!

It was already past dawn. The sparrows were starting their morning choir practice. Sunlight streamed in softly through the mosquito netting that covered the front of the tent. Bev got out of the sleeping bag quickly and started pulling on some clothes. Her skin was clammy with sweat. She felt dirty, like a slug had crawled all over her. Her nose still felt numb. "I must be going crazy," she muttered as she pulled on her bra. "These dreams are too fucking real!"

Bev crawled over to the front of the tent on her knees. The sun peeped shyly over Mount Blanchard, bathing the valley in a soft, even light. Bev walked over to the nearest bush and squatted. It didn't look like George had come back yet. The flap of his tent was wide open. Bev emptied her bladder and peeled some toilet paper off of the roll. Her genitals felt sore this morning, and there were a few spots of blood on the tissue. Funny, she thought, I'm not due for another week yet. She pulled up her panties and jeans then walked over to George's tent. "Anybody home?" Nope.

Bev opened the metal cylinder of the Coleman stove and poured in some fuel, using a plastic funnel. When the cylinder was full, she replaced the cap firmly, pumped up the pressure with the thumb pump, and then mounted the cylinder back on the stove, opened the value, and gave the flint a squeeze. The gas ignited with a whoosh. In a few minutes, she had some water boiling.

Bev poured a cup of coffee from the pot. Her hands trembled slightly as she took a sip. She was having it black this morning. No milk or sugar to get in the way of the caffeine kick that she so desperately needed. She hadn't bothered cooking breakfast; the thought of eating made her want to gag. She pulled out a Black Cat plain from the package and gave the Bick a flick. George had stashed a carton in the grub pack. Bev had never really been a smoker, though she had tried it a few times, but today seemed like as good a day as any to start. The first puff made her cough. The second puff started her head spinning and her stomach doing flip flops. The raw tobacco burned the end of her tongue, George didn't believe in filters. The smoke seemed to help though. She felt the panic subsiding slightly. Bev sat on the makeshift log bench and considered her predicament. This trip's been a disaster, she thought, ever since we came out here, it's been one bad scene after another, first the hoodlums nearly kill us on the lake, then these awful dreams, and now Paul's gone! Bev could feel the tears welling up under her eyelids, but she fought them back. No need to get emotional, she told herself, stay calm, use your brain. Bev snuffed out the cigarette with the heel of her boot and lit up another one. "I've only been a smoker for a whole five minutes and already I'm a chain smoker." She went back to the tent and got a change of clothes, soap, shampoo and a towel. She needed a bath. Her body felt like it was growing scales. "If only I could wash away the dreams so easily," she wished out loud as she walked down to the edge of the lake.

The water was cool and totally refreshing. Bev lathered her body from head to foot and dove back in to rinse off, swimming underwater for as long as she could. She surfaced about fifty feet from shore and flicked back her long wet hair. Treading water, she looked out over the lake. There wasn't a single boat in sight. All of the fishermen and water skiers were probably still asleep in their dome tents or back at the Pitt River landing in Winnebago's or campers on pickups, getting ready for another day of high speed boating and fun in the sun, or laid back, but equally serious, sports fishing. She turned back towards the shore. Their camp was just visible through the thick growth and driftwood that lined the high water mark. Somebody's watching me, she felt. Somebody's hiding in the bush and watching me take a bath.

"Don't be so God damned paranoid," she chastised herself. Bev slipped back into the quiet luxury of the blue green water and swam back in towards the shallow shelf. She had been hovering over the edge of a steep underwater cliff, the stone face disappearing into the inky darkness below. The smooth rocks in the shallower water were coated with a thick layer of brown mulch, the remnants of bark and other decomposing plant life. Bev ran up onto the beach and grabbed her towel. Her heart was beating briskly from the exertion of the swim and her skin was covered with goose bumps from the cool air. She couldn't shake the feeling of being watched. Somebody is still there, she thought, as she patted herself dry, I just know it—Bev donned her clean clothing—he's still there and I'm not crazy. Bev rolled her dirty clothes up in the wet towel and slipped on her thongs. She started up the short, narrow path to the campsite.

IT TOOK RANDY three-quarters of an hour to find the trail again. He had about given up and decided that he was completely lost, when he stumbled onto it by sheer chance. He immediately headed back towards camp, hoping to find someone there, the old Indian even. Anyone.

He had gone about a mile when he heard something. Randy stopped. There it was again. He held his breath and listened. A faint rustling sound broke the silence. "Anybody there?" he called. No answer. He continued walking towards the lake. He had been hiking non stop now for over two hours. Randy was tired, hungry and worried sick.

There is was again, louder this time. The sound seemed to

come from the left side of the trail, behind a thick tangle of bramble bushes. "Hello?" Randy was still in shock. All that he could see was the image of Kevin's body toppling off the side of the hill, falling and falling...

"Help me, please. My friend fell off a cliff. He, he's—" Randy stopped in mid sentence. The rustling was louder now, accompanied by muffled thuds that sounded like heavy footsteps on soft ground. "Hey, is anybody there?" A strong whiff of burning assaulted his nostrils. It smelled like burnt toast.

"Hello, darling." The voice came from directly behind him. Randy spun on his heels. There stood his mother Elaine.

"We missed you." Aunty Velma was there too, wearing one of the long black dresses that were her trademark. "We've been waiting to chat with you for such a long time now," she smiled, a look of pure malice, "my dear, sweet nephew."

"You're not real, you're dead!" Randy screamed at the ghosts.

"Yes, we're dead, but did you really think that little bonfire of yours would keep us away forever?"

"Leave me alone!"

"Now, you mind your Aunty Velma," Elaine added, waving a stern finger at his nose.

"Just leave me alone!" Randy shouted again.

"Do you still piss on the floor like a dog?" Velma sneered. "Your mother should have cut off your peter when she had the chance. We could have had ourselves a weenie roast."

"Go away!"

"You've got an X on your forehead," Velma croaked and spat out a mouthful of ashes. Smoke started to come out of her nostrils, "You're going to burn, boy," and then her ears. Velma's eyeballs melted like two marshmallows, and ran down her cheeks, leaving a trail of white goo and two black holes, a couple of bottomless pits. He caught a glimpse of eternity in that void.

"Why are you here?" Randy asked. He was so scared, he pissed his pants, but didn't seem to notice. "Go away!"

"Peek-a-boo, Randy." That evil smile again. "Surprise, I can still see you!" The flesh on Velma's cheeks started bubbling turning a brownish yellow, the color of nicotine. Her lips blackened and shriveled back, leaving a toothy skeletal grin. "Trick or treat, come and give your Aunty Velma a big kiss!" Velma opened her mouth, spilled out a huge clump of worms.

"NOOOO!!"

"I loved you!" Elaine screamed. Her dress exploded in a shower of sparks, the hungry flames licking up her legs. "Why did you kill me?" The inferno dissolved her clothing into soot and the wind carrying away the ashes, leaving a black, cratered landscape of blistered skin. Maggots began crawling out her nose. Her hair sparked and sputtered, stinking up the air with the smell of burning. "Why, Randy?"

"I, I didn't mean to, mommy. Honest! I didn't want to go into the closet anymore. No! No, please, mommy. Don't put me in the closet. I'll be a good boy. I promise," Randy sobbed.

Velma interrupted Randy's mewling with a swat across the side of his head that send him to his knees. "Why, you sick little snot-nosed brat!" Her face kept changing back and forth. Randy's eyes had trouble deciding on which image to focus, the unscathed Aunty Velma, her lips pursed tight in rage, or the tar zombie with black holes for eyes. "Now you listen to me, you little twerp. You let that limp-wrist faggot and his half-breed slut make a real fool of you. Are you going to let that Whore of Babylon and her fornicating atheist friend go right on sinning?"

Randy stopped crying and looked into Velma's eyes. The entire universe was consumed in that microcosm of Hell.

"They're fornicating right now, the two of them. I can hear them rutting like a couple of pigs." Velma's coal black finger touched the end of Randy's nose, sending an icy cold shiver down his spine. She traced a sooty X on his forehead. "Do you want to be forgiven, Randy? Do you want the blood of the Lamb to wash the X off of your forehead?" Velma grabbed his arm and squeezed, her fingers leaving five distinct yellow patches on his skin. "Do you want to go back in the closet?" she shouted. Randy shook his head frantically back and forth, too afraid to speak. "Good. Then go forth and do the Lord's work. Cleanse the world of sin, kill the fornicators!"

Chapter 24

KEVIN GRADUALLY FLOATED back into consciousness. His first thought was one of surprise—surprise that he was still alive—and the second, that he hurt badly all over. He opened his eyes slowly.

He was lying in a heap at the bottom of a slide of loose shale. His left leg veered off at a weird angle, it was broken in at least two places. When he tried to move his left arm, he couldn't. This caused him to panic for a second, thinking that he was paralyzed, but he soon discovered that he could wiggle his fingers. His collar bone was broken. Kevin surveyed the damage: compound fracture of the left leg, broken collar bone, his side was on fire too, probably some bruised ribs. All in all this didn't worry him too much, broken bones would heal.

He rolled over with some difficulty and touched the side of his head with his good hand. Behind the temple above his right ear, it felt like a squashed pumpkin. That reminded him of the TV commercial advocating motorcycle helmets, the one where the car runs into a pumpkin, splat! His biggest fear at this point was that he had a serious concussion or internal bleeding. His second biggest fear was that even if his injuries were not life threatening, he would probably die of exposure if he had to spend the night here alone. Where the hell was Randy? He had left his jacket. Had he gone to get help? The third and by far biggest fear came when he heard the low growl.

It was a huge, scruffy looking brown bear, staring at Kevin from about fifty feet away, sniffing the air and emitting a low grunting growl. It was preening the loose shale with its long claws, throwing chunks into the air.

I'm in deep shit, Kevin thought as the bear started towards him. Kevin rolled back over and laid there face down. Play dead, don't move, Kevin decided. That was easier said than done. The bear sniffed his back then prodded him with its paw. This went on for a few minutes: sniff, prod, and then another sniff. Kevin tried to breath as shallow as possible, but the bear kept prodding the side where his ribs were broken. Each time the hot flash of pain came back, Kevin held his breath and wished he could scream. The bear pawed at his shoulder, trying to flip Kevin over onto his back. Its warm breath smelled like rotting fish. Kevin was sure that his whole body was trembling from the shock of his injuries and the fear. After a few more tries at flipping Kevin, the bear gave up and backed off a few paces. He's trying to decide whether I'm dead meat or fresh enough to eat, Kevin mused. He knew that the bear was still watching him, could sense the animal's eyes boring into him, but he dared not move his head even for a peek. He could still hear its heavy breathing. The bear was playing a cat and mouse waiting game, you move, you loose. Kevin was feeling waves of nausea, it was all that he could do to keep from puking, but he knew that if he did, it would be the last thing he ever did. For the first time in his life, Kevin prayed. Then he prayed some more.

Kevin had read about bear attacks. They were rare, usually the bear was more afraid of humans than the humans were of it, but they did happen. Often it was an older bear, one that was lame and having trouble gathering food, or one that was just plumb crazy. From the size and looks of this guy, Kevin thought, he could be both. Sometimes, they didn't even bother to kill their prey first, just ate it alive and squirming. Kevin remembered reading about a little girl who had had her buttocks chewed off, and survived. The bear had dragged her from her campsite, hauled her off into the bush and then ate her ass off. Her parents found her just in time. The bear was tracked and shot by wildlife officials.

Kevin's dad had been an avid hunter. He had told Kevin about seeing a black bear clearing six inch windfalls out of its way like they were matchsticks. "One swipe of its paw would take half your head off, boy!" his father had told him. "And if a bear ever decides to come at you, worst thing you can do is run. A bear can run a whole lot faster than any man. Best thing to do is to lie down and play dead. Only time you got a hope of out running a bear, is going down a steep hill. You grab a tree and do a quick ninety-degree switcheroo, and the bear will just keep on going. You see, their front legs are shorter than their back legs, and they've got a whole lot of body mass, so if they try and turn or stop quickly, they start doing somersaults. And don't think climbing a tree's going to help you either. A bear can climb a tree a whole lot better than you can. Best thing is to just lie still and think of something else. Worst thing is to be afraid. The bear will smell the fear on you, and that just gets its adrenalin going."

Kevin thought about what his father had said years before, and tried to let his mind wander to other things. He thought about working on his car, imagined pulling off the carburetor, taking it apart piece by piece. In a few minutes he was daydreaming.

The bear eventually decided that Kevin was not worth eating and wandered off in search of livelier game.

"Excerpt, from the journal of Dr. Paul Gregory, PhD and royal fuck up," Paul dictated to the wind. He was thoroughly disgusted with himself and starting to get more than a little scared by the whole predicament.

"It is now day three of our little misadventure.

"Last night, I got myself lost while taking a piss. Hopped out of the tent, watered a tree, and then couldn't find my way back those long thirty feet to the tent. A real fucking boy scout, I am. Oh, and let's not forget, I had a long conversation with the ghost of a dead priest." Paul shook his head in disbelief.

He was walking along a dark overgrown trail, trying to find his way back to the camp. He was cold. All that he had on was his buckskin coat, a remnant from his hippie days, but it was tough and water repellent—the reason he had brought it along on the trip—and a pair of hiking boots without socks. Other than that, he was bare balls to the breeze. His legs were numb from the cold. "When you're just leaving the tent to take a leak, you don't exactly dress up," he mused. "So either I am hallucinating or dreaming."

And there in the middle of a small break in the tall salal and thick brambles, looking surreal and totally out of place, was the old freezer he had found so long ago in a field beside the Robert's house. It looked exactly the way he remembered it. Dull white paint, flaky rust spots, the long slash in the lid with pink fiberglass poking out. Paul approached it apprehensively, like he was reliving the steps of a strange dream. It had to be a dream, didn't it? It couldn't be real. No one would bother to haul a freezer way out here. And what would be the odds of it looking exactly like the one he had discovered as a kid? A million to one?

Paul gave the tarnished chrome handle a tug. The feelings of deja vu and inevitability overwhelmed him. Maybe there's something bad in there, Paul thought, maybe there's something REALLY bad in there. He stepped back a bit to consider this further. "Aw, don't be silly," he scolded himself. "You're a grown man now. This is just a funny dream, that's all. And there's nothing in that box that could possibly harm you either." Paul grabbed the lid with both handles and slowly pried it open, the hinges groaning in protest.

"Holy Shit!" Paul gasped. The bottom of the freezer was covered with thousands of gold nuggets. He had to squint to look directly at them; the glare of reflected sunlight hurt his eyes. Paul leaned in and scooped up a handful. They sure felt real.

"I'm rich! I'm rich!" Paul shouted happily as he climbed into the freezer. He got down on his hands and knees and started stuffing every available pocket with nuggets until they were overflowing. The seams of the old buckskin looked ready to explode.

The lid slammed shut hard. It struck Paul of the top of the head and drove him face down in the slime at the bottom of the freezer. The gold nuggets were gone. His pockets were wet and oozing the same goop he was laying in. Paul clutched his aching head, rolled over onto his back and gave the lid a good kick. It didn't move one iota. "Let me out of here!" Paul screamed. "Let me outta here!!" The foul air smelled like the inside of a tomb, and the slime seemed to be getting deeper, growing around him like something alive and hungry. "HELP!!" He started kicking and punching the lid like a three year old throwing a temper tantrum. "Sweet Jesus, Please! Somebody help me!"

Paul exhausted himself, and fell back into the slime, sobbing. "Get a grip on yourself," his inner voice commanded, "this is just a bad dream, that's all. Any minute now, you're going to wake up beside Bev in a nice warm sleeping bag and laugh about this stupid dream."

"Yoo-hoo. Paul?" The muffled voice came from the outside. "Anybody home in there?

"Let me outta here! Help me, please!" Paul shouted again, someone was there to rescue him.

"What's the matter, Paul?" the voice asked. "Is it too dark in there? Huh, Paul? Is the slime too yucky?"

"Who the hell are you?"

"I'm a friend. Don't you want to come out and play with me?"

"Let me out of here!"

"Oh, yes! I'd like that very, very much."

"Please, please, whoever you are," Paul pleaded. "Just let me out of here, now!"

"Anything you say, Paul. Here I come, ready or not!"

The first blow shook the freezer violently. The concussion from the noise in the confined space made Paul's eardrums feel like they were going to pop.

"It won't be long now, folks!" The second impact dented the interior lining, crumpling it like a squashed beer can.

"Hi-ho, hi-ho, it's off to work we go..." The third hit exploded through the lining, letting in a bright stream of sunlight.

Paul suddenly realized what had made the long gash in the freezer years before.

"I've been looking forward to meeting you for a long, long time now," the voice droned on as the lid began to rise.

"No. No! NOOO!!!"

There stood Stevie Roberts, grinning at Paul, yellow pus

dripping from the empty holes where his eyes should have been. He was holding a long handled, double bladed axe, its sharp head, caked with dried gore.

"Hello, Paul," the monster drooled. "I just know we're going to be fast friends." Swoosh— Paul dove from the freezer and rolled. The axe missed him and made another dent in the side. Paul was up and running in a flash. Swish— He felt a breeze on the back of his neck as the axe missed his head by inches.

"Care to join me for dinner, Paul? You can be the main course." Swoosh— "Ha, ha, ha!"

Paul backpedaled across the grassy clearing and leapt into the knee high salal that braced a young stand of cedars. The stems thrashed his thighs, slowing his momentum to a crawl. He fell forward and continued on, dragging himself forward on hands and knees.

Swoosh... The axe blade cut leaves loose near Paul's heels. "Come here you little bugger," spat Stevie Roberts. He charged into the thicket like an angry grizzly. "I'm going to chop off your balls, boy!" Swish— Swoosh— The axe-head grazed the back of Paul's leg and embedded itself in a recent deadfall. Stevie Roberts stopped to jack-knife it out. Paul scrambled madly to his feet, high jumping an alder snag in the process, and then crashed down onto a bed of damp moss by the main trail.

"Owww!!" Paul winced. His arm had caught a root on the way down, grazing the skin on his forearm from elbow to wrist. "Jesus." Paul struggled to his feet. Stevie already had the axe-head clear. Here he comes again, no reprieve.

"You're really starting to piss me off, boy!" Stevie Robert's empty eye sockets glowed dull red.

"Get fucked, you freak!" Paul screamed back. Then he beelined it straight for the trail, clutching his right elbow to stop the bleeding, his heels throwing up moss and decaying fir needles. Stevie Roberts was no match for the slender Paul. After a minute, Paul looked back and saw the monster falling further and further behind on the trail.

"I'm going to chop your dick off when I catch you, boy!"

Paul gave Stevie the finger and kept on running.

"First your dick and then your head!"

The monster's voice was getting fainter. Paul raced towards an embankment where the creek had cut back the top soil, exposing layers of clay and a massive outcropping of bare roots, rotting in the weather. There appeared to be a cavity at the base of a huge stump that had once grown on the side hill. Paul squeezed in between hunks of bark and shale. The wet earth stank of mold and decay.

A large black beetle popped out of the ground near Paul's mouth. The beetle eyed the intruder with suspicion, and then burrowed its way back into the soil. Paul tried to stop hyperventilating long enough to get his wind back under control. Surely, Stevie Roberts would hear Paul's breathing if he didn't quiet down really soon. Paul envisioned Stevie's axe crashing on the top of his skull. He could almost feel the bone exploding as he pictured the cold steel parting flesh and grey matter. Is that how I'm going to die, he wondered.

Paul held his breath. His knees were trembling. He put his hands on his legs and tried to will the shaking to go away, but it just got worse. His chest felt like a balloon ready to pop. It felt like he was going to black out any second.

This is ridiculous, thought Paul; I've got to breathe sooner or later. He held his nose and breathed out slowly through his mouth. He tried to remember his training from meditation classes.

Paul had been attracted to transcendental meditation in the

early seventies. A speaker at the university had enticed him to join, though rather reluctantly as there was a hefty initiation fee. After the first session, Paul was given a mantra, a secret word, by his instructor. He was not supposed to share this word with anyone. It sounded sort of like 'sharon,' only with a strong emphasis on the *ron*. Paul had forgotten the full significance of the word, but it had something to do with the rain. Paul let his mind go blank, and soon his breathing slowed as did his heart rate. His consciousness, fear and anxiety were slowly washed away by the lapping of waves on an imaginary beach. He could feel the cool, white foam rushing across his toes. The sky was blue with a few puffy, white clouds and the sunlight danced like a million jewels on the crests of the waves as they rolled in . . . one after another . . . the air, that moist rich smell of the ocean. Everything was calm and peaceful until a seagull flew by and let out a loud squawk.

"Paul." The voice jarred Paul back to reality. It was soft, yet close. Paul backed further into the crevice. He was trapped. The only way out, was the way he came in. Stevie Roberts wasn't likely to let Paul leave alive, let alone in one piece. The gory vision of the axe, crashing into his head, came back. Death. The end. Al Fine. But—

"Paul?" There was something about that voice that didn't jive. Paul felt a lump come to his throat. His heart was beating very fast again now. It couldn't be. Could it?

"Are you in there, Paul?" That voice. It was on the tip of his tongue. It was—

"Hey Paul, come on out. It's me!"

"Billy? . . . Billy!"

KEVIN'S HEAD WAS still pounding. He was laying face

down, his arms tucked underneath him. I hope that bear has split, he thought. Everything seemed kind of fuzzy. The inside of his head felt wooly like it was stuffed with cotton batting. And the shale felt soft now, like a blanket. Kevin opened his eyes and examined his surroundings.

I'm in jail he realized with surprise, what the fuck am I doing here? He remembered the bees and the fall from the cliff. He remembered the bear. He remembered dreaming about working on his car. After that, everything was a blank, like someone had erased the tape. I must be losing it, Kevin mused, this has got to be another dream, just one mother of a bad one after another. Or maybe I died and this is Hell, he thought with some horror.
Kevin sat up on the cot. He didn't seem to be injured any more; everything seemed to be in working order. He flexed his arm, nothing broken there, then rubbed his leg, it seemed to be okay, his side was fine and so was his head.

The cell was small, two walls faced in red brick—one inset with a barred window—and thick metal bars that defined the corridor across the front and divided the side from two identical cells beside it. They were both empty. A rusty bucket in a corner stunk to high heavens, it was full of human waste, and another near the cell door had a ladle sticking out of it. Stale looking water, Kevin discovered. There were two cots in each cell, topped with a thin mattress and a grey blanket. The mattresses were old and damp, the stuffing poking out of them all over the place. Not exactly the Holiday Inn, Kevin decided. He picked up an empty tin plate from the floor and started banging it on the bars.

"Hey, let me outta here! I haven't done nothing wrong." His voice echoed down the hallway. "Open up!"

"Jesus H. Christ! Will you cut the racket, son? I'm trying to sleep off of a drunk. And you're disturbing my peace. A sin, that is." The cell next to him wasn't empty after all. One of the cots was occupied by a thin old man.

"Where am I? Why am I here?" Kevin demanded. The shock was starting to wear off, and he was starting to panic. Kevin had done a year in Okalla prison, and more than a few nights in the drunk tank on Main Street. He hated being locked up. It made him feel helpless, trapped. He was not normally claustrophobic, but there was something about being locked up which made him feel like he was suffocating, like someone was strangling him with a plastic bag. "Answer me!" Kevin screamed at the old man. "Why am I here?"

"You ain't gonna let me sleep, are ya?" the old man sighed and threw off the blanket. He sat up and scratched his coarse, grey hair. "Damn mites. They itch worse than a boy's balls in a whorehouse. What was I sayin'?" The old man hobbled over to his bucket and spat out a thick ball of yellow-green mucus. Kevin noticed with mild interest that the old man's pants were buttoned, not zipped. The old man labored to get them undone with his bony old fingers. "Ahh . . . Yes!" The old man relieved himself and gave it a good shake. "I can't screw worth a damn any more. The doc says it's the booze, but it still feels awful good to take a piss." The old man took a sip from his ladle. "They brought you in here last night, must'a been, oh, 'bout ten o'clock. You were fighting 'em every inch of the way, son, screamin' and kickin'. Hee, hee." The old man walked towards Kevin and put his leathered skin up to the bars. His face was covered in white stubble and his mouth looked like it had collapsed. Kevin saw when the old man started to speak again, that he didn't have any teeth. "You're in deep shit, son." The old man cracked a toothless grin. The red veins in his eyes looked liked forked lightening on a pale yellow sky.

"Why am I here? What jail is this?"

"One question at a time, lad." The old man's breath stunk like spoiled meat. "To answer the last one first, these luxurious accommodations," he gave a sweep of his gnarled hand, "are provided free of charge, courtesy of the Queen's City." The old man stopped to rub his chin. "As to the latter, they say you were playin' poker over at the Merchant Saloon. A well known and well liked chap by the name of Jerry Barker, caught you cheating. Next thing a fight broke out and you blew his head off just like that. Hee, hee. One shot from your .45 and they were scraping his brains off of the bar stools. Hee, hee." The old man's eyes opened wider. "You're gonna dangle, son. Sure as the Lord made them little green apples, you're gonna swing from a noose. Hee, hee, hee." The old man puckered up his shriveled mouth. "Can I have that funny looking skirt yer wearin'?" He was pointing at Kevin's black Harley-Davidson motorcycle jacket. "I ain't never seen one like that before. And you sure won't be needed it where your going. I dare say, it's warm enough down there. Hee, hee." His eyes glanced at the planked floor. He shook his head. "Bad business."

Kevin reached through the bars and grabbed the old man by the throat. "Look. I don't care what the fuck you say! I don't belong here. And you're full of shit you old geezer, I didn't kill anybody!" Kevin squeezed harder until the old man's eyeballs seemed to be popping right out of their sockets.

"Leave him alone!" A horse whip cracked and Kevin felt his shoulder catch on fire. He released the old man and turned. The jailer was almost as big as Kevin. His eyes looked mean and cruel, they sparkled with malice. The jailer had the whip in one hand and a ring of keys in the other. An ugly looking revolver dangled from the holster on his side. "And don't try nothin' funny. I could pick your eyes out with this before you blinked twice." The jailer gave the whip another crack, this time in the air. "And what are you doin' picking on old Percy? He's just a harmless drunk, he wouldn't harm a flea. Aren't you in enough trouble already?"

"But, but, I didn't do anything!" Kevin stammered. "I'm innocent."

"Sure you are." A second jailer had appeared beside the first. In his hands were a set of leg-irons. "You can tell that to Judge Drake."

"I'm Mr. Burr," the jailer holding the whip, said. "And that's Mr. Conner." He gestured to the new arrival. "But you can call us, sir!" Conner nodded. "It's time to get you ready to go to court. I'm sure Judge Drake will have a few choice words to say to you. They don't call him the hanging judge for nothing. Ha, ha, ha."

The second jailer laughed too, and then grabbed his own throat mockingly. He stuck out his tongue and made his eyeballs go big. "I'm gonna love watching you hang," he said after the charade. "Jerry was a good guy, a personal friend of mine."

"But I'm innocent," Kevin whined.

"That's what they all say."

"But, I am innocent. You've got to help me. I, I . . ." The jailers ignored Kevin's pleas and continued their preparations in silence.

PAUL FELT A surge of relief as they walked together down the hill. Everything was going to be okay now. The Dynamic Duo was together again, Billy and Paul reunited, the A-Team, Mission Impossible. Paul had a million questions of course, maybe a zillion, but he kept quiet, afraid of talking Billy's ear off. Instead, he just savored the moment for what it was, old friends walking side by side again after a long absence. The fact that Billy had died in 1975, and had been rotting away in Mountain View Cemetery ever since, didn't matter. In fact, nothing seemed to matter anymore. The memory of the freezer and Stevie Roberts had faded away like somebody spun a dial in Paul's head and changed the channel. No homicidal monsters here, just Paul and Billy setting off on a new adventure, buds forever. That was all. An adventure! Onward and upward; one for all and all for one.

Someone had dropped the final piece into a cosmic jigsaw puzzle and set the wheels of this alternate universe tumbling forward: a world where Billy climbed down from the transmission tower and chided Paul for his concern. "No need to worry," Billy patted him on the back, "Billy boy knows which side his bread's buttered on. Com'on, let's party!" A world where Paul and Carol spent the rest of the evening fucking their brains out in the back seat of his dad's car, instead of at the RCMP station on Minoru Blvd, sobbing and crying as they told the police for the nth time what had happened to Billy. This time, the instant replay was different. Billy looked just fine. No burnt skin, no cooked eyeballs, just a plaid red and black work shirt, a pair of black stovepipes with white socks and a pair of points—"nut pickers," Billy liked to call them—the kind with the black plastic finish that you could spit polish until they were as shiny as the boots on the S.S. officers in war movies. Billy and Paul had always loved war movies. Their favorites were the Great Escape and Sink the Bismarck, the former had them singing the theme song for weeks after. As they walked along now, both of them started singing it at once. They were like that, tight, cosmically connected.

"Oh, we have to sink the Bismarck to the bottom of the sea. We got the decks a running, we spun our guns around . . ." Paul and Billy walked with their backs to the setting sun, heading deeper in the forest.

Chapter 25

Bev had a strange feeling; she felt funny all over, but in a good kind of way, the swim had refreshed her, the warm sun and cool breeze felt delicious on her skin. Her apprehension about Paul had faded into a kind of blind optimism. Sure, he was missing, but George would find him soon, no problem. It would be alright, there was absolutely nothing to worry about. After all, George had told them he was the best guide in the valley. She butted out another cigarette on the side of the fire-pit and picked up a small knapsack. She had packed a little lunch and a canteen.

Bev left camp and headed out one of the trails. It began with a gentle slope that wrapped around the small hill that rose from the beach. Most of the trees were second growth, fir and alder with the odd cedar. The shores of Pitt Lake, with easy access by boom and barge, were logged off at the turn of the century. There were a few flowers in the denser sections of bush, buttercups, trilliums, and every so often, the forest would open onto a small meadow alive with a sea of swaying daisies, their happy yellow faces capped in white bonnets. Bev picked a bouquet and threw them away one by one as she skipped up the trail. She felt like Dorothy in the

Wizard of Oz. Any moment she would come across the Scarecrow or the Tin Man. Or maybe the Lion would come crashing out of the woods roaring in his quest for courage.

"Ding dong, the witch is dead, the witch is dead, the witch is dead.

"Ding dong, the wicked witch is dead . . ."

Bev could almost hear the munchkins singing. She must be getting stoned on the fresh air and sunshine. Or maybe the nicotine from all the cigarettes she had smoked that morning. It felt like she didn't have a worry in the world. Everything was A-okay. She couldn't remember the last time she had felt this carefree, probably not since childhood.

"Follow the yellow brick road. Follow the yellow brick—Oh!"

There was a fork in the trail, and instead of a scarecrow to point the way, tied to one of the trees that formed the point of the intersection, was a bright yellow balloon. It bobbed and weaved in the breeze like a fighter trying to slip the jab of some unseen opponent. Printed on it in black, was an arrow pointing to the left, towards the smaller, more overgrown trail, and underneath the arrow was printed: LOST MINE, THIS WAY!

Bev pinched her arm. She didn't wake up. Next she pinched the string that held the balloon and gave it a tug. She pulled the balloon towards her and touched it gently with the tips of her fingers. It seemed real enough. Weird, must be somebody's idea of a joke, she thought. There was a small circle on the balloon, it said: COOL. Wait a minute, I got it, George must have found Paul—that's it—she thought. They were back. And they had set her up good, ha, ha. One of them must have snuck out here and planted the balloon. A joke. That's all.

"Those guys!" Bev shrugged and started down the narrower footpath. Curiosity is difficult to deny, and harder still to satisfy, so off she went. But I won't go far, she decided, I don't want to get lost.

It wasn't long before she came to another balloon. This one was blue and it said: THE END OF THE RAINBOW IS NEAR! The arrow pointed down the trail and in a small circle was printed: WARMER.

"Those guys!" Bev exclaimed again. It seemed like an innocent game. She might as well have some fun and go along with it. I wonder if they're watching me, she thought, and immediately felt eyes peering at her from the bushes. "Aw, I'm just psyching myself out. There's nobody in these woods except for many the odd squirrel or raccoon."

The next balloon was red, and it said: THESE NUGGETS AREN'T CHICKEN! That one sent Bev into a fit of giggling. There was of course an arrow on the balloon and this time a circle that said: HOTTER.

Then she heard it. Music. It seemed distant though, far away. Carney music? A carousel? This didn't jive with the conspiracy theory, not unless they had hidden a transistor radio or a portable tape recorder somewhere. But wait a minute, realization dawning on her; Paul had his little Sony Voice-O-Matic with him, that's what it is. And they're probably out there now, watching me from the bushes, trying not to laugh their heads off, Bev decided.

Suddenly, it sure felt like someone was watching her. But it wasn't a nice feeling. Bev pinched herself again but still didn't wake up. She felt like she was in the crosshairs of a sniper's scope. Alone and vulnerable. Easy prey.

The euphoria wore off quickly. Doubts followed by anxiety, followed by more doubts. Bev felt her stomach tighten as her mood shifted, the gay playfulness no longer disguising the fear and apprehension. This game was no fun any more. Bev felt like a child who suddenly decided that it was time to take her marbles and go home. The forest seemed to get darker, gloomier. And there was a different feel to it now. It was subtle, like an odor that seduces you at first, and then turns when you get a good whiff of the base note, sweet, yet rotten at the same time.

Bev continued down the trail like a boot camp graduate getting his first taste of the jungle in 'Nam. She heard a quick rustle behind her and screamed, "Yiiiii!!"

But it was only a cute, little squirrel. He stopped in the trail with his bushy tail held high in an S-shape. His tiny brown eyes seemed to say, "Hey lady, you look like you've seen a ghost. If I were you, I'd go straight home, take two aspirins and go right to bed." He scampered off into the ferns without collecting a fee for his diagnosis.

Bev pushed on. The trail wrapped around a rock bluff then leveled out in a small clearing. Somehow, she knew that it would be there even before she saw it. The tent.

It was a large tent with brown canvas and fancy trim, a carnival tent. A sign above the entrance, where the ticket booth sat empty, read: SEE SLUMACH'S HISTORIC GOLD MINE, $1 (CHILDREN ONLY 50 CENTS).

There was a drum roll, and the tent flap opened all by itself, followed by a loud trumpet cue. Then an unseen barker began his spiel. "Step right up, ladies and gentlemen, boys and girls, solve the mystery that has baffled the world for over a century! See for yourself one of the great secrets of the universe . . ."

Bev felt like she was being sucked forward by some invisible force; slowly, and with much apprehension, she entered the tent.

RANDY WATCHED HIS mother and Aunty Velma fade

into the afternoon sun, disintegrating like Kirk, Bones and Spock did on the transporter in Star Trek. Scotty had locked onto the two demons from Hell and was beaming them somewhere else, hopefully to the other side of the galaxy.

Randy stood there staring at the spot where the two corpses had just been standing. They were gone, but Aunty Velma's voice still rang loud and clear in his mind, a twisted dirge, "Kill the fornicators. Kill the fornicators." He slowly struggled to his feet. His head hurt where she had smacked him, it was still throbbing, but the imprints of Velma's fingertips on his forearm were gone. Randy wiped his own fingertips across his forehead. No sooty remnants clung to them. Was that real, he wondered, or am I going crazy kuku?

BEV FELT HER blood go cold. There stood Bobo the clown, a magician's top hat in one hand and a straight black cane with an intricately carved gold head in the other.

"Step right up folks!" the clown invited the trees. "See the great whore, Beverly Dayton, also known as Mystery, Babylon the Great, the mother of harlots and abominations of the earth." Bobo stuck the top hat on his stringy mop of orange hair and with a puff of smoke, the hat turned into a raven; its eyes as red as a harvest moon. The clown stuffed the cane down the front of his pants, where it seemed to disappear without a bulge.

"Hi, Bevy! Long time no see, eh?" The raven flew off of Bobo's head to a perch in the corner. "Surprised to see me? Huh? I know your name now, a little birdie told me, hee, hee." The raven shifted from foot to foot on the perch and let out a couple of loud squawks. "I'm sure you remember me," Bobo continued, "We met in Spokane at the carnival. You were just a tiny little thing then, but I see that you're a big girl now, all grown up, hee, hee." A stream of drool ran down the corner of Bobo's mouth, washing off some of the white makeup. "I've got something that I want to show you; something that I've been dying for you to see for a long time." Bobo grinned showing a mouthful of dazzling white teeth. "What do you say, Bevy? Do you wanna see my thing? Do you? Wanna touch it? Hmmm?" The clown pulled down its suspenders. The bright red pants dropped onto the ferns and covered the oversized black clown shoes. His 'thing' was huge and black. It didn't look real.

"Oh, yes! Bobo's gonna make you laugh. He's gonna make you scream with delight!" The clown gave his penis an affectionate tug; it bounced back and forth like a huge rubber dildo.

Bev started to back away slowly, keeping her eyes glued to Bobo in case he made a sudden move.

"I know you're a slut, Bevy. So do half of the guys on the West Coast. No fooling ol' Bobo, no siree!" The clown started coming towards her. "I hear you're not too choosy about who you drop your panties for: Tom, Dick, Harry . . . Joe, Jim, John. I bet you don't even know most of their names, do you, Bevy?" The raven flew off of the perch and landed back on the clown's head where it turned into a black bowler. "You can't help it, Bevy. It runs in your blood. You're part Injun and everybody knows that squaws screw like rabbits. Give 'em a few drinks and come on down! Coo-coo, all aboard!" Bobo winked at her. "And your mother Marie, the Injun lover, why she was the biggest slut in Yakima county. For all we know, you might not even be George's kid."

"You're a liar! My mom loves my dad. She wouldn't do anything to hurt him!" Bev yelled.

"Oh, I don't thing so, and from the look of it, neither do you.

I bet you can't wait for me to stick it in you. Or how about your mouth? Wanna suck on Bobo's popsicle, Bevy? Or would you rather take it up the ass? No matter to me. We can do it all three ways if you like." Bev had almost backed out of the clearing, but Bobo followed, keeping an even distance. "I bet you haven't had a good fuck in a long time. I mean that professor guy? He may have a lot going on upstairs, but between the legs? Kind of a joke isn't he?"

"He's more of a man, than you'll ever be!" Bev hissed.

"Now, now. No need to get testy. Does Paul know what you're really like? Hmm? I don't think so. Did you ever tell him about the dorm party in your sophomore year? How many guys went home with smiles on their faces that night? Huh, Bevy? How many? Can you count them on one hand? Two hands? Two hands and one foot?" Bev just stared at him with her mouth slightly open. "Getting warm, aren't I?"

"I was just a kid," Bev sobbed. "I was drunk."

"Just a kid, eh? Does Paul know that you sucked your first cock when you were only twelve years old? Or that your Uncle Sam made you—"

"Stop it! Stop it! It's not true. I, I'm not like that. I've changed!" Bev exploded. "Leave me alone!" She clamped her hands over her ears, but she could still hear him.

"Aw, I'll leave you alone, Bevy. But first I want to taste some of that sweet stuff you've been giving away all these years. Bobo wants his turn too. No sloppy seconds tonight!"

The clown's sad sack face underwent a complete metamorphoses, like peeling layers of transparencies off of a police composite drawing and exchanging them for a new ones with completely different features. The down turned mouth was replaced by a grin that seemed to stretch from ear to ear. The oversize pointed teeth were dazzling white. The clown's eyeballs bulged out of his head like a couple of golf balls ready to explode.

"Yee haw! Let's boogie! Bobo's gonna fix you up real good, little lady." The clown started to lick its eyebrows. His tongue was long, thin and forked like a snake's. Bev turned and ran.

THE COURTROOM WALLS were red brick with windows set high along the side, letting in light, but not allowing spectators to peer in from the outside. The benches and dockets were all made from dark mahogany, and they had that uncomfortable look like church pews. Judge Drake was definitely not a preacher, but he was known to give rather long lectures to the incarcerated and condemned.

The spectator seats were about a third full, non-descript faces in dull colored clothing. In the era before TV and soap operas, the courtroom provided one source of entertainment for the bored. A small group near the front showed more emotion, the relatives of the victim. They were here for revenge. And blood.

Burr and Connor dragged the prisoner in through the side door, and over to the prisoner's docket. The shackles jangled as they dragged along the floor behind his feet. This woke the crowd up, and they came alive with a solid chorus of boos that seemed to say, "Thumbs down, no need to waste any more time, we've reached our verdict, let's have a necktie party!" Someone had to restrain the brother of the deceased. He was prepared to shell out justice with his bare hands.

"All rise, order in the court!"

Judge Drake entered the courtroom from his chambers. He surveyed the gathering sternly before taking his seat. His robes were black with red trim and he wore the traditional blond wig.

"Be seated."

Drake twisted his handlebar moustache and waited for the murmur of the crowd to die down. One loud bang of his gavel called the session to order.

The charge was read: "Kevin Allan Macarthur, it is charged that on the 21st day of June, 1891 in the township of New Westminster, you did willfully murder Jerry Barker. How do you plead?"

"Sir, there must be some mistake, I . . ."

A loud bang of the gravel cut him off. "How do you plead, son? I want a simple answer, guilty or not guilty."

"But, I . . ." This brought another bang of the gavel, this one much louder. "Er, not guilty."

"Is the prosecution ready to proceed?"

"Yes, Your Honor."

"You may call your first witness."

The trial lasted for twenty minutes. Four eyewitnesses, who had been in Merchant's Saloon at the time of the shooting, gave damning testimony. The guilt was overwhelming. The jury took only five minutes to return a verdict of willful murder.

"Kevin Macarthur, you have been found guilty of willful murder. Do you anything to say before I pronounce sentence?"

"Sir, I, ah . . ."

"Very well," Drake cut him off.

"You're going to hang, boy. Yes, siree. They're going to put a big thick rope around your neck and a black bag over you head. You're going scream and cry, but it won't make any difference in the end. No one is going to listen. You're dead meat, son." Judge Drake seemed to be enjoying this immensely, berating the condemned, waving his gavel at Kevin's face.

"Now you might be hoping that this is only a nightmare and

that you're going to wake up soon, but it's real, boy. As real as the piss I see on your pants. As real as the fear in your eyes. Oh, yes! If you've got something to say to your Maker, you'd better start praying. And pray really hard, son, 'cause when they take you out to that scaffold and that old noose snaps your neck like a dry twig," Judge Drake snapped his fingers, "you're going to shit your pants. No fooling! The last thing you'll ever do in this world is crap your drawers." The whole courtroom roared with laughter. The gavel banged twice. "Then they're going to cut you down, lay you in a cheap pine box, nail on the lid and plant you in the ground. The worms are going to have a feast! Eat the flesh right off of your bones."

"No."

"You got something to say, boy?"

"No. This isn't real. You're not real, none of you!" Kevin screamed.

"Take him away!" Drake commanded banging his gavel again and again for order. The crowd cheered enthusiastically as Burr and Conner dragged the screaming prisoner from the courtroom.

Chapter 26

THERE SHE WAS! The hot bitch herself. Randy stared with disbelief. She had just walked into the clearing where he was standing. She was a beautiful harlot, no denying that. She looked gorgeous in jeans and a button up shirt, the sleeves rolled up to her elbows, and her hair hanging in two long braids. Finally the Whore of Babylon spoke:

"Why, you're the prick who almost ran us over!" Her eyes were cold slits of anger. "You could have killed us! Asshole."

"It was an accident," Randy replied, feeling his own anger building.

"Like hell, it was!" The woman was right in front of him now, eyeball to eyeball. "You should be locked up." She pushed his shoulder.

"Fuck you. Bitch," Randy fired back at her.

"Oh, tough guy." She started laughing at him.

"Stop that."

She covered her mouth with her hand, but kept right on laughing.

"Quit laughing at me," Randy demanded. He hated to be

laughed at. It was humiliating. The kids used to laugh at him all of the time in the foster home, the poor little orphan boy. They had teased him constantly. He was an outsider, not really part of the family.

WHEN TRAGEDY HAD struck—the terrible fire—taking Randy's mother and aunt, the Leblanc's had done their Christian duty and had taken the boy in. He got a roof over his head and three healthy meals a day. And they made sure he had discipline when he needed it too, which was often. Spare the rod and spoil the child, was their motto. Like Aunty Velma and his mother, they belonged to SOG. Randy went to church three times a week whether he liked it or not. Rain, wind, ice or snow, nothing kept the Leblanc family from their God.

The Leblanc's own two children, Ronnie and Kate, blamed everything on Randy. And of course, they were always believed over him, the outsider. Randy got caned so often, the bruises never healed. Ronnie and Kate devised every kind of torment and humiliation possible. They never grew tired of seeing Randy in tears. And at night, when the lights were out and everyone else was sleeping, Ronnie would visit Randy's bed and torture him in an entirely different manner.

"**I** BET YOU have a tenie-weenie dick, don't you?" the Whore of Babylon spoke again, holding her thumb and forefinger about an inch apart and laughing even harder. "You're just a pathetic, little guy, aren't you?"

"Shut the fuck up!"

"Oh, baby has a temper! Didn't your momma teach you

anything?" The laughter again, on and on and on, ringing in his ears like a broken record. The woman began to back away.

That's it, thought Randy, enough abuse. He decided then and there, to take Aunty Velma's advice, and kill the fornicator.

BEV RAN OUT of the tent with Bobo in hot pursuit. She sprinted further down the trail, not knowing where it would take her, and not really caring. All she wanted to do was put as much distance as possible between herself and the nightmare in makeup. But the clown kept up with her, his oversize shoes plopping along like a couple of snow shoes. The trail narrowed as it entered a ravine. Branches tore at her arms as she ran by. Bev rounded a corner and long jumped a small creek. One foot caught the water in a splash and soaked her boot.

The trail ended in a rocky embankment. She was trapped. The only escape was up. Bev scrambled desperately on the steep slope, trying to reach the more level ground on the ridge, but the dry moss kept peeling off in her fingers and her hiking boots failed to find a foothold on the smooth granite beneath the moss. She slid backwards.

"Keep away from me!" Bev screamed as she clawed frantically at the ground above her.

"Bobo won't hurt you." The clown jumped, just missing her foot with his outstretched arm. "Please, come and play with me."

Bev's fingers found a small bush and locked around it, she began to slowly pull herself up. "Not likely, sick-o!" The roots held the weight. Bev inched her way up the slope. Time seemed to stop and take a holiday as she made it up those last few feet. Almost there. She began to feel a wave of hope wash over her fear. She was going to make it! Then the hand closed around her ankle like a vise.

The two of them tumbled down the face of the hill, and landed roughly in a heap at the bottom. For a moment, neither the hunter nor the hunted had enough energy to move. Bev was the first to recover, but as she struggled to her feet, she discovered that she had sprained her ankle. As she tried to limp away, Bobo lunged and caught her waist in a flying tackle. Bev clawed at his face as he climbed on top of her, but the clown countered with a knee to her stomach that knocked the wind out of her.

"See, mommy, see! I'm a big boy now, mommy!" Bobo squealed as he tore at Bev's shirt. "I'm a big boy!"

"I'm not your fucking mother!" Bev screamed, and then spit in his face. The clown ripped open her blouse and pulled at the bra.

"You crazy bastard! Why don't you just whip out your little prick and get it over with!" Bev hissed.

It was the wrong thing to say. Bobo stopped sucking and glared at her—the scream hung in the valley for an eternity—then he sat up and spat out the end of her nipple. He was crying too.

"No, mommy, no!!! Don't cut off my pickle. I'll be a good boy, mommy, I promise!" The blood oozed down her side onto the grass, dyeing it scarlet.

Bobo the clown was gone. In his place sat the maniac from the speedboat. Drool dripped from the corner of his mouth, his vacant eyes glazed over like those on the trophies in a taxidermy shop. Two robot hands closed around Bev's throat and began to squeeze. She struggled against his weight, pulled on his wrists, fighting for her life, but slowly she lost consciousness, her struggles got weaker and weaker, then stopped. Everything faded and went white.

PAUL WOKE UP lying on the ground. The grass against his cheek was damp, and a hard root had been jabbing into his back for so long that it felt like it was growing there. His body was stiff and sore all over. "Billy." Paul looked around. Billy was gone. He was alone again. Or maybe he had been alone all along, and Billy had just been a mirage, a vision brought on by shock and exhaustion. Who knows anymore?

Paul realized that he was in a very bad situation. He needed food, water and a warm fire. And he needed them soon.

Paul crouched up in the small clearing. It was completely surrounded by thick undergrowth. He pulled out a book of matches from the buckskin pocket. It said, "Greek Village Restaurant" and "Please come again," on the cover. That seemed like so long ago now, that relaxing dinner with Bev, another place, another life. The thought of food made his mouth water.

There were only a couple of matches left in the package. Paul scooped up a handful of dry grass and piled them in a small heap. He added a few pieces of wood from a cedar windfall. That should burn for sure, he thought as he struck a match. It sputtered briefly, and then went out. "Fuck!" Paul cursed, feeling more and more desperate. He pulled the last match from the book. The black striker strip on the cover was damp, probably from the dew. Paul took a deep breath, muttered a prayer, and dragged the match head across the safety strip. The match sputtered, looked like it was going to go out and then burst into flame. "Com'on, baby," Paul encouraged as he guided the flame to the grasses. They began to burn. "Alright!" Paul cupped his hands around them and blew into the embers which glowed brighter. Just when it looked hopeful, the cedar was starting to catch now too, a sudden gust of wind extinguished the whole fire. Paul blew on the pile. It was still smoking. There was hope. "Please. Come on." Paul blew and blew. Nothing. The embers had turned black, even the smoke had ceased. "Oh, no," Paul gasped. He threw down the match cover. He was disgusted with himself, some boy scout he was, he couldn't even light a measly little fire when his life depended on it. Paul sunk to the ground. There was nothing left to do, so he cried, thought about his predicament, and cried some more. Finally he stopped crying, and shrugged it off. He climbed to his feet. He had to go somewhere, anywhere, and do something, anything. If he just sat there, he would surely die. As long as he was moving, he was still alive, be it barely.

THE TRAIL ENDED in a rocky embankment. Randy had her trapped now. There was no way that the bitch was going to get away. She tried to climb up the rocks, she was getting away! Randy lunged forward and stretched out his arm. Almost. He lunged again with all his strength. Success! He grabbed her ankle and pulled hard.

She crashed down on top of him and they both slid to the bottom of the rock face. She struggled to her feet first and began to limp away. Randy dove at her. They went down in a heap again, with Randy on top. She tried to claw his eyes out, so he kneed her hard in the groin. It worked. She stopped struggling for a minute. Randy tore open her shirt and grabbed her bra. Might as well have a little fun, he figured.

She yelled something, and spit in his face, but he was to busy to notice. Her nipples looked very pink against her smooth bronze skin. He took one in his mouth and began to suck like a child.

"You crazy bastard! Why don't you just whip out your little prick and get it over with!" the Whore of Babylon screamed at him.

That got through, he glared at her angrily. Then something snapped in Randy, and his mind went blank. He clenched his teeth down hard, and then sat up. Something was in his mouth. He spat it out. There was blood everywhere.

Randy's hands locked around the harlot's throat, Aunty Velma's voice urging him on. "Kill the fornicators!"

PAUL WALKED SIX miles in four hours, no small feat in the dense bush and steep terrain, especially in his weakened condition. He was running by instinct alone, no cerebral cortex required for this journey, and he had long since given up trying to figure out which direction he was going in, he was so lost by now that it didn't make the slightest difference. For all he knew, he might have been going around and round in circles. Each tree and rock looked just like the next one and the one before it. "Keep moving. I've got to keep moving."

A trail led down the side of a steep canyon. Paul followed it like grease on a frying pan, ending up at a narrow gorge on the bottom, where a small creek ran through the glacial rocks.

"Water! Water!" Paul cried as he ran over to the edge of the creek. He was incredibly thirty, his mouth and lips so dry they stuck together. He got down to his knees and put his whole face in the water. It was cold, sweet and delicious. Paul sucked it up like nectar. "Ahhhh . . ."

Paul straightened up and shook his wet hair. He felt refreshed, so much better. Now all he needed was something to eat. He looked around hopefully. It was only then that he noticed the color of the bedrock, yellow. His eyes opened wide and his mouth dropped open. "I found it," were his last words.

The axe head cut the air silently in a deadly arc, imbedding itself easily in the soft target. The gold nuggets at the bottom of the creek were quickly obscured by the blood.

BEV WAS FLOATING on a warm wind. She had no sensation of weight, no body. Below her, the darker greens and browns of forest, the canopy broken in spots by a small meadow or outcropping of rock, rolling hills and valleys. The forest melted into scrub and wetlands, several geese making long trails on the smooth surface of a small lake. Now she could see farmland, a checkerboard pattern of green fields and crops, a river snaking through the symmetry, pockets of mist hanging on its banks, and then she began to recognize the terrain, the lay of the land at first, and then a barn that looked familiar, a farmhouse, and finally, a church with a tall, white steeple, nestled in a grove of Garry oaks.

Bev floated down towards the church. A single tan colored SUV was parked in the gravel driveway below stained glass windows and white cedar siding.

It was fall here and the leaves had already fallen, covering the ground in a rusty red and yellow blanket. Bev floated amongst the tall oaks, weaving in and out of their gnarled branches.

The small graveyard was at the rear of the church, a wrought iron fence overgrown with ivy, monuments of all sizes and shapes paying tribute to its permanent residents. In one corner a man wearing a heavy coat with a fur collar and a black Stetson, knelt in front of a small tombstone. As Bev floated closer she could hear his sobs.

She wanted to touch him, to hold him, let him know that everything was alright, because she knew this man, it was George Dayton, her father.

But he looked too old, his hair was nearly all gray now, and the long, hard lines on his face told a sad story. George had a single long stemmed red rose in his hand. He laid it by the tombstone, put one hand on top of the marble, and knelt there in silence for a few more minutes. Then he got up and walked away, stooped slightly and head hung low, heading back towards the church and his vehicle.

Bev felt his sadness lingering in the air, a fragrance of grief and pain. Then she floated closer to the grave, reading the words inscribed on the smooth dark surface: BEVERLY JEAN DAYTON, 1969 - 2002, Beloved Daughter.

Bev read her epitaph again, and then floated back to the oaks. The branches were swaying in a light breeze. Bev drifted higher, riding the currents.

The farmland was now far below, the sparse buildings appearing as tiny dots. She could see the bluish gray coastal mountains rising up in the distance. In the west, the sun was bright, heading towards the endless blue Pacific Ocean, and a thick blanket of clouds rolling in towards the coast, bringing rain. Soon she was higher than the highest clouds, the gentle curvature of the earth perceptible. The land below was now just a blur of colors.

Bev was being drawn up, higher and higher, heading towards to the sun, the source of all light and warmth. She stared at the bright, white ball. It was all she could see now, all that mattered, the light, drawing her in, closer. She was hurtling though space, past the moon, picking up speed, faster and faster, in seconds she would become one with the light.

THE BULLET STRUCK Randy at the base of his neck, near the shoulder blade, passed down through his heart, right lung and exited out his mid-back in a gapping hole. The force of the impact didn't send him flying through the air like in the movies, instead his body just hung there for a few seconds before collapsing beside Bev. Glazed, lifeless eyes pleaded with the sky, as the thunder of the loud report echoed up and down the hills and valley. A raven, perched high in a dead tree, watched in silence.

Bev's eyes gradually began to focus, she gasped for air—her throat was badly bruised—then she saw him. Someone was standing there at the top of the ridge she had tried unsuccessfully to climb. He was tall and very old. His white hair fell in two braids on the ragged, red hunting shirt, and a wrinkled hand held an ancient percussion rife resting on the ground. His brown skin was dark and extremely weathered.

A pair of intense dark eyes caught Bev's own, held them for a brief moment, then his lips smiled ever so slightly. Bev felt like she was looking back at the beginning of time itself. Then the man shouldered his rifle, turned and disappeared from sight.

The raven left his perch on the snag, circled the ridge three times, and then flew off without making any comment.

Epilogue

After an autopsy, Randy Smith was buried beside his mother in Mount Pleasant Cemetery. Including the pastor, seven people attended the brief memorial service.

Charges of manslaughter against Simon George were dropped after a preliminary hearing. George testified that he had never fired a single shot, which was confirmed by a forensic examination of his rifle. He also stated that he had not been present at the time of the shooting but had heard the shot from a distance. When he arrived on the scene, Randy Smith was already dead and Beverly Dayton was barely conscious.

The autopsy revealed that Randy Smith had been killed by a single slug fashioned out of a gold nugget. The verdict at the inquest was homicide by person or persons unknown, another mystery.

Now in his seventies, George still likes to tinker with cars, and once in a while, he will take a party of hunters or fishermen on a little adventure. And he can still out hike the average twenty year old, even with a full pack.

Two days after his fall, Kevin Macarthur was found by a search and rescue team, who air lifted him to Vancouver General

Hospital. The doctors attending his injuries described his slow, but full recovery from the fifty foot fall as nothing short of miraculous. His mother Cloe, now a widow, visited Kevin nearly everyday during the long healing, and they spent many hours talking about life and God. A provincial court judge let Kevin off easy on charges of possession of stolen property: the boat and outboard. He got six months probation and a small fine.

Kevin is now a born again Christian. He works as a cement finisher and odd jobs as a mechanic evenings and the odd weekend. And he stays out of trouble, keeps his nose clean, no more scams or get rich quick schemes, no more hot cars or stolen property, and definitely no more gold fever, just honest hard work and clean living. He has settled down now, and is living with a pretty divorcee and her two children in a Surrey townhouse.

Beverly Dayton was treated for shock, minor injuries, and then released. Several months later, she underwent plastic surgery on her breast.

Bev finished her PhD and accepted an assistant professorship at the University of Texas in Dallas. She is now married to Michael Johnson, a senior analyst with the EDS Corporation. They are expecting their first child.

No trace of Dr. Paul Gregory was ever found. He is listed as missing and presumed dead. After Randy Smith, Paul became officially, the twenty-seventh person to die or disappear while searching for the Lost Mine—the unofficial list is a lot longer—but still the quest goes on.

Every spring, gold fever returns to the Fraser Valley and dozens of treasure seekers and adventurers begin the rugged, and sometimes dangerous, trek up to the head waters of Pitt Lake, each one confident that they will be the lucky person to unravel the mystery that has baffled seasoned prospectors and tenderfoots alike for nearly a century.

Does the Lost Mine exist? No one really knows for sure. And the dead don't speak, or do they?

"Nika memloose . . . Mine memloose."

Acknowledgments

I would like to thank to my wife Debi and our good friends Holly and Francie, for editing and proofreading this manuscript.

When I was just a small boy, my father told me a colorful tale about an Indian and his lost gold mine. The story stuck in my subconscious and many years later, I decided to write this book.

My father was born in 1899, and he moved to the Vancouver area in 1906 when he was just a boy himself. Only fifteen years had passed since Slumach walked to the gallows in New Westminster. When I began my research for this book, I discovered that the legend has changed little in the last century.

The search for the Lost Creek Mine in my book is entirely fictitious—the people and events described herein are not meant to portray anyone living or dead—however much of the background of the story is based loosely on a mixture of historical fact, local folklore and Salish mythology.

The writing of this book stretched over twenty years. The first few chapters were written in 1983, and there were major additions in 1989 and 1995. I finished the bulk of the writing in 2003.

I would like to take this opportunity to thank the Vancouver Public Library and the British Columbia Provincial Archives in Victoria, for making the research of this book possible. There have also been many magazine and newspaper articles on Slumach and the lost mine, several books including <u>Slumach's Gold/In Search of a Legend</u>, edited by Art Downs (Heritage House Publishing Company Ltd., 1981)—which was invaluable—and a couple of television documentaries. To all of these sources, I am truly grateful.

-Edgar Ramsey
Sonora, California 2006